FOR WHOM THE SPELL TOLLS

Also by HP Mallory:

THE JOLIE WILKINS SERIES:

Fire Burn and Cauldron Bubble
Toil and Trouble
Be Witched (Novella)
Witchful Thinking
The Witch Is Back
Something Witchy This Way Comes

Stay Tuned For The Jolie Wilkins Spinoff Series!

THE DULCIE O'NEIL SERIES:

To Kill A Warlock
A Tale Of Two Goblins
Great Hexpectations
Wuthering Frights
Malice In Wonderland
For Whom The Spell Tolls

THE LILY HARPER SERIES:

Better Off Dead

FOR WHOM THE SPELL TOLLS

Book 6 of the Dulcie O'Neil series

HP Mallory

FOR WHOM THE SPELL TOLLS

by

H.P. Mallory

For Dulcie's Fans

Acknowledgements:

To my mother: Thank you for everything you do.

To my editor, Teri, at www.editingfairy.com:
I always appreciate your fantastic edits! Thank
you.

To my husband:
I love you.

To my son:
Thank you for making me laugh every day.

To my beta readers Evie from Paromantasy and
the Eaton sisters, thank you!

To the winner of my "become a character in my
next book" contest,
Rachel Wallace: Congratulations! I hope you
enjoy reading about yourself!

To Mary Stadter:
Thank you so much for entering the contest to
come up with the title for this book.
I really love it!

A Note From HP:

To all my readers,

I hope you've enjoyed Dulcie's adventures as much as I've enjoyed writing them.

As this is the last book in the Dulcie series, it's with a heavy heart that I write this note but I do hope you've enjoyed the series and you're happy with the ending!

I will certainly miss writing about Dulcie, Knight and the gang but I'm also very enthusiastic about new projects that are currently underway. (Be sure to read the first chapter—at the end of this book—of "Better Off Dead," the first book in the brand new Lily Harper series!)

Thank you so much for all your continued support. As an indie author, I can't tell you how much it means to me.

Love, HP

ONE

The decision was made.

And now that the decision was made, I could somehow think a little more clearly. It was like the proverbial fog was lifted from my eyes, revealing the reality that we were going to invade the Netherworld.

The decision to invade the Netherworld was both complicated and not-so-complicated. The not-so-complicated part was that the decision *had* been made so now it was just a matter of planning the strategy for the invasion. The complications arose with regard to invading the Netherworld, itself, because we, The Resistance, intended to dethrone my father, who was not only the head of the Netherworld, but also a ruthless tyrant. Given our father-daughter relationship, some people might have considered the whole situation complex but as far as I was concerned, it wasn't.

"You good with this?" Knight asked as he sat behind the wheel of a Chevy Suburban. He kept alternating his piercing blue gaze between the road and me.

I nodded immediately. "I'm good with it." And that was the Hades-honest truth. I mean, only moments earlier, I'd announced that we needed to stop wasting time and invade the Netherworld *now*. Truth be told, I was concerned that we'd waited too long already. Why? Because I'd just discovered that my father had tricked the head of The Resistance, Christina Sabbiondo, into revealing many of our secrets which had, in turn, completely compromised everything we were planning. At this point, all we really had on our side was the element of surprise. And from where I stood, banking on the element of surprise wasn't necessarily a good bet.

Knight offered me a smile. Even though he simply raised the corners of his lips—not even into a full-fledged grin—it caused butterflies to rise up into my stomach all the same. Maybe it was because Knightley Vander's photograph could have been posted beside the headline "So incredibly gorgeous, it feels sinful just to look at him" in good ol' Webster's Dictionary. Or maybe it was his personality—the quintessential flirt who could basically undress you with just a glance. But he was also incredibly dedicated and devoted to people and ideas he believed in. All in all, Knight might appear the rogue and, in many ways he was, but he was also a good guy. A really good guy.

"You realize what this will mean?" he continued, eyeing me with his black eyebrows drawn together in an expression of speculation. His pitch-black hair and olive complexion imbued him with a certain Mediterranean air, but those crystal blue eyes muddied any hunches about his ancestry. I knew what he was though—a Loki, a creature born from the fires of Hades and created in Hades's own burly, large and stunning image.

"What *what* will mean?"

"Dulce, we're going against your father with the intention of bringing him down, no matter the costs." He took a deep breath and seemed to zone out on the road before he returned his gaze to me. "And the costs could be your father's life."

I felt my jaw tighten at the mention of my father, Melchior O'Neil. Glancing down at my clenched fingers, I found my knuckles were white. I relaxed my hands and shook them out as I turned to face Knight. "As far as I'm concerned, I don't have a father."

Knight took a deep breath and exhaled loudly. "He's all you have left."

Unfortunately, Knight was right—my father was the last of my kin. My mother had died a long time ago and my father had only come into my life recently. But it definitely wasn't a family addition that I welcomed or invited, by any stretch of the imagination. Melchior O'Neil, my father, was basically Enemy Number One, as far as I was concerned. He'd created an illegal narcotics Utopia in which street potions from the Netherworld were transported to my city of Splendor, California, (as well as many neighboring cities) through portals. My father had been importing these street potions for centuries. As an elf, he had the ability to control his own aging, and in the process, he was able to grow incredibly wealthy, thereby gaining even more power. The irony of the whole damn situation was that I'd dedicated myself and my life to fighting crime as a Regulator for the Association of Netherworld Creatures (ANC) here in Splendor. Funny how life sometimes kicks you right in the nuts … well, if you have any, that is.

"He's not all I have left," I countered. "Sam, Dia, Quill, Trey and … you … you're my family. And you all are way more family than Melchior ever was to me."

Even though Knight and I had experienced our fair share of issues during our relationship, there was no denying that we were absolutely in love with each other and always had been. Despite trying to talk myself out of being in love with him on numerous occasions, it was a complete waste of time. When it comes down to it, you just can't rationalize emotion, much less try to control it.

I probably shouldn't have been surprised that I couldn't convince myself not to be in love with Knight. Every time the man so much as looked at me, I felt my insides melt. What was more, a fire began to brew in my core—a fire that felt very much like yearning. It was a sexual ache the likes of which I'd never experienced with another man. But that was no surprise because sex with Knight was, in one word … addictive.

When confronted with my own thoughts, I felt heat burning my cheeks and shifted uncomfortably, trying to clear my own mind. Thinking about sex with the Loki

3

wasn't going to solve the issue of invading the Netherworld. All it would do was get me flustered, which was something I really didn't need to add to the overwhelming list of emotions already plaguing me.

"You're the strongest woman I've ever met," Knight said thoughtfully. He didn't look at me, but continued driving. "I admire you more than words can express."

"Hey, you aren't so bad yourself," I said with a slightly embarrassed laugh. I wasn't really comfortable with compliments and mushy stuff. I never had been. It was one of the things I envied about Knight—he didn't have a problem balancing his funny, sociable or tough side with his caring, romantic and emotional side.

He glanced over at me and there was no expression on his face. It was just a blank canvas of male beauty. "I *am* your family," he said simply. "And I would gladly give my life if it meant saving yours."

I swallowed hard, not able to face the truth in his eyes. I didn't want to think about him trading his life for mine because it was a trade I would never accept. I would never allow Knight to die for me or in my name.

"Don't talk like that," I said softly, hating the image of him still and lifeless. I crossed my arms against my chest and felt my chin starting to jut out in defiance. "We're going to take my father down and that's that."

Knight nodded with a slight smile as he studied me. After another few seconds, he glanced back at the road, as if to make sure we weren't veering into oncoming traffic. When we were safely traveling in our traffic lane, he looked at me again. This time, there was something in his eyes that wasn't there before—a certain twinkle like he was pleased to know something I didn't.

"One thing I do know for sure," he started, but seemed to swallow his words. Instead, he just wetted his lips with his tongue.

"What do you know for sure?" I asked, sounding less than interested.

"Once this shit with Melchior is figured out," he continued, sparing a few seconds for the road before returning his intense gaze to mine, "I'm locking both of us in my bedroom for at least a week; and at the end of that week, you won't be able to walk."

My stomach dropped down to my feet as the butterflies that were already causing a quiet flurry inside me suddenly intensified, feeling like a flock of angry crows. The yearning I mentioned earlier became an all-out conflagration of need, so intense my heartbeat raced and my breath started coming in short gasps. Yep, this was exactly what Knightley Vander did to me. At the mere mention of sex, I became a slobbering dog.

"Oh … okay," I said dumbly. But it wasn't my fault—words had completely escaped me.

"I need to taste you, Dulcie," Knight whispered, and his eyes began to glow like they did whenever he was turned on or … jealous. He shook his head and tightened his grip on the steering wheel. Meanwhile, I felt like my insides were succumbing to an avalanche of craving. "I keep replaying a memory of you in my mind and I think it's slowly driving me crazy."

"A memory?" I repeated in a mousey voice as I felt my own hands gripping the leather seat more tightly.

I could see his eyes flaming white, their glow his way of telling me that his body had selected me as his mate, and I was his for the taking. It was something innate to Lokis—in order for a Loki to procreate, the woman with whom he mated had to be strong enough to bear his seed. And Knight's body had illustrated the fact that I was strong enough by glowing whenever Knight and I were being intimate or if another man ventured anywhere near me.

"I'm on top of you," Knight started in a deep, but breathy voice. Thank Hades he wasn't looking at me, and instead watched the road, because I feared I'd melt into a sticky mess if he so much as even glanced my way.

5

"You're naked and your hair is spread all over my pillow and all over your breasts," he continued, still staring straight ahead. "I wrap my hands around your tiny waist, trying to force myself to go slowly with you, to savor every inch of you. But there's something primitive in me that keeps yelling at me to … to plunge myself into you as hard and deep as I can, to make you realize you're mine."

Without any warning, he suddenly slammed his hand against the steering wheel. I instantly realized that whatever this primitive thing inside of him was, he didn't like it. He finally pulled his attention away from the road and looked at me with what appeared to be anger in his eyes. "There's something in me, Dulcie, something I'm always at odds with. I think of it as a sort of instinctual beast and the beast tells me to take what I want. Most of the time, I can keep it in check, but with you, I'm always teetering on the edge."

He paused and I could see his jaw visibly tightening. "Um, go on," I whispered, thinking to myself that I wanted nothing more than the beast to make its appearance. At this point, Knight was teasing me as much as himself, and even though it was torture, there was no way in hell I would let him stop.

"I remember pushing my finger into you and you arching up against me and moaning." He stopped talking and faced forward, the glow of his eyes obvious, even in his profile. "The beast nearly took complete control of me then, Dulcie. I wanted nothing more than to spread your legs wide and thrust myself into you. I had to close my eyes and force it back." He took a breath and chuckled. "And then you told me you needed me inside you."

I remembered this particular incident—it was probably one of the most intense sexual episodes Knight and I had ever experienced together. It was relatively early on in our relationship and I was over at Knight's house. We'd just taken a shower after an especially long motorcycle ride. As soon as we were out of the shower, Knight had carried me to his bed and the rest was history, as they say.

"I couldn't control myself once you said those words," he continued, the chuckle dying on his lips. "The beast took over and I had to be inside you." He was quiet for a second or two and when he started talking again, his voice was suddenly raw. "I remember looking down at your beautiful body while I spread your legs and wondered how a woman could turn me on so much." He shook his head as if he still didn't have an answer to his question. "And the feel of your tight slickness when I pushed into you ..." His voice trailed into soft quiet again as I silently begged him to continue. I'd never been so turned on by words before. But it wasn't that surprising because this was how sex with Knight was—completely mind-blowing.

"What's funny is that the memory is so clear, it's like it happened yesterday." He chuckled again. "Maybe it's because I've replayed it so many times in my head, it keeps its novelty." He paused as he appeared to contemplate it, finally shaking his head. "I don't really know why."

"Tangent," I snapped, surprised by the irritation in my voice. "Back to the point."

Knight gave me a raised brow and a smirk that was, even now, broadening. "Excuse me, Ms. Demanding."

"Ahem, back to the story, please," I corrected myself, adding a pleasant smile.

He suddenly pulled the Suburban to the side of the road, and the uneven terrain caused my teeth to chatter in my head. A few rocks pelted my door as a dust storm circled the car, manifesting the fact that Knight was driving too fast. He turned to face me, making no motion to do anything other than stare at me, but it felt more like he was staring right through me.

"The part I can't erase from my mind and the part that I keep replaying over and over again is the feel of you. How wet and tight you were when I pushed myself into you. I remember a voice inside my head telling me to take you even faster, to push into you harder and deeper. I couldn't fight the beast, Dulcie. As soon as I watched your beautiful

7

breasts bouncing up and down, the beast won. Even though I wanted to close my eyes and fight my urges, I couldn't stop staring at your stunning body. I couldn't stop staring at myself going in and out of you." He sighed long and hard. "The only other time I lost myself to the power of the beast was that time in the Denali on the side of the road."

That was another incident when our sex got rough. At the time, Knight and I weren't getting along. Even though I told him things were too ugly between us for us to have sex, he could read my body language, which shouted that I wanted him … badly.

"I think the beast needs to be released every now and then," I whispered, following his gaze to my breasts. I noticed the line of my nipples standing out against my shirt in an obvious broadcast of my own arousal.

Knight reached over and took my right nipple between his thumb and middle finger, pinching it slightly. There were a good few seconds where I completely forgot to breathe. I couldn't help it as my gaze drifted south to his lap. And, just as I imagined, he was already straining against his jeans, the outline of his penis more than obvious. I felt a stinging between my thighs and knew my body was preparing itself to receive him.

He didn't say anything more, so I brought my eyes from his erection back to his face, only to find him staring at me.

"I'm about a second away from tearing off your pants and burying my face between your legs," he said with calm resolve.

"Um," I responded, but again lost the ability to form words.

"But I'm not going to," he finished, dropping his hand. He glanced in the rearview mirror, then his side mirror, and finding the coast clear, pulled back onto the road, leaving another cloud of dust in his wake.

There was a definite sense of disappointment welling up within me. "Why?" I asked the obvious.

8

"Because I've got a team meeting to orchestrate," he said with a lofty smile. Then without waiting for my response, he pressed a button on the steering wheel and said: "Dial Dia." The sound of dialing filled the car as I tried to put a lid on the intense desire to jump him.

"You are such a tease," I muttered to which he smiled a broader grin. The bastard was proud of himself!

"Unless you're callin' to tell me you've decided to take a ride on the goblin train, I'm not interested," Dia's voice rang out.

Dia, a *somnogobelinus*, was a specialized type of goblin who could influence people's dreams. If that doesn't sound especially impressive, Dia's abilities allowed her to insert herself into people's dreams and if she harmed or killed them during sleep, they would also die in real life. But, luckily for us, Dia was more interested in rescuing people. She headed the Association for Netherworld Creatures in a neighboring city of Moon and was also one of the board members (for lack of a better word) of our Resistance team.

The Resistance team comprised five Netherworld creatures who were specially chosen to help our former head, Christina, plan an attack against my father. But now Christina was no longer a viable leader because my father had subjected her to an illegal potion which forced her to divulge any and all information regarding The Resistance. As such, Knight was now in charge, and I was his second in command.

Knight chuckled. "I need everyone at the cabin, pronto."

"Roger that," Dia said with a hearty laugh. It was one of those contagious giggles where you can't help but smile or laugh yourself.

"Everyone needs to arrive in less than twenty minutes," Knight added with authority.

"I want Sam and Trey there as well," I interrupted.

"Hi, girl," Dia piped up. "Phew, I'm glad to know you're with the Loki 'cause I was gettin' worried."

After my father tried to assassinate Knight and me, I had to go underground with a "friend" of mine named Bram. At the time, I didn't know Bram was in cahoots with my father for the past couple of centuries. But, as with most Netherworld creatures living on Earth, Bram also wanted to renounce his ties to Melchior. According to Bram, he was now firmly entrenched in The Resistance camp.

"Hi, D," I answered. "Yeah, I'm fine."

"Amen ta that, sistah!" Dia said with a laugh. "Okay, Sam and Trey, I'm on it."

Samantha White was my best friend and an incredibly gifted witch. She worked alongside me at the ANC and I considered her a devoted ally both to the ANC and to The Resistance. Trey also worked with me at the ANC as a fellow Regulator. He was a hobgoblin, who had the ability to see the past, present and the future in dream-like vignettes that had helped us crack many cases. Just as he was a boon to the ANC, I knew The Resistance could also benefit from his talents.

"And Quillan needs to be involved too," I added, even as I realized my comment wouldn't go over well with Knight.

Knight immediately shook his head, but I was steadfast in my belief that Quill should be part of our preparations to invade the Netherworld. "He was my father's right-hand man, Knight," I argued. "Quill knows the way my father thinks and without him, we'd be doing ourselves a huge disservice."

"I don't trust him," Knight answered, his jaw tightly clenched. I noticed he refused to even glance my way and, instead, kept his eyes trained on the road ahead of us.

"Your fairy's got a point," Dia said. "Quill could help us, Knight."

"And what if he still maintains ties to Melchior?" Knight demanded. "What then?"

10

"He has nothing to do with my father anymore," I said in a soft voice, knowing Quillan was a sore subject where Knight was concerned. It wasn't just because Quill once worked for my father, either. Quill had been my boss at the ANC before we discovered he was working for my father. And once upon a time, I'd even had a big crush on him, a crush which he'd returned and now made no attempts to hide. If the truth be told, I believed Knight was a little jealous over my friendship with Quill. "He took the tests of his loyalty to The Resistance just like everyone else did," I argued. "And what's more, he passed every single one of them."

Knight swallowed hard, sighing deeply as his left eyebrow arched in what could only be described as a lack of enthusiasm. "Quillan too," he said simply.

###

The "cabin" was a fitting name. Ensconced in myriad enormous, snow-decked Linden trees (which sort of look like poplars), the lodge was completely constructed from hewn logs. It took Knight and me about ten minutes to get here, during which time we traveled through three portals. Not surprisingly, we were the first to arrive.

I opened my door and shivered in the cold wintry air. "Where are we?" I asked, glancing around to find we were in the middle of basically nowhere. There wasn't another cabin, house or lodge within view, just the refreshing smell of ice and earth permeating the otherwise still air. A few lone birds sang out dolefully, and the snow flurries dropped from the boughs overhead to find a final resting place on the ground.

Knight reached behind his seat and produced a black, down coat, which he handed to me. "Here, this will keep you warm."

I accepted it eagerly and threw it on, zipping it up as I realized it was a woman's coat and also my size. "Do you always carry around random women's clothing?"

Knight chuckled. "I know your size, silly." Then he looked me up and down appraisingly. "And, no, I don't just carry random clothing around. I knew we'd be coming here." He smiled from ear to ear. "I planned."

"And where is here again?" I reminded him of my first question as I tried not to notice how his grin lit up his entire face.

"Southern Germany, in Bavaria," Knight announced, almost proudly. "The town is Garmisch."

I shook my head in wonder as I took in my surroundings again. It looked like we were at the base of the Alps, the mountains beyond the trees incredibly steep by anyone's account. "Ten minutes to Germany. Portal travel is the way to go," I said.

Knight laughed and started for the door to the lodge, unlocking it and opening it wide. From my viewpoint, I could make out dark wood floors and a fireplace that occupied one entire wall. Knight stepped over the threshold and faced the fireplace, as flames began to erupt in the firebox. Then he eyed me as if seeking praise for a job well done.

"Another of your Loki abilities?" I grumbled, sounding less than thrilled. It was an ongoing joke between the two of us—as a Loki, Knight had myriad abilities, abilities which he kept under lock and key. The only reason I knew he was capable of anything at all was because I simply stumbled upon them the more time we spent together. What number this latest ability was, I had no clue—I'd lost track a long time ago.

"Forged from the fires of Hades," he answered with a self-impressed smile.

I was spared the need to respond when the sound of wheels crunching snow caught my attention. I turned around and watched Dia arriving in a scarlet red Cadillac Escalade,

12

complete with spinning rims. I could hear the beat of Rihanna's "Diamonds" blaring, even though the windows were all rolled up. Sam was sitting beside Dia and I could make out Trey and Quill in the backseat.

"The party can now officially start, y'all," Dia shouted as she opened her door.

Dia is very tall and curvy with the most beautiful smile you've ever seen. Her skin is the color of hot chocolate and paired with her fire-engine red snow jacket, she was a sight to behold.

"Dulce, you're okay!" Sam said as she stepped out of the car and hurried toward me, with Trey and Quill right behind her. Sam threw her arms around me and beamed happily. "It's so good to see you." She hugged me again. "I was so worried since no one heard from you and Knight couldn't reach Bram."

I started to respond, but was interrupted by the sound of another car pulling up. I turned and watched someone I didn't recognize pull up in a silver Land Rover LR4. Sitting beside her was Erica Comacho. I didn't know Erica well, but what I did know of her, I liked, even though our relationship hadn't exactly begun on good terms. It was sort of hard not to like her because she was so closely related to me, ancestry-wise. As a nymph, she was separated from fairies by just a few branches in the evolution tree. Layman speaking, she was a distant cousin. Similar to fairies, nymphs also possessed magic, but only when they were in the natural environment because their magic came from natural elements. Given how natural this environment was, I imagined Erica was going to have a field day with her magic.

The driver killed the engine and opened the door, stepping outside. She was strikingly pretty and looked like she was in her late twenties. She wasn't much taller than I was, maybe 5'3" if I had to guess. What sun there was lit up the caramel highlights in her otherwise brown hair which was maybe two inches past her shoulders. Her brown eyes

13

had a sweetness to them and with her plump lips, she was definitely a looker. She was dressed in tightly fitting blue jeans and a tighter black sweater, both of which revealed her naturally curvaceous body. A pair of nude, platform peep-toe heels peeked out from beneath her jeans.

"MJ!" Knight called out from beside me as the woman faced him with a huge grin. They instantly threw their arms around one another as I was left wondering how in the hell they knew each other.

"It's great to see you, Vander," she said to him, once they'd separated.

Knight glanced at me and motioned for me to join them, so I walked over, trying to force jealous feelings from my gut. It would just have been so much easier if Knight decided to surround himself with women who were less than attractive. Really, was that too much to ask?

"Dulce, this is Rachel Wallace," he said as he glanced back at his "friend" and smiled at her. "MJ, this is Dulcie O'Neil."

Rachel extended her hand and smiled at me warmly. "I've heard so much about you," she said with a grin. "It's really great to finally meet you."

"You too," I said and forced a smile. "Though I'm not sure how you and Knight know each other?"

She started to color a bit and dropped her chin as if she was embarrassed.

"We used to date," Knight answered as I felt my eyes widen and the jealousy that had been threatening me earlier suddenly amplified tenfold.

"Oh," I said, not really knowing what else there was to say.

"That was a long time ago," Rachel added quickly, as if to assure me that neither of them had feelings for one another anymore. Something which waited to be seen …

"Oh, I found MJ for you, Knight," Erica said as she faced Knight with a smile.

"Thanks," Knight said, before turning to face me. "MJ worked for me as a Regulator before I came to Splendor."

Hmm, so I wasn't the only employee he'd ever dated. Interesting. Not so much interesting, actually, as it was irritating.

"She was a very good Regulator so I thought it would behoove us to have her on our team," he finished, obviously realizing it was important to explain exactly why he'd decided to include his ex-girlfriend.

"The more, the merrier, right?" I said with a forced smile. "So should I call you Rachel or MJ?" I asked, facing her.

She blushed. "Most people call me Rachel. MJ is just a nickname I've had since I was little."

"Ah," I said and nodded. "What does it stand for?"

"Minnie Jean," she said with a quick smile.

Not wanting to focus on the fact that Knight and she had been close enough for him to refer to her using her nickname she'd had since she was a kid, I instead decided to focus on Erica as she took a deep breath and grinned broadly. Her red hair stood out in stark contrast to the snow-covered ground. The first two times I'd met her, her hair was aqua blue and then canary yellow. Today, it was still cutely bobbed and just as red as Dia's jacket.

Erica closed her eyes and held her hands up on either side of her, inhaling deeply. When she opened her eyes again, they appeared to be backlit green. She opened her palms wide and a glowing white light appeared in each of them. The tail of the light seemed to push up from the snow-covered ground, through her palms, and shattered into a beautiful display of prismatic light. She threw her hands upward and the air suddenly responded with a deluge of falling snow. It landed on all of us and looking at the horizon, I realized it was snowing as far as I could see.

I glanced at Erica again and she dropped her hands as she smiled. "It's good to be a nymph," she said simply. Then she turned back to face the Durango and frowned. "Dude,

Fagan, get a move on!" she called to the man still sitting in the backseat. What in the hell he'd been doing back there was anyone's guess.

She faced me again and rolled her eyes as Fagan obediently opened the door and stepped outside. He appeared less than pleased when the snow starting dusting his head and shoulders. Fagan was a Drow, and just as his species dictated, he seemed forever in a bad mood, a scowl tightening his otherwise blasé features. Drows were in the same family as elves, but more like their grumpier cousins.

He took a few steps forward, looking austere but regal with his immense height (he was probably six feet, four inches, if I had to guess) and his navy blue sweater. He was incredibly skinny and the dark rings beneath his eyes along with his sallow complexion gave him the overall look of someone malnourished.

"Where the hell have you been?" Quill asked, grabbing my attention as he intercepted Sam and me. He grabbed both of my shoulders and I could see the pain in his eyes. Quillan Beaurigard was probably tied with the second most handsome man I'd ever laid eyes on. Tied only with Bram. First place was still reserved for Knight. Quill was tall, though not as tall as Knight, but his dark golden hair and amber eyes that matched the olive tone of his skin, definitely made him a looker.

"Hey," Knight warned, glaring at Quill as he took a step forward. "Take your hands off her."

"It's fine," I started, spearing them both with my less-than-thrilled expression.

"Do you really think I'd hurt her?" Quill asked, frowning at the Loki.

"Boys, boys, boys," Dia interrupted. "There is plenty of the fairy to go around, so just cool yer britches."

"She is so damn lucky," Erica said to Dia, her eyes plastered on Knight. "What I would do with that much deliciousness all rolled into one hot ass Loki …"

16

"Get in line, honey," Dia responded. "Right behind me."

I just shook my head as I faced Sam and Quill again. "I'm fine," I said, smiling apologetically. "I've been with Bram the last couple of days."

"Whoever came up with the idea to leave you with Bram was a fucking moron," Quill spat out, his gaze resting on Knight. I didn't have the wherewithal to inform him that the idea wasn't Knight's but Bram's. Apparently, Knight was also past the point of useless conversations because he didn't say anything either. He merely eyed Quill with daggers.

"This sistah's goin' inside, y'all," Dia sang out in her melodious voice. "I'm about ta freeze the diva outta me!"

TWO

"Nice digs," Erica said as she glanced around the inside of the lodge and chomped on a piece of what smelled like strawberry bubble gum. She took a seat on one of two brown-and-grey upholstered chairs in the living room, while Fagan grabbed the matching chair beside her. Rachel sat on the arm of Erica's chair, both of them obviously friends.

I shivered as a cold wind forced itself through the front door, wrapping its icy fingers around my body. Trey closed the door behind me as I looked through the windows and noticed a dark grey sky attempting to obscure the otherwise snowy white horizon. The longer I watched, the darker it became until I realized dusk was already falling upon us. The flurries of snow increased and came down faster. I wasn't sure if Erica might have somehow affected the natural progression of daylight with her little magical stunt that she'd performed earlier, but it definitely seemed like dusk had arrived too soon. Or maybe the incredibly shortened day had something to do with our traveling through portals? Either way, the daylight hadn't lasted as long as it normally did.

Abandoning my curiosity as to why evening was fast approaching, I turned my attention to Knight. He was standing in front of the daunting floor-to-ceiling fireplace, leaning one beefy arm nonchalantly on the mantel while he waited for the rest of us to take our seats. Both sides of the enormous hearth were flanked by twin, knotty alder bookcases. Along with the two lounge chairs, there was also a tan leather couch placed in front of the fire, where Dia and Sam sat. Trey had already plopped himself on the hearth beside the fire, at Knight's feet.

"Girl, there's room here," Dia sang out when it became apparent that I still hadn't found a place to rest my butt. She made an exaggerated show of moving to the far end of the couch and patting the empty space between Sam and her encouragingly.

"Thanks, D," I said with a smile as I took the proffered spot. Sensing someone behind me, I glanced up and noticed Quill. I gave him a quick but friendly smile but he didn't return it. Instead, he just gazed at me, wearing an expression I couldn't place.

"Christina sure knows how to live the high life," Erica commented as she eyed her surroundings again before blowing an enormous pink bubble.

"You can say that again," Rachel agreed.

"*I* own this place," Knight corrected them. I couldn't mask my surprise since I had no idea that Knight had even been to Germany, let alone bought a cabin (or was it termed a chalet?) here. The Loki cleared his throat, which I assumed was a sign that he wanted our meeting to commence.

"As I'm sure you're all aware, I'm subbing for Christina," he said.

"I can't believe Melchior fed her *Blueliss*," Erica whispered to Rachel, who shook her head in agreement to the latest revelation. *Blueliss* was an illegal narcotic capable of voiding the user's memories. In the process, Melchior managed to imprint his own will upon Christina, thereby coercing her into revealing all our secrets.

"I'm afraid to say that the time for staging a game plan is over," Knight continued. "It's now time to take action."

"What does that mean?" Fagan inquired accusatorily.

"It means we must invade the Netherworld now," I answered.

"Balls!" Trey exclaimed, his eyes wide as he shook his head in apparent surprise.

Dia nodded while Sam's mouth dropped open and Erica's gum bubble snapped against her lips.

"Are we ready for this?" Fagan continued.

19

"We have no other choice," Knight replied, his lips in a steel-like line and his eyes discouraging argument.

"MJ and I can rally our soldiers as soon as we need to," Erica offered. Seeing as how she'd stopped chomping her gum, I half wondered if the shock of Knight's announcement made her accidentally swallow it.

"I believe an enforceable draft should be demanded of all eligible creatures," Fagan added, holding his chin up high in a rendition of "I'm right and no one better argue with me."

"A draft?" Dia repeated.

Fagan nodded. "Anyone of age, who can use his or her magic must be recruited; otherwise, we have no chance in Hades of defeating Melchior."

"When this meeting is dismissed, Erica and MJ, please rally the soldiers," Knight said, then turning to Fagan, he continued, "A draft should be instituted immediately." Knight took a deep breath. "And I agree; any creatures of age who are capable enough should be recruited."

"When are you planning this attack?" Quill suddenly piped up from behind me. At the same time, I could feel his hands on my shoulders as he began massaging them. I was so surprised, I didn't even react.

Knight didn't respond right away. Instead, his eyes settled on Quill's hands like a hawk on a field mouse. Half a second later, his eyes narrowed and a familiar, whitish glow started to eclipse his irises. I could see his hands closing into fists.

I managed to wiggle my way out of Quill's hold and leaned forward a bit in an effort to deter him from touching me again. It was a strange show of affection on his part, since he'd never rubbed my shoulders before. It just felt awkward and forced—like he was deliberately going out of his way to piss Knight off. I glanced back at Knight, who was still glaring at Quill, and cleared my throat, urging Knight to get on with it.

He dropped his murderous gaze from Quill and seemed to study the floor for a second or two. Then, after apparently remembering what he was in the middle of discussing, he glanced back up again. This time, his eyes returned to normal and his hands were no longer balled into fists.

"We have two days," he said simply.

"Two days!" Fagan exclaimed in disbelief.

"That's not much time," Rachel said, eyeing Knight with worry.

"Double balls!" Trey choked, a definite look of trepidation in his eyes.

"Two days isn't enough time," Quill protested. He walked around the couch and took a seat on the armrest, just beside Sam. "You're planning on fighting the Netherworld Guard. Do you have any idea of the threat they pose?"

Knight continued to glare at the elf. "I am very aware of the threat they pose. Let me remind you that I spent the majority of my life training in the Netherworld."

Quill quirked an unimpressed brow. "Then it should be obvious that this is a complete fool's mission."

"Quill, we have no other choice," I said and swallowed hard, seeing how this wasn't going exactly well. "Melchior already knows too much. The longer we wait, the greater the risk for us."

"We act now," Knight repeated with fortified resolve. "And if you aren't with us, you're against us, as far as I'm concerned."

"Lose the attitude, beefcakes," Quill shot back. "I'm on your side."

At the term "beefcakes," I winced because I knew Knight wouldn't appreciate the title.

"For your information, Beaurigard," the Loki started as he took a step forward. His tone of voice was frostily reserved. "The only reason you're here is because Dulcie insisted on it. If I had things my way, you'd still be behind bars."

21

I could only eye Quill's profile from where I sat on the couch, but I distinctly saw his furrowed eyebrows, which only intensified the scowl on his face. "Well, then, I guess I have Dulce to thank, don't I?"

"Enough," I said, holding my hands up in surrender. "These conversations are tiresome, and they don't get us any closer to our goal."

"You're both manly men, okay? We get it," Erica added, shaking her head in frustration. She turned to Rachel and added, "Men! Chicks never pull this much crap."

"I guess some things don't change," Rachel said as she glanced at Knight and shook her head. Yep, the familiarity between the two was definitely irritating to say the least.

"Woo-hoo is there some testosterone in the room!" Dia said with a smile as she fanned herself with her hand. Then, turning to Quill, she said, "I'm sorry, Mr. Sexy Elf, but my money's on the Loki."

"As I was saying," Knight continued, even though he slipped Dia a quick smile, "we have two days to rally the soldiers and get the draft into effect. It shouldn't be too great a feat, Fagan, considering everyone is already assembled in the Compounds."

"Don't concern yourself with the particulars," Fagan replied stonily. "I was aptly chosen for my post, and you will have your drafted participants when you require them."

Knight didn't say anything more, but simply nodded.

"Quill, we're going to need you to help us too," I said in a soft voice, glancing at my old friend. "You need to teach us to think like my father thinks."

He looked at me and smiled warmly, lending his handsome face a soft expression. "I will help you however I can. You know that, Dulce."

I nodded. "You play a big part because you know my father better than any of us. That's why I insisted on your participation."

Quill sighed as he rubbed the blond stubble on his chin. "Well, I do and I don't know your father well. Yes,

22

I've been working for him for many years, but your father is a master in the art of surviving and that's not by accident. He knows how to keep people close without letting them get too close."

I was spared the chance to respond when there was a loud knock on the door. I immediately eyed Knight, since I had no clue who would be calling, especially so late at night. But the Loki also wore a blank expression. When I scanned the other people in the room, I noticed everyone shared the same general look of bewildered surprise. As far as we knew, with the obvious exception of Christina, The Resistance team was already present and accounted for. Furthermore, we were assembled out in the middle of nowhere, so who in hell would be visiting now?

I stood up, intending to answer the door, but Knight's voice stopped me. "No, Dulce," he said in a tone that forbade me to argue with him. Then he walked past me, to see to our visitor himself. Abandoning any argument, since it wasn't worth waging, (hey, it was *his* house) I just sighed and watched him open the door.

"What a shame that I was not invited to your little rendezvous," Bram's accent rang out. The dashing vampire sidestepped Knight and showed himself into the living room. He was wearing black slacks and a navy blue, knitted sweater that looked especially impressive next to the pitch black of his hair. As soon as he entered the room, a draft of air followed him, which enveloped me in Bram's unique scent. It was something very clean, but with a hint of earthiness.

"How the hell did you find us?" Knight asked in an acid tone. He closed the door behind him, though, so I figured he figured Bram's visit wouldn't be a short one.

Bram took turns smiling at each of the women in the room, his eyes settling on Rachel a little longer than was polite, before addressing the furious Loki. "Quite simple, my brutish friend."

23

At the mention of Knight as Bram's "brutish friend," I had to laugh. Hearing Sam and Erica also giggling from the corner of the room, I wasn't the only one to see the humor in Bram's description of Knight.

"I tracked my phone, which still resides in our lovely fairy's possession," Bram finished. He extended his manicured hand, inspecting his nails as he smiled with visible pride.

Damn, I'd forgotten about the fact that I'd put Bram's cell phone in my pocket. I reached down to feel the lump in my jeans pocket, the sure reminder that it was really still there. And, yes, it was.

"You aren't welcome here," Knight said.

"I realize you and I do not run in quite the same circles," Bram answered with a phony smile. He turned away from Knight and began approaching all of us. When he strode past Erica, she wolf-whistled to Dia, who just nodded her silent agreement that even though Bram was more than aware of it; he was pretty hot.

Bram walked over to the fireplace and pretended to warm his hands in front of the fire. It was really all for show, because as a vampire, he was perpetually cold. No amount of outside warmth had any impact on his internal temperature. He stopped walking when he was just beside Trey. The hobgoblin remained seated on the hearth, gazing up at Bram with what appeared to be admiration.

"Hiya," Trey said with a bucktoothed smile.

Glancing down at Trey, Bram half-smiled, doing little to conceal his distaste. He then patted Trey on the head as though he were a trusted, St. Bernard wearing a little, red, emergency tankard of Schnapp's secured to his collar. I rolled my eyes at Bram's nerve, but spared a comment when his piercing eyes found mine.

"I have information that all of you will, no doubt, find useful," he said, his English accent sounding particularly heavy. He again allowed his gaze to settle on Rachel, his expression one of: "How you doin'?"

24

"Where is Christina?" Fagan demanded with a skeptical frown, making it more than obvious that Bram wasn't surrounded by any supporters.

Bram arched an irritated brow in Fagan's direction before facing me again. "Your leader is safe, you may all rest assured. She is recuperating from the effects of the drug Melchior forced upon her." Then, shaking his head like the whole situation was a big shame, he pretended to give a damn about Christina's well-being.

"Don't think any of us trusts you for one second," Knight continued, his eyes narrowed and angry. "I have a mind to tell you just what I think about you working for Melchior this entire time."

"*With* Melchior, kind sir, not *for*," Bram corrected him immediately, wearing a placid grin although his eyes burned. "I have never worked *for* anyone, save myself."

"Regardless, Dulcie trusted you, and you not only lied to her the whole time, but you lied to all of us," Knight continued, studying the vampire with undisguised aversion. "The ANC doesn't regard liars and manipulators well."

Bram averted his eyes from Knight's less-than-thrilled countenance and looked at me again. "I have always valued Dulcie's trust in me, and I have never harmed my sweet," he replied. "And as to the ANC, I come here now with my proverbial tail between my legs."

"Ha! Your tail between your legs?" Dia laughed as she shook her head. "That'll be a fine day when Bram's tail goes between his legs."

Yep, I had to agree. If there was one thing I knew about Bram, it was that any and everything he did never included his tail between his legs. It was more appropriate to say that Bram didn't participate in anything that didn't suit his own ends. He was and always had been a narcissist, around whom the world revolved, in his opinion anyway.

"I realize the time for choosing sides is now upon me," Bram continued and winked at me, hinting to the fact that I was the one who forced him into finally revealing his cards and choosing which side he was on—ours or my father's. "My appearance here this evening, I hope you all realize, is testimony that I have chosen you."

"What the hell does ...?" Knight started, but Bram interrupted him.

"And now, as I strive to benefit my brethren from the Netherworld, I come bearing gifts—gifts in the form of privileged information."

Beware of Bram bearing gifts echoed through my head.

"Then out with it," Knight said. "Whatever the hell you have to offer us, you better get to it because I'm not a patient man." He took a deep breath, and his lips curled angrily. "And when it involves spineless, manipulative bloodsuckers, I'm even less tolerant."

Bram smiled at Knight as if the Loki had just announced Bran won the title of "Sexiest Man Alive" (or Not Alive in Bram's case). Then slapping his hands together with an eager expression, he faced me again.

"Very good, my dear, sweet Dulcie, please accompany me." He held his arm out as he approached me. At the same time, Knight stepped between both of us, confronting Bram. Less than three inches of air separated the two, and they were about the same height, although Knight was definitely broader.

"She's not going anywhere with you," Knight spat out. "Whatever you have to say, say it now and make it quick. You've already overstayed your welcome."

Bram chuckled lightly before tsking and shaking his head. "As the information I possess remains mine, I shall divulge it, when, how and to whom I see fit."

"Knight, just let him tell me whatever he needs to tell me," I argued dejectedly. Bram was about pomp and circumstance and the sooner everyone realized the only way to get what they wanted from him was to play his game, the better.

"No," Knight said, shaking his head. "I'm tired of allowing him to play his little games." He faced Bram. "You're in my house now and you'll play by my rules."

"Your home, is it?" Bram looked around himself, with a feigned mask of surprise. "Although I find it a bit barbarian for my taste, it certainly seems to suit you nicely."

"Enough!" I said for the second time that evening. I shook my head in exasperation because both men were, in a word, maddening. "Bram, whatever you have to say to me, say it quickly. I've had to deal with more machismo than I can handle today."

Bram nodded and sidestepped Knight, offering me his arm again. "Please allow me to escort you to the door, my dear."

Knight grumbled something indecipherable as I walked with Bram to the door. When we were out of earshot, Bram stopped walking and held the doorknob as he faced me. "You continue to breach our contract," he started.

I sighed long and hard, remembering the contract we'd made prior to visiting the Netherworld. I'd pledged to dine with Bram five times in return for his accompaniment (and protection) in the Netherworld. I still owed him three dinner dates.

"You want to do dinner?" I asked with a frown since I didn't feel like I had enough time period, let alone wasting it on Bram.

"Yes, my dear, I would like that very much."

As he glanced down at my jeans and long-sleeved shirt, his expression turned to one of repugnance. "Unfortunately, I failed to remember to procure a gown for you. I suppose that … outfit will have to suffice." Then another idea occurred to him and he suggested, "Unless you would prefer to dine naked?"

"Holy Hades no," I grumbled, shaking my head. Yes, I could have created anything Bram wanted with my magic but if he didn't remember as much, I wasn't about to remind him. "When do you want to leave?"

"Now, Sweet. I hunger for your … company."

I turned to Knight who was fast approaching me. "What does he want?" he asked, glaring viciously at the vampire.

"I have to go to dinner with him."

"What?" Knight ground out. "What the fuck for?"

"Because I agreed to do it a long time ago and if I don't, I'm in breach of contract."

Knight shook his head. "Who the fuck cares? As far as I'm concerned, any pacts you made with that bastard aren't worth shit."

"And he has information for us that he won't give us any other way," I reminded him, throwing my hands on my hips.

Knight shook his head and rubbed the back of his neck the way he did whenever he was frustrated. He sighed as he walked past me and addressed Bram. "You touch her and the only thing left of you will be your fangs."

"You are so poetic, my primitive friend. I ardently assure you I hold Sweet's safety in my uppermost regard."

"Dulcie, keep that phone on," Knight said, before he returned his full attention to Bram. "You have one hour, bloodsucker, and if she's even half a second late, there will be hell to pay."

Bram nodded. "Very well. Sweet, it seems you must eat rapidly."

As he offered his arm again, I accepted it with stoic resignation.

I took my seat across from Bram in the closest "restaurant" we could find, something that reminded me of a diner, only German-style. The plastic booth seats were red, to match the red, black and yellow tablecloths, the colors of the German flag. Due to our severe time constraints, we'd ended up here, but it was so busy, we had trouble getting a seat. After relying on his vampire persuasion, Bram accepted the hostess's offer of the only available booth in the place. It happened to be in the corner of the restaurant, on the way to the kitchen. Consequently, Bram was inadvertently nudged in the shoulder twice by the hurried wait staff. After a bowl of scalding hot soup was nearly dumped over Bram's head, the hapless waiter brought him an extra large serving of Spaetzle, and announced it was on the house.

Of course, Bram, as a bloodsucker, was unimpressed by the Spaetzle. Instead, he began picking and examining it as if he were a finicky five-year-old inspecting a bowl of asparagus. For me however, I took great pleasure in witnessing the pretentious vampire crammed into a plastic booth with the sounds of Oompah music in the background. The icing on the cake, however, was the diner sitting at the table nearest us. Our tables were so close, the woman was less than five feet away from Bram. She looked like an Amazon: so tall, she dwarfed her chair, the table, and her dining partner, who was a small, mousey woman. She was easily the tallest woman I'd ever seen, and also incredibly broad. Her colossal size (I would have bet she was even taller than Bram) was owing to large bones and strong muscles though, and not from fat. Her platinum-blond hair was confined to a bun behind her head, pulled so tightly, it appeared to slant the corner of her eyes up. She had the look of someone whose hair had gotten caught in a pair of double doors.

What pleased me to no end, however, was when this mammoth woman decided she liked Bram. She kept smiling and making doe eyes at him, stealing glances his way whenever the opportunity arose. As Bram continued to pick at his Spaetzle, and for all intents and purposes, ignored the enormous woman, I watched her lean forward and whisper to her female acquaintance.

"Ich wette er wuerde lieber meine Spaetzle essen."

Being unfamiliar with the German language, I figured Bram, who was very cultured and refined, probably understood. "You speak German, right?" I whispered.

"Unfortunately, yes," he grumbled as he folded his arms across his chest and eyed me with a drawn brow, revealing an overall expression of someone less than enthusiastic.

"So what did that woman just say about you?" I asked in another whisper, unable to hide my growing smile.

Bram sighed, looking like a tragic Shakespearean hero, and answered, "She told her friend that I would prefer eating her Spaetzle rather than this one." He glanced down at the dumplings and frowned as he added, "And on that subject, I most vigorously assure you that such is definitely not the case."

I erupted into a fit of laughter, which only further irritated Bram. I just couldn't help it though and I also couldn't remember the last time I'd laughed so hard. As soon as I regained my self-control, the German woman glanced over at Bram. With a diminutive wave, she batted her eyelashes profusely. I took one look at Bram, who was now pretending extreme interest in his Spaetzle, and burst into another fit of euphoria.

"It pleases me to no end that you find this situation so entertaining," he said, still frowning. "I envisioned our evening quite unlike what it has turned out to be."

"Sorry," I replied as sincerely as possible. When another eruption of laughter threatened to emerge, I wasn't sure how, but I managed to subdue it. Taking a deep breath, I turned to the question of why we were sitting here in the first place. "Okay, no more humor at your expense. I apologize." I took another deep breath. "So what's this information you have for me?"

Bram was spared the need to respond when the waiter returned and brought with him my dinner—bratwurst with a side of fried potatoes. I thanked the man and cut a piece of my sausage, spearing it on my fork before bringing it to my mouth and chewing, all the while thanking Hades I wasn't a vampire because German food was damn good.

"Have you agreed upon a strategy as to how you will invade the Netherworld, Sweet?" Bram asked as he leaned back into the booth and stretched his long legs out so they butted up against mine. Clasping his hands behind his neck, he studied me purposefully as the woman beside him giggled and gushed to her companion. For all the ennui he pretended to assume, I was more than sure that he was lapping up all the attention.

"I guess we'll have to force our way through the portals," I answered non-committedly. I honestly wasn't exactly sure of the best way forward. I considered it a problem for Knight to figure out because it wasn't like I knew much at all about portal travel to and from the Netherworld to begin with.

"Sweet, do you honestly believe Melchior would not have guards posted at every portal entrance to the Netherworld?" He didn't wait for me to answer his question and instead shook his head as he tsked me. "Come now, Sweet, your father is no fool."

"I never said he was," I barked back. "And as to your question, no, I don't know what defensive measures Melchior has taken, because last I checked, I wasn't a mind reader."

Bram nodded, his expression one hinting that he hadn't taken my words as a slight. Instead, his attention moved to the foot of the German woman who was feebly attempting to play footsie with him. Instantly, he sat up straight and pulled his legs back from under the table, refusing to so much as incline his head in her direction. Meanwhile, she giggled as she whispered to her companion something about him "playing hard to get."

Now focused on my face, Bram seemed to be attempting to remember where our conversation was headed. Seeing the perplexed expression in his eyes, I said in a hushed tone, if only to foil any would-be eavesdroppers,

31

"You asked me how I intended to invade the Netherworld; and I said we would try the portals, to which you responded by tearing my answer apart."

"Ah, yes, now I recall. To answer your admission that you have no idea what defensive measures your father has taken, I do possess that knowledge, my dear. I am more than well aware of the obstacles that lie before you in the Netherworld."

"So what's the answer then, Bram?"

"The answer, my sweet Dulcie, is to use the element of surprise to your distinct advantage."

"Which means what?"

Bram arched a brow, frowning at me as if the answer was apparent. "Enter the Netherworld via a portal at which Melchior will not have guards posted," he finished. He acted as if it were no big deal at all to find some random portal that my father either didn't know about, or didn't post guards to, for some unknown reason.

"I hope you're also going to tell me you know the locations of these portals?" I asked and then paused to chew my food, which I swallowed down with a hefty swig of beer.

"Not locations of existing portals, my dear; but yes, I do have a suggestion for you."

Spearing a potato with my fork, I took a bite, feeling my tolerance level for Bram nearing its limit. "So what's the answer?"

Bram didn't respond right away, but reached inside his pants pocket and produced something that looked like a can opener. It was maybe four inches tall and an inch wide, and made from some sort of metal that gleamed in the low light. He handed the gadget to me and I was surprised by how little it weighed.

"What is this?" I asked.

"This, my dear, is a portal ripping device."

"A what?" I demanded.

Bram smiled, even chuckling slightly as if to show his amusement. "This handy little tool will allow you to cut a portal anywhere you desire."

I glanced at him in disbelief for a second or two, trying to understand just what he meant. "So if I wanted to, I could use this thing to create a portal right here?" I asked, inclining my head to include the immediate space around us. Bram simply nodded. "And that portal would take me to the Netherworld?" I finished.

Bram nodded again. "This ripping device will cut a portal wherever you intend it. You simply program it to the location of wherever you desire to go."

"How?" I continued.

Bram smiled that patronizing grin of his and opened his hand in a charade of "give it back to me and I'll tell you." I dropped the can opener looking thing into his palm and watched as he thought to himself and hummed annoyingly.

"Well?" I demanded.

"I am just deciding on a location, my dear," he answered. "Perhaps something arbitrary," he said more to himself than to me. Then he turned what appeared to be a handle on the devise clockwise four ticks and then counter clockwise five ticks.

"What was that?" I insisted.

"I programmed it forty degrees north by fifty degrees west," he answered smugly. Then he glanced down at the implement, smiling at it as if impressed, before returning his gaze to me. "If this were not a tutorial, I should simply rotate the device so the edge is furthermost from me and then I would draw it toward me as if I were slicing through the air." He smiled more broadly. "And then a portal would appear between here and there."

He then turned the handle a few more times, apparently clearing it before handing it back to me again. "So I just program it with my location and then slice the air and that's it?" I asked doubtfully.

33

Bram nodded. "Quite simple. You must always begin with the northern or southern coordinates. Turn the handle clockwise for north and counterclockwise for south. Once you have entered those coordinates, you enter the western or eastern coordinates. Clockwise for east and counter for west."

"And the number of clicks dictates the degrees?" I asked.

He nodded. "You simply multiply the number of clicks by ten. Two clicks equals twenty, four clicks equals forty and so on."

"What if my coordinate is forty-three?" I asked, sharing the first example that occurred to me.

"You would click forward four times and then turn the handle one click in reverse before proceeding to the three clicks which would symbolize forty-three." Then he grinned boyishly.

I glanced down at the portal ripper in my hand, replaying Bram's directions in my head to make sure they were committed to memory. Once I was satisfied they were, I looked up at him again. "Where did you get this?"

Bram shook his head. "That is unimportant."

"Does Melchior know you have it?"

"No, this is a mere prototype. Melchior does not even know it exists."

My eyes grew wide as I realized what this portal ripper could mean for us. "When you mentioned the element of surprise earlier," I started, but Bram interrupted me.

"I was not speaking in abstracts." He leaned forward and eyed me purposely. "This tool could be the single advantage leading to victory over your father."

THREE

When Bram and I returned to the lodge, I noticed Dia's red Escalade and Rachel's Land Rover were nowhere to be seen, so I figured the meeting was adjourned. Knight's Suburban still sat in the driveway, only now it was covered with maybe two inches of snow. Bram pulled up beside it, in one of his many vehicles—this one a black Lotus. After killing the engine and making a big show of opening my door, he insisted on walking me to the front door, like he was sixteen years old and trying to make a good impression on my folks. We said our good-byes, but when he attempted to kiss me on the cheek, I pulled away. It wasn't that I was particularly opposed to a pretty harmless kiss on the cheek, but I imagined that such a seemingly innocent act could, and most probably would, inflame Knight. And that was a situation I wanted to steer clear of by all means. Apparently realizing that kissing me anywhere near my face was a no-go, Bram reached for my hand. He bowed in a great show of affected and outdated gallantry before bringing his ice cold lips to the top of my hand.

"As always, I have enjoyed our time together, Sweet, however short it had to be and," he cleared his throat, frowning "fraught with … distractions."

I laughed and assumed he was referring to the German woman who'd taken a shine to him, which turned out to make my evening. Speaking of the woman, after eating as much of my dinner as I could, Bram paid the bill, and we both stood up with the clear intention of leaving. What happened next is forever etched in my mind, albeit shrouded in hilarious infamy. As soon as Bram stood, the woman also shot to her feet alarmingly quickly (after lazily making idle small talk with her mousy companion, both of whom had already finished their food at least ten minutes earlier). In her rapid response to our departure, she nearly knocked her table over. Just as expected, she towered over Bram (who was tall, in his own right, well over six feet). Then she theatrically announced she had to find the "*toilette,*" evidently assuming Bram was en route to the lavatory because she made it a point to brush against him. Well, "brushing against him" doesn't accurately describe what happened. Really, it was more fitting to say she pretended to trip and chose Bram to break her fall. With arms flailing, she thrust her enormous breasts into his face while he looked on in absolute horror. Then her boobs simply engulfed Bram's head as his face disappeared into her doughy mounds of flesh, lending him an uncanny resemblance to the headless horseman, minus the horse.

The only thing that crossed my mind at that moment was the line "That's a huge bitch!" from *Deuce Bigalow*.

It was an evening I doubt I could ever forget.

I felt a smile curling my lips at the recollection of Bram's adventures with the German woman, but managed to dispel it. I figured it wasn't something he would want to recount anytime soon. And besides, he *had* supplied me with the portal ripper …

"Thanks, for … uh, everything, Bram," I said and offered him a genuine, heartfelt smile before raising my hand to knock on the front door of Knight's lodge, lest I freeze to death on the doorstep. Before I had the chance to make contact with it, the door opened on its own accord, revealing a very unhappy Loki looming before us.

"You're a minute late," he grumbled at the vampire, crossing his arms against his chest and looking pretty pissed off.

Bram's eyebrows reached for the sky in a practiced but feigned expression of surprise. "How odd. According to my timepiece," he said as he fished out a pocket watch from another era, "I am a minute early." Then he shrugged, smiling broadly. "I suppose we should respectfully split the difference and assume I was on time."

Knight muttered something I couldn't understand while holding the door wide open for me. With a wave to Bram, I squeezed past the Loki, and relished the warmth of Knight's house as it settled into my bones, thawing the cold harshness of the elements.

"We shall soon be in touch, my dear," Bram called out behind me. "And I should appreciate it if you would put in a good word for me with the brunette."

I just shook my head, forever surprised by his nerve. I took off my down jacket and draped it over the chair Erica had formerly occupied, turning to face Knight as he closed the door behind him. Seconds later, the lights from the Lotus reflected through the windows and I heard the sound of the engine purring as Bram backed up, his tires crunching the snow. Moments later, he faded away down the driveway.

"How was your date?" Knight asked with a scowl as he approached the fireplace and stepped onto the hearth.

"It was hardly a date," I answered, figuring he was going to start a game of twenty questions. "You heard him, he has the hots for MJ," I said her name in a dreamy-like way. "Apparently he's not the only one."

Knight raised his eyebrows at me, smiling. "Someone sounds jealous."

"Well, when one of your ex-girlfriends randomly shows up, it's a little off-putting."

Knight chuckled. "I would hardly call MJ my ex-girlfriend. We dated very briefly and ended up being much better friends."

"Oh, and why was that?" I asked, my hands on my hips.

"Because she was in love with someone else who she ended up marrying," he finished with a smile.

"I see," I said and couldn't help feeling stupid. "But it sounds like you were into her?"

Knight shrugged. "At the time, yes I was. But that was before I met a feisty little fairy who made me stop thinking about other women altogether."

I couldn't help but smile at him. Sometimes he knew exactly the right things to say.

"So going back to your date with Bram," Knight started.

"It wasn't a date!"

Knight had never liked Bram, and at one point in time, he'd been convinced that I was dating the vampire, something which I never had, nor ever would. Although not exactly his nemesis, Knight definitely wouldn't call Bram a friend.

Sitting on the leather couch, I reached down and untied my shoelaces. I took off my shoes and socks to make myself comfortable because I had an inkling this lodge would probably be our refuge for the remainder of the evening. Propping a pillow against the arm rest of the couch, I curled up against it, and stretched my legs out.

"Tell that to Bram; he clearly thought it was a date," Knight continued with tightened lips and eyes still narrowed. But as angry as he appeared to be, he managed to keep his temper and/or jealousy in check—owing to the fact that his eyes weren't glowing. Well, not yet, anyway.

"Bram would call coasting through McDonald's drive-through a date," I answered.

Knight smiled at my joke, but it was a rushed smile hinting that he was keen on acquiring more information. "So was it a complete waste of your time? Or did he actually come through on that information he promised earlier?"

I stifled a yawn, feeling increasingly tired with my full belly and the radiant warmth from the fireplace. "He delivered," I said simply, reaching into my pants pocket, where I'd placed the portal ripper for safekeeping. I withdrew the small instrument from my pocket and offered it to Knight. He took the few steps separating us and grasped it in his large hand, flipping it as he examined it curiously. It was obvious that he'd never seen one before.

"What is it?" he asked finally, continuing to study the tool in the low firelight.

"Bram called it a portal ripper," I answered and sat up, afraid I might accidentally surrender to my body's need to sleep if I remained sprawled on top of the couch.

"A portal ripper?" Knight repeated absentmindedly as he continued to rotate the device in his hands.

"Apparently, it can cut a portal to the Netherworld wherever we want it to," I told him. "Bram said it could be the single advantage for defeating my father."

"And Bram also exaggerates," Knight was quick to respond as he placed the portal ripper on the mantel and faced me squarely.

"I don't know, seems like a handy gadget to have, if you ask me."

He nodded. "Yes, it seems handy, but that's if you buy what Bram is selling."

"What do you mean?"

Knight shrugged, as though I should have instantly followed his line of reasoning. "Considering Bram worked for your father …"

"*With* my father, not *for*," I chided him with Bram's own words, but added a sly smile.

"As I was saying," he frowned, giving me the feeling that he wasn't in a very good mood. I was already more than certain it was because of my "date" with the vampire. "Since Bram worked with your father all those years, it seems a no-brainer to distrust him. Who's to say that he's not setting us up?" He took a deep breath. "As far as we know, he could be your father's newest mole."

"At this stage of the game, my father would prefer to have us assassinated if he or someone who worked for him knew where to find us. To Melchior, we are worth a lot more dead than alive." I took a deep breath. "Once you, Christina and I are out of the way, there goes The Resistance."

Knight nodded as he ran his hands through his hair, and eyed his boots before bringing his attention back to me. "You make a good point, but I still don't trust Bram."

I shrugged and sighed, having already considered the question of whether or not Bram could be trusted. "I can't say for sure if Bram is completely truthful." I sighed, looking at the fireplace and watching the flames dance along the log before consuming it. I brought my eyes back to Knight's, and was awed as the firelight reflected in his beautiful blue eyes, making them appear almost red. "But I also know that sometimes you have to take a chance in life. Without Bram, we could be headed down a one-way street with no chance of escape. "

"Then it's a chance you're willing to take?" Knight continued, narrowing his gaze on me as he cracked his knuckles.

I shrugged. "I think the answer to your question is pretty obvious."

"You're going with yes, you do trust him," he said, exhaling a pent-up breath. "Then I guess it waits to be seen."

As if to signal the termination of the conversation, he lifted the fire iron and poked the log in the fireplace, which crumbled into embers. Reaching for another large log, he bent over and plopped it onto the fire grate, stoking it with the iron. Standing up, he wiped the debris from the log on his pants before holding his hands behind his back to warm them. The flames of the fire fanned and flickered behind him, creating an aura that silhouetted his swollen deltoids, broad shoulders, and accentuated his trim waist and shapely thighs. I suddenly flashed on the sexual torture he'd inflicted on me in the Suburban while we were en route to this lodge.

Maybe it's time to prove just how much of a bitch payback can be, I told myself. It probably also didn't help that the embers of jealousy were still smoldering inside me.

Silently, I came to my feet. I could feel Knight's eyes on me and saw the question in their depths, as if he insisted on finding out what I was up to. But I just stood there, staring at him boldly, with no trace of bashfulness or shame in my gaze. Then, as seductively as I could, I grabbed the top of my long-sleeved shirt and simply pulled it up and over my head, allowing the tendrils of my hair to snake back around my shoulders, and fall across my collarbone, adorning the black lace of my push-up bra.

"You're not the only one who can replay memories of us in our more … carnal moments," I said quietly, with a cunning smile.

Knight chuckled, but there was a fire in his eyes that burned even more brightly than the fire behind him. I watched his eyes travel down to my breasts, where they loitered on my cleavage. After a few seconds, he brought his attention back up to my face again.

"Is that so?" he asked, another chuckle dying on his lips, but leaving a slight smile in its wake.

"It is," I said simply.

"So tell me all the naughty thoughts swirling around in that head of yours," he demanded.

"All in good time." I unbuckled the button of my jeans, pulling the zipper down as slowly as possible. Knight's eyes never left my body as I slid the jeans down the lengths of my legs. I felt his gaze penetrating my black lace underwear and a blush started to creep across my cheeks. Refusing to allow any timidity or hesitation to consume me, I forced the anxiety aside, and chose instead to channel my inner femme fatale.

I approached him, adding an extra sway to my mostly naked hips. I stepped onto the hearth and glanced up at him, the top of my head only grazing his shoulders. Somehow, the fact that he was so much taller and bigger than I was, not to mention that he could snap me like a twig if he wanted to, turned me on … a lot. There was just something about him—he just made me feel so feminine. I ran my fingers up his shirtfront, dipping my index finger into the recess of his clavicle. With a simple shake of my hand, I could feel a pile of my fairy dust already manifesting in my palm. I opened

41

my hand and allowed the dust to rain down Knight's
shirtfront. At the same time, I walked my index finger down
the center of his chest, while imagining the fabric of his shirt
separating beneath my fingers. I watched as the image I held
in my mind played itself out in reality as Knight's shirt
divided in two, revealing his stunning chest.

Knight's chest never failed to impress me with its deep
valleys and sumptuous peaks of pure muscle. His
exceptionally broad shoulders are definitely something to
write home about and his biceps are probably the size of my
head. Sinking my face into the ropey muscles of his lats
below his arm, I kissed a soft trail, feeling him wince when I
touched an especially ticklish spot. Somehow, knowing this
enormous man was ticklish—someone who was bred to
defend the Netherworld and exterminate any would-be
threats—was sexier than sexy.

"My daydreams always begin with a memory of this,"
I said as I spanned my hand across the soft skin of his naked
chest. I outlined the pale pink, raised scar that started at his
collar bone, and crossed all the way down through his right
pec. He'd told me a long time ago that he'd earned the scar
in a battle with a werewolf, and although some might
consider it a blemish on his otherwise flawless chest scape,
to me, he couldn't be any more perfect.

He started to reach out to touch me, but I shook my
head and firmly pushed his hand back down to his side. I
intended to assert my own right—I was in charge now, and
just like he'd formerly done to me, by teaching me the true
meaning of sexual frustration, I was anxious to return the
favor. But I was going to one-up him.

"Your rules, huh?" he whispered.

"My game, my rules."

I stepped away from him and unclasped my bra, letting
the straps drop down my arms. I crossed my arms against
my chest, cleaving my breasts together so the mounds
appeared even larger, but I shielded my nipples with my
arms.

"No fair," Knight whispered.

I smiled as I dropped my hands to my sides, the bra falling until it landed unceremoniously on the floor. I glanced up at Knight, and relished the fact that his eyes were riveted on my breasts. To be able to possess such power over him gave me a rush, in and of itself.

"You have the most beautiful body I've ever seen," he said in a hushed tone. I could feel my nipples hardening as he scrutinized them.

"That's nice," I answered, trying to sound as indifferent as I could. I had to remind myself not to get too caught up in my own lustful thoughts, since the whole point of this game was retribution. I brought my fingers to my breasts and outlined my alert nipples, feeling goose bumps starting as my nipples hardened even more. I pinched one rosy bud between my index finger and my thumb, rolling it gently. "Whenever I think about your fantastic body, something… happens to me," I continued, remembering I had a story to tell.

"Something happens to you?" he repeated, his voice coming out incredibly breathy. I could see the outline of his penis already straining against his pants. I had to resist staring at it because every time I glanced at it, my giddiness exploded and threatened my delivery, my payback.

"Something that makes me want to … touch myself," I finished, savoring every second of the control I had over this incredible man, this unparalleled creature. As a soldier created in Hades's own image, Knight was the strongest they came. He was brawny and powerful and now this enormous beast hung onto my every word, unable to tear his eyes away from me. And it was so painfully clear that any power he might have had was useless against my own—the age-old wisdom of womankind.

"Where does it make … you want to touch yourself?" he whispered.

I cocked my head to the side, pretending to ponder his question. "Here," I said, lazily looping my index finger

43

around my nipple. "And, maybe here too," I added, encircling my other nipple. "But, mostly down here," I finished as I slid my finger down my stomach before rubbing the outside of my lace panties. Feeling the soft lace, a stinging sensation started from deep down within me.

Knight's eyes fastened on my panties. I continued to graze my fingers across the lace, gasping whenever I strayed too close to the sensitive nub cresting my thighs. Suddenly anxious for more than playful wandering, I pulled my panties to the side, baring myself to Knight. I watched him inhale deeply as the pulse quickened in his neck.

I slid my finger down my vagina, feeling how wet I was. As soon as I skimmed my nub, I moaned out in response, while my knees threatened to collapse. I snatched my finger away as if I'd just been scalded and inwardly chastised myself. I was getting too caught up too fast, too turned on.

"I want to taste you," Knight ground out.

"Hmm, that sounds like a personal problem," I said with a haughty laugh, never having imagined I would so enjoy playing the role of the dominator but the truth of it was that I did.

Knight's eyes narrowed. "You're deliberately trying to torture me."

I didn't say anything right away as I backed up until the leather couch touched my calves. With my eyes still locked on his, I hooked my finger through one side of my panties and drew them down my naked thighs, letting them fall on the floor. Stepping out of them, I sat down on the warm leather.

"You're getting me back for the car ride, aren't you?" he inquired with a powerful stride forward as he stepped off the hearth.

I cocked my head to the side. "Maybe, and maybe not."

Then, prepared for the grande finale, I took a deep breath, and seeing that his eyes were still locked on mine, I opened my legs. Even though it was a simple act—a mere parting of the thighs, I sensed my own power emanating through me. It was as if the single motion of spreading my legs wide open and allowing Knight to behold my naked flesh channeled the enticement of Aphrodite, the goddess of love, herself. I felt like I alone possessed the key to Knight's libido. His eyes traveled the length of me before resting on the space between my legs, and I could see them change. They seemed to go from being sexually charged to ravenously hungry.

At that moment, I had complete mastery over Knight.

"Whatever game you're playing," he panted, "I give up. You win."

Closing my thighs, I laughed, savoring the command I had over him. "That was easier than I imagined."

I started to sit up from the couch, but he was instantly in front of me, his eyes glowing in that weird and wonderful way. Putting his hand against my shoulder, he pushed me back down onto the couch.

"Don't think you're getting off that easily," he grumbled. Removing his shirt, he let each side slowly slide down his muscular forearms. Dropping to his knees, he faced me again, and the irises of his eyes were completely eclipsed by the white glow.

"Feeling slightly threatened by Bram?" I asked, even while wondering if I was taking this game too far.

Knight narrowed his eyes at the mention of Bram and I wasn't sure but it looked like they burned a little more brightly. "Not threatened," he answered. "But let me remind you that I have something Bram doesn't ..."

"And what is that?"

"The beast," he answered with a low, animal growl. It was as if the beast were speaking through him. I felt myself throbbing, my sensitive parts swelling at the thought of the beast within Knight and what it was capable of. I didn't say anything, but noticed the rise and fall of my chest increasing as my heartbeat began to race.

"And it might be more fitting to say you're the jealous one," Knight continued.

"What?" I replied, pretending offense.

"So what's MJ to you," he mimicked, even going so far as to use a girl voice. I threw a sofa pillow at him. He caught it and threw it on the floor, the smile dropping from his face. "Spread your legs," he commanded in a voice that told me not to argue.

With my former power diminishing, I simply obeyed his demand and opened my legs to him. I watched his eyes shift from my own as they settled on my swollen female flesh. The pulse in his neck sped up to match his shallow panting.

He didn't say anything as he studied me, but simply allowed his eyes to devour me. Despite the sensation of being vulnerable, almost like I was being displayed to him in the most exposed fashion, the sexual goddess within me allowed me to vanquish the feeling immediately. Once again, I savored the intensity of the power I still held over him.

With another growl, he buried his face between my legs and the feel of his tongue sucking and pulling at me was almost too much for me to endure. Just when I thought I was about to orgasm, he pulled his tongue away before plunging it deep inside me, causing me to moan out.

"I can never get enough of this," he groaned. His tongue again found my nub and he thrust two fingers inside me as I arched up against him, screaming out my surprise. He pulled his mouth away, but continued plunging his fingers inside me, burying them as high as he could.

"Open your eyes and watch me feel you," he commanded.

Even though it was difficult, I opened my eyes to find him staring at me. Then he averted his gaze to his busy fingers and together we watched as he pushed them in and out of me. I felt him curving his fingers to follow my inner channel as he drove his hand deeper inside me, deeper and

46

faster. That was when he found my G spot. I grew wetter as the smoldering ember deep in my gut turned into an incendiary. My legs were trembling and I clamped my eyes shut tightly, knowing an orgasm was imminent.

"Look at me or I'll stop," he barked.

I opened my eyes just as blissfulness exploded within me and I ground my pelvis against his hand. I cried out, as he impaled me even harder. Without another word, he pulled his fingers out and ripped off his pants, his erect penis bouncing behind them. Grabbing both of my legs, he positioned them above his shoulders as he coaxed himself to me. I felt the head of him at my opening and wrenched myself away in an effort to retain some sense of control. Glancing up at me, he growled again before gripping my thighs and pressing my hamstrings against him. He leaned forward until I could feel him at my opening as he smiled down at me. Ultimately, he knew we'd both won. With that recognition, he thrust inside me as deeply as he could. I screamed out as I buried my nails into his back, feeling him pull out of me again. Gripping his taut rear cheeks between both of my hands, I sunk my nails into his soft skin at the same instant that he penetrated me again. This time he seemed to delve in even deeper than before. He wrapped his hands around my ankles and widened my legs further above his shoulders, pulling slightly away from me so he could watch himself entering me. He put his fingers on the nub between my folds of feminine flesh and started rubbing it back and forth, and then in circles.

"You're going to come for me again, do you understand?" he asked, but it was more like an order.

I simply nodded, at a loss for words. While his fingers continued dancing against me, he put his other hand on my right nipple and pinched it. There was only a slight pain before something began blossoming in my stomach, and I cried out in the throes of another orgasm.

Knight chuckled and pulled out of me. "Get on your knees."

I dutifully turned over and felt him gripping me by my upper thighs as he yanked me backwards. Seconds later, he slammed himself into me as I screamed out.

"I could stare at you like this forever," he said in a tight-lipped voice.

His thrusts suddenly gained momentum as he pushed himself into me as deeply as he could. I bucked beneath him so he wrapped his arm around me to anchor me in place, while reaching around to touch my sensitive spot again.

"Third time's a charm," he whispered into my ear.

His wish became my command and I bucked as another orgasm seized me. As soon as I came down from the high, he thrust into me with renewed vigor. He clutched a handful of my hair and wrapped his hand around the back of my neck as his breathing came in short gasps. A few moments later, he arched against me stiffly.

Now relaxed, he pulled out of me as he collapsed on the couch with a wide grin.

"You are temptation's finest," he said, panting softly.

FOUR

One night gone, one night to go. Then we would invade the Netherworld.

For the first time since deciding on a plan, I could feel my stomach tightening with anxiety and I felt sick. I had no idea why these feelings of apprehension and uneasiness hadn't hit me earlier, but now it seemed like they were trying to make up for lost opportunity.

"Great, good job," Knight said out loud, speaking to Erica through the Bluetooth in the Suburban. We'd already left the lodge in Garmisch and traveled through two portals, so I had no idea where we were now. I glanced outside my window to view miles of rolling hills, complete with white picket fences and nondescript houses. Since we were still driving on the right side of the road (well, according to American custom, anyway) we could still have been in Germany or maybe we were now back in the States.

"Everyone is motivated and ready," Erica continued. Her tone was so chipper, she might as well have announced that her kindergarten class was ready to put on the school play. "I've moved all the soldiers to Compound One, and all the civilians are currently staged at Compound Two. Fagan is also orchestrating the draft so all eligible recruits will be relocated to Compound Four."

"What are we doing in terms of weapons for those creatures who are less than magically inclined?" Knight asked, concentrating on the road ahead of him. I studied him, trying to get any sort of indication as to whether this whole thing was making him nervous or not. But there was nothing in the inflection of his voice nor his posture that even hinted to fretfulness. Instead, he appeared as always—calm, cool and collected, like the serene Loki I knew so well.

49

"Well, we're supplying all the weres, elves and goblins with Op 6s and 7s," Erica's sing-song voice rang out. "We debated doing the same for the vampires, but concluded it would ultimately be a waste of time since they can retain their speed as well as their strength in the Netherworld."

"Yep," Knight said as he nodded. "All creatures will become stronger in the Netherworld, but don't forget the Netherworld Guard is about as strong as they get."

"I know," Erica answered, with an inflection that said she didn't appreciate lectures.

"What's the count so far?" Knight asked. He depressed the accelerator and took a right on a street whose sign was obscured by a nearby tree, maybe a poplar or something of that sort.

I heard the sound of shuffling paper coming through the Bluetooth and guessed Erica was searching through her notes for an answer to Knight's question. "Um, let's see … our top Resistance soldiers number roughly about three hundred. Last I heard from Fagan, he managed to draft another two hundred able-bodied civilians. So that puts us at around five hundred in total." She took a breath. "Not too bad considering you only gave us the go-ahead yesterday."

"Not too bad," Knight agreed, but I couldn't read his expression to detect whether he was pleased with the information or not. "At last tally, the Netherworld Guard numbered well into the upper four hundreds, which tells me this will be a difficult battle for us to win."

"But we *can* win it," Erica interjected quickly. "We outnumber the Guard when you look at the totals. Besides, the Netherworld civilians won't fight so that's another plus on our side."

Knight cocked his head and I could see the disappointment in his eyes. "I guess it remains to be seen."

"So what does that mean?" Erica asked, sounding somewhat crestfallen. "If you don't think our odds are good, we shouldn't even try to invade the Netherworld."

Knight sighed. "I didn't say the odds are against us. I just meant it's not going to be any picnic." She didn't say anything more so Knight continued. "Good job with everything, Erica. Check in with me when you have more information."

"Will do, hot stuff."

He chuckled as he pressed a button on the steering wheel, thereby disconnecting the call. The resulting quiet became pervasive, but since Knight seemed absorbed in his own thoughts, I didn't think I should interrupt him with mine. Once he started to shake his head though, my curiosity to know what he was thinking grew impossible to subdue.

"What are your thoughts?" I asked, almost afraid for his answer. I didn't want to hear him say we should abandon our plan, or abort our mission to dethrone my father.

He tilted his head as if he were pondering my question and took a few seconds to respond. "Our soldiers are just as capable as the Netherworld Guard, but we have much smaller numbers."

"But what about the soldiers Fagan drafted?"

He nodded halfheartedly. "Depending on what types of creatures they are, that could be meaningless. If they possess their own magic, that's great; but if we're talking about a bunch of inexperienced, eighteen-year-old wolves, that's something entirely different." As he glanced over at me, he reached for his cell phone, which lay in the cubby hole beneath the CD player. "Do me a favor? Text Fagan and ask him what the breakdown of all the creatures that he drafted is, will you?"

I nodded and took his phone, doing as he instructed. "If he gives you an answer you don't like, what will that mean?"

"It won't mean much of anything. We've set our wheels in motion and we need to act soon. But, at the same time, I need to know what my team is comprised of so I can make sure I prepare them as best as I know how."

51

I finished texting Fagan and put the phone back into the cubby as an idea occurred to me. "Do you really think we need to regard this as an invasion?" I asked, turning to face him.

He eyed me quickly before returning his gaze to the road. We were on a single, paved lane in the middle of nowhere, with what looked like endless miles of verdant farmland on either side of us. A few cows and sheep punctuated the otherwise monotonous green.

"Is that a rhetorical question?" he asked.

"No," I quickly responded just as Knight's phone began to beep. I picked it up and recognized Fagan's name on the screen. "Vamps, warlocks, witches and wolves," I read Fagan's text out loud.

Knight shrugged. "I guess that will do."

"Okay, going back to our previous conversation," I started as I put the phone back in its cubby. "Just hear me out for a second." I took a big breath, hoping the thoughts circling through my head would make sense when put into words. "The Netherworld Guard answers to my father, right?"

"Yes."

"And from my understanding, it seems the civilians of the Netherworld don't intend to fight either for or against my father; but at the same time, they aren't exactly thrilled with having him as the Head of the Netherworld, right?"

"Yes, most won't fight. But whether or not they would like to see your father deposed? That's anyone's guess."

"Okay, so my point is, why risk the safety of our soldiers and civilians, when all it really takes is the removal of my father from his position as Head of the Netherworld?"

Knight glanced over at me, furrowing his brows. "You mean someone to assassinate him?"

I nodded. "That's exactly what I mean. If we successfully dethrone him, who is next in line to command the Netherworld Guard? And furthermore, would whoever is next in line try to quash us?" I didn't wait for him to respond. "*Who* is second in command?"

Knight narrowed his eyes as if he weren't following me, or didn't think I was on the right track. "Caressa is second in the hierarchy, but that's only for show. As to how much power she actually wields ... she really has none."

"But that's only because my father won't allow her to fulfill her role in the hierarchy." I cleared my throat, excited by the fact that I thought I had a very good point. "Think of it like this, if my father's office is usurped, the Netherworld population will expect Caressa to assume power, right?"

"Yeah, I guess so. I mean, that's how it's set up."

"So Caressa steps in, and since she abhors everything my father represents, she obviously won't allow his legacy to continue."

Knight nodded, but his eyes remained narrowed, which meant he wasn't completely in accordance with the idea. "It makes a lot of sense in theory. In practice, however, there would be a whole lot of potion smugglers and thugs just chomping at the bit to overtake Caressa and slip into your father's place, which puts Caressa's life in imminent danger ..."

"So we beef up the Netherworld Guard to protect her."

He shook his head. "Half, if not most, of them are already involved in the potion smuggling rings."

"Then we throw them in jail and protect her with our own soldiers."

"Again, it sounds good in theory."

"Why not in practice?" I interrupted snidely. To me, the answer was so crystal clear, he was just being pig-headed by refusing to try it my way.

He frowned. "First of all, how are we going to find your father?" He didn't wait for a response but quickly continued while barely glancing at me. "It's not like he's going to be sitting around, waiting for us to come for him. Second, wherever he is, he's definitely surrounded by the best guards. It won't be as simple as just showing up and pointing a gun at him."

I nodded, having already considered this point. "What if we create a diversion?"

"How so?"

I shrugged. "First off, my father has no clue as to when we're going to act, right?"

"Yeah, but now that Bram and Christina are missing, he'll no doubt figure we're going to act soon, so we can't entirely rely on the advantage of surprise."

"Good point, but I think my idea still could fly." I took a breath and swiveled my entire body around to face him, pulling the seatbelt out to give me more space. "Let's say we create some sort of diversion at one or more of the portals that currently exists between here and the Netherworld—like the main one at the airport. What's the first thing that would happen?"

"You got me."

I frowned. I was well aware that he knew where my idea was going, but the anal manager in him insisted that I spell it out detail by detail. "Obviously, Melchior would send the Netherworld Guard to investigate."

Knight nodded and offered me an encouraging smile, even though his eyes quickly dropped to my bustline.

"Pay attention!"

He chuckled. "Okay! Yes, you're right, Melchior would probably send the Guard, but he wouldn't send all of them."

I nodded, having already assumed that much. "Of course, he wouldn't send *all* of them. But the goal of the exercise is to reduce their numbers and give us a better chance against them, right?"

"Get to your point, Dulce."

"My point is: if we create a diversion and get maybe a third or so of the Guard involved in it, we can use Bram's portal ripper to create entry points wherever we need them.

Then we can use the element of surprise to our distinct advantage."

Knight was quiet for a few seconds. I could see the wheels spinning in his mind. Finally, he turned to face me. "There are some holes."

"Okay, lay them on me."

"The biggest obstacle is that we don't know exactly where Melchior is. It will only be a matter of time before any secret entry points that we create with Bram's portal ripper are discovered, which would put us on a huge time crunch." He was quiet for a couple more seconds. "The only way your plan could work is if we know where Melchior is before we go in. Then we simply cut a portal into the Netherworld, take him out, and be done with it." He cleared his throat and looked over at me. "But I'm sure you'll agree, that's a huge 'if.'"

I nodded. "That's where Quillan comes in."

"How?" he asked, his eyes narrowing at the mention of Quill.

"He knows precisely where Melchior's homes are, as well as his hangouts, and what's more, Quill knows how Melchior thinks."

Knight shook his head. "Your father won't be that stupid. Whatever Quill knew has already been invalidated by your father. I'm sure he realizes that Quill is no longer a trustworthy ally."

"My father still doesn't know Quill joined our side," I argued. "All he knows is that Quill got arrested during the skirmish with his men when you busted the *Draoidheil* delivery." I took a breath. "That's it."

"Don't you think Quill's loyalty would have been one of the first questions your father demanded of Christina when she was on the *Blueliss*?" Knight asked, frowning at me.

"We don't know that for sure," I said, even though I had to admit (if only to myself) that Knight did make a pretty good point.

"The point is that your father makes it his business not to trust anyone, which is the primary reason why he's stayed in business for so long." He shook his head. "And besides, he's also well aware that Quillan is in love with you. Because of that alone, he knows that Quillan's ties to you are stronger than they are to him."

I shook my head with a sigh, feeling frustration all the way down to my toes. "Quill is not in love with me."

Knight eyed me with raised eyebrows. "Keep telling yourself that." He faced forward again just as a sucking sound interrupted the air, shaking the Suburban as if we'd just driven over a cattle grate. It was the sure sign that we'd just traversed another portal.

"Where are we going, anyway?" I asked, frowning because I was annoyed he still didn't see the beauty in my plan. Sometimes he was just so pig-headed.

Knight smiled at me. "That's for me to know and you to find out, my sexy, love kitten."

"Really?" I asked, cringing at the appellation.

With another quick smile, Knight sighed. "Going back to our conversation: your father isn't an idiot and creating a plan in which you *must* rely on his trust in Quillan won't fly."

I nodded, since I knew he had a point—about Quillan's loyalty, that is, not about Quill being in love with me. "Okay, what about Bram?"

"What about Bram?"

I shrugged. "Maybe Bram knows something about my father's whereabouts."

"What makes you think Bram would have that information?"

"Because Bram knows a lot more than he ever lets on. He gave us the portal ripper, and he knew about my father forcing Christina to confess our secrets. Bram is our wild card."

"I won't be placing any bets on him."

Just as I was about to respond, Bram's phone buzzed in my pocket. I pulled it out and glanced at the caller ID, which said "Private Caller."

"Is that Bram's phone?" Knight asked, regarding it with disdain.

"Yeah, I wonder who's calling," I answered, unable to mask the surprise in my voice. Who would be calling and why? I had no clue. The phone rang again, and after wondering if it might be Bram, I decided to answer it. "Hello?"

"Guten morgen, Sweet," Bram's English accent purred into the receiver.

"What are you doing awake?" I asked immediately with a quick glance up at the sky. Although it was still early morning, and the sun had not quite risen to the center of the sky, it was still undeniably daytime.

"I am in the Netherworld, my dear, where I do not fear any hour of the day."

"You're in the Netherworld?!" I repeated incredulously. Knight speared me with a pointed expression, but I refused to acknowledge him, since it was more than obvious that Knight wanted nothing to do with Bram. But what he didn't realize was that Bram was the answer to my plan and I needed him. Scratch that, *we* needed him.

"What the hell is he doing in the Netherworld?" Knight demanded.

"What are you doing in the Netherworld, Bram?" I asked, suddenly sincerely worried for his well-being. "Are you in trouble?" I took a breath. "Are you sure it's safe to talk? What phone are you calling me from?"

Bram chuckled for a few seconds, sounding as if he had all the time in the world. "I appreciate your concern, my pet. As to your questions, no, I am not in trouble. And, yes, I am quite certain the line is safe."

"What are you doing in the Netherworld?" I asked finally, my tone of voice sounding harsher because I wasn't in the mood to play detective.

57

"I have more information for you, my dear," the vampire responded. "I am contacting you to request the privilege of your presence this evening so I can reveal my latest findings to you."

"Tonight?" I repeated. This was my last night to spend with Knight before we invaded the Netherworld. Was it too much to hope for one last romantic evening?

"What the hell does he want?" Knight commanded.

"Just a minute, Bram," I said, muffling the receiver in my shirt as I turned to face Knight. "He says he has more information for me and asked me to have dinner with him tonight."

"Like hell you're going to have dinner with him again," Knight said, with a tight jaw and rage in his eyes. "Whatever he has to tell us, he can tell us right now over the phone. I'm sick to death of playing by his rules."

I shook my head. "You know he will only ignore our demands, Knight. If we want information from him, we *have* to play by his rules."

Knight took a deep breath. "Give me the phone."

Assuming I had no choice, I handed the phone to Knight and watched his whole demeanor stiffen as he prepared his side of the argument that was destined to ensue. "What game are you playing, Bram?" he asked in an acid tone.

"Ah, my brutish friend," I heard Bram reply. "It surprises me to hear your voice when I thought the lovely fairy was speaking to me."

"Cut the crap. What information do you have for us?" Knight demanded.

I could hear Bram chuckling. "Forgive me, but I have no information for you."

"Yeah, that's what I figured. Do us both a favor and …"

"I repeat that I have information for my sweet, which will no doubt benefit The Resistance." After a few moments of silence, he added, "However, I do have something to say to you. Your fair leader has been purged from the toxic effects of the *Blueliss* and now wishes to reunite with you."

At the mention of Christina, I realized Bram was firmly on the road to getting his way. "Give me the phone, Knight," I said with steely resolve. "We're going to play this his way."

Knight said nothing as he passed the phone to me. In reading his frown and furrowed brows, it was pretty apparent he also realized Bram had won, at least, for now anyway.

"You say the kindest things, Sweet," Bram said as soon I held the phone up to my ear.

"Where are we meeting and what time?" I asked just as something else occurred to me. "And you better not expect me to come to the Netherworld."

Bram chuckled again. "Of course not, Sweet, of course not. I realize the Netherworld is not yet a safe destination for you. I shall arrive to pick you up at eight o'clock."

"I don't even know where we're going so how will you?"

"I can always track my mobile phone, in case you forgot," Bram responded.

There was a sudden feeling of concern that welled up within me at his words. Bram could track us anywhere as long as I carried his phone …

If Bram or Melchior wanted you dead, you would already be dead, I reminded myself. *Bram's partnership with your father is history, and he's trying to help you now. You have to trust him.*

"Eight tonight," I repeated, suffering pangs of angst in my gut.

I met Bram at exactly eight p.m. in the lobby of the hotel Knight booked for us. After traveling through two more portals, we arrived in Lucerne, Switzerland. We checked into the *Hotel Des Balances* which looked like something out of a period French movie. The hotel was beautifully located right on the river, Reuss. Knight reserved one of the suites, which was an enormous room, with a living room area off to one side. The other half of the room was dominated by a king-sized bed in the center, surrounded on three sides with a chiffon curtain. Adjacent to the bed stood a lone bathtub, along with a bottle of champagne chilling in a stand beside it. The room boasted views of the ancient city from one window, and the river from the balcony.

It was by far the most romantic hotel I'd ever seen, and I couldn't dislodge the sorrow in my stomach over the fact that Knight and I wouldn't be able to enjoy our stay here like the other couples would. Instead, I had to go on a date with a vampire, and when I could reunite with my Loki, I knew we'd both be occupied by daunting thoughts of the impending battle.

"Sweet, how lovely you look this evening," Bram said as he turned from where he'd been pretending to warm himself by the lobby's fireplace.

Glancing down at my jeans, sneakers and sweatshirt, I was far from looking lovely, but I figured that was a conversation for another day.

"Where are we going?" I asked as soon as he offered his arm. He proudly escorted me to a white Rolls-Royce that awaited us beyond the double entry doors.

"For a nice drive, if it pleases you," Bram quickly responded.

I didn't say anything as I allowed him to open my door and took a seat in the ridiculously expensive vehicle. Neither of the valet attendants came anywhere near us or the car which didn't surprise me too much since I figured Bram had probably just warded them away either with a few snippy words or his vampiric powers of persuasion.

As he sat down in the driver's seat, he glanced over at me and smiled, reaching behind my seat. He produced a white box about three feet long and two feet wide that was tied with a wide, red satin ribbon. He placed the box in my lap as he pulled out of the hotel driveway.

"What's this?" I asked, already dreading what lay beneath the lavish wrapping.

"A gift for you, my dear. I would like you to wear it for me this evening."

I grumbled something unintelligible, but figured I had to play by his rules, so I might as well comply. I pulled the ribbon off the box and opened it. After wrestling with the tissue paper, I reached inside and felt the silky material rubbing across my fingertips. It was a floor-length, electric blue, satin gown with a cleavage-exposing halter top bodice. I was surprised to find it floor-length since Bram was so explicit that I wear only short dresses. Well, my surprise diminished when I further inspected the gown and found a slit straight up on one side, so high as to bare most of my upper thigh.

"Thanks," I muttered.

"You are most welcome, my dear, most welcome," Bram answered. Then the car began to shudder and the air popped, signifying that we'd just crossed through a portal.

"Where are we going?" I asked, unable to conceal my anxiety.

"We shall dine in the French Alps, Sweet," he answered dismissively. "At one of my favorite homes."

"I didn't realize you owned a home in France."

Bram glanced at me and chuckled. I guess I should've realized he was wealthy enough to own property anywhere and everywhere. A silence descended on us when we traveled through yet another portal. Moments later, we found ourselves atop an incredibly steep mountain. Far below us appeared to be a tiny village. The lights flickered and glowed through a mist of fog imbuing it with the appearance of a backdrop to some horror movie. How ironic that I should be on a date with a vampire …

The road continued to climb the incredibly sheer cliff side until it leveled at the top before starting back down again. The road finished in a cul-de-sac at an ornate, wrought- iron gate, complete with inlaid lilies and curlicues. Bram depressed a button near the sun visor of the windshield and the gate opened inward automatically. The Rolls' headlights revealed an ancient-looking, cobbled driveway.

The "driveway" could have been called a road really, because it stretched in a serpentine pattern farther than I could see. On either side of us, an ancient wall surrounded the drive, its vanilla-colored stucco peeling in some places, while in others, it was completely obscured by lush vines. Beside the manicured olive trees that were planted equidistant at twenty-foot intervals, were sculpted, white rose bushes. They hugged the wall, and it soon became pretty obvious that this place was going to blow my mind.

Although I was semi-prepared for it to blow my mind, my jaw involuntarily dropped open on its own accord when we started over a bridge to a moat that protected the front of the estate. The cobbled driveway circled back across the moat and continued into the same winding entrance from whence we'd come.

As to Bram's estate, it was unparalleled. Awe-inspiring couldn't describe it. It had to be four stories high, and looked like something straight out of a story book. It reminded me of Sleeping Beauty's castle at Disneyland. The façade of the building was rough, cream-colored stone, which gave it a medieval-looking finish. There were black shutters on each enormous, beveled-glass window. As to how many windows it had... I lost count after the first bazillion.

Bram parked in front of the mansion, but I didn't give him the chance to open my door. Instead, I quickly unbuckled my seatbelt and jumped out as I dropped the box with the blue gown on the passenger seat. Then I simply stared at my surroundings, rapt in complete and total wonder.

There was a courtyard in front of the estate, with a fountain that featured a Rubenesque, life-sized woman holding a bucket of water over her shoulder. The water trailed over her naked breasts, and pooled into the V of her thighs, before trickling down her legs suggestively. The fountain was illuminated with white lights that reflected off the water like the twinkling stars overhead.

"You *live* here?" I asked, barely able to find my voice.

Bram chuckled as he held out his arm, inviting me to walk with him. "I *live* nowhere, Sweet."

"You own this?" I corrected myself, accepting his proffered arm and allowing him to lead me to the front of the house. He, however, changed course and we followed a grass pathway, flanked by peach rosebushes on either side, at the right of the house.

"I do own this chateau," Bram answered simply. "It has belonged to me for over two hundred years." Then he sighed longingly. "I do not spend as much time here as I would prefer, though, Sweet. I am certain you can deduce the reason why."

I thought the reason was because he didn't want to alert the townspeople that they were living alongside a vampire. Even though most Netherworld creatures were out of the so-called "closet," in remote areas such as this, it didn't matter. Small town people were much more narrow-minded and quick to judge when it came to anything supernatural. In places like this, it wouldn't have surprised me to hear that witch hunts still occurred. And I could just imagine what they'd think about Bram.

"I hope you will join me for a walk around the garden before retiring into my home?" Bram asked, smiling at me hopefully. The moonlight enhanced the whites of his eyes and teeth, imbuing them with a glow.

"As long as you tell me why you brought me here," I started.

"Yes, yes," he interrupted, waving his hand impatiently. "I give you my word that we shall spend the majority of our time together discussing business. For now, however, I prefer to enjoy your company amidst the beauty of nature."

I didn't say anything more since I knew I could and would humor him for as long as necessary if it meant getting his privy information. I also couldn't deny being curious to see the rest of the incredible establishment he called his home, which to me looked more like a dream.

FIVE

"So what were you doing in the Netherworld earlier today?" I asked Bram. We'd just finished his tour of the "garden," which equated to a sprawling four-acre (well, the ground we covered anyway; Bram made a point to tell me the entire estate sat on thirty acres) horticulturist's dream. There were various orchards, an ornately hedged maze, a thirty-foot-wide walkway, which included an overhead pergola that was woven with wisteria, as well as a fish pond the size of a swimming pool.

And the interior of the marvel, which Bram simply referred to as his "French countryside home," was just as extraordinary as the exterior. Every room featured original distressed walnut floors, the planks of which had to be more than a foot wide. The family room, which Bram termed a "great room" (which was fitting since it *was* pretty great) was dominated by a limestone fireplace that stretched from the floor to the twenty-foot ceiling. The ceiling was edged with elaborate white crown molding that looked like it belonged in the Vatican. The library took the walnut floors a step further, by adding antiqued walnut doors and floor-to-ceiling bookcases, all constructed of centuries-old walnut. When our tour came to an end in the dining room, I found it just as impressive as the rest of the house with distressed paneling that ran halfway up the walls, a grand stone fireplace, and a wine cellar at the north end. The wine cellar came complete with a terra cotta tile floor, massive stone arches, vaulted ceilings, and hand-hewn, wrought-iron light fixtures. The irony? Bram didn't drink wine.

After our tour of the incredible grounds, I begrudgingly changed into the gown Bram so thoughtfully supplied for me and met him in the foyer of the chateau.

When I walked through the stone archway, en route from the restroom, Bram turned to face me. He was speechless for a few seconds, and just gazed at me as if he'd never seen a woman before. As for me? I couldn't say I was exactly comfortable in the shrink-wrap that he referred to as a gown. Just as I'd expected, it was skin tight and slit so high up on my leg, if it happened to shift to the side, my hoo-ha could be visible to anyone who cared to take a look. The bodice was also ridiculously tight, as in corset tight, with a plunging (think: bungee jump plunging) neckline. The halter top amplified the swells of my breasts to such a degree, it looked like I'd chewed one of Willy Wonka's experimental sticks of blueberry gum, and was beginning to inflate like a balloon, boobs first.

"Your loveliness never fails to amaze me," Bram said finally. His tone was low and his expression pensive.

"Well, at least one of us is impressed," I grumbled as I attempted to walk the few steps separating us. Due to the constraints of the dress, however, I only ended up waddling side to side like a penguin.

Bram offered his arm and I accepted it. I allowed him to "walk" me into the dining room as I inch-wormed alongside him. "You didn't answer my question," I pointed out as we crossed the threshold to an enormous wood table that was stained a rich, dark chocolate and dominated the room. Bram pulled out the chair closest to me and I plopped myself down on the velvet seat, which was the color of fresh milk.

"And thus begins our business discussions?" Bram asked, peering at me in a disappointed manner. He took the seat beside me at the head of the rectangular table that looked like it could seat about forty people.

"Yes, I kept my end of the bargain and now it's time for you to keep yours."

He nodded, but didn't say anything for a few seconds. Instead, he just kept staring at me in a bizarre, almost vacant manner.

"Earth to Bram," I muttered, waving my hand before his eyes to regain his attention.

"I have forgotten what your question was, Sweet," he admitted with an unapologetic smile. "I must confess that your beauty has captivated me, and unfortunately, mere words were lost on me."

It was more fitting to say he was so taken aback by my cleavage, that he space-cadetted out, but I didn't feel like arguing. Not while we still had lots of business to discuss and I still wanted to make it back to Knight at a reasonable hour. I definitely needed some one-on-one time with my Loki. "I asked you what you were doing in the Netherworld," I repeated.

"Ah, yes, of course." Then he took a big breath. "Before we begin our adventure into business discussions, would you care for something to eat?"

"No," I answered quickly, hell-bent on sticking to the subject. "I'm not hungry."

"Very well," he said, with tightened lips. "I am quite hungry, myself."

I felt my left eyebrow arching of its own accord. "I'm not on the menu."

He chuckled, his eyes revealing the fact that he hadn't been lying: he *was* hungry, ravenously so. "I am quite well aware of that, my dear."

"So stop procrastinating and answer the question."

Bram leaned back into his chair and tapped his long, perfectly manicured fingernails against the tabletop. "I was visiting a friend of mine."

"A friend?" I asked, narrowing my eyes. It immediately occurred to me that the only person Bram would have visited in the Netherworld would have been my father, owing to their prior business relationship. If such were the case, however, I could only wonder on what side Bram was truly allied? Was Knight right that I shouldn't have trusted the vampire? Maybe Bram *was* still working for my father? If he were, I was as good as dead now ... "Were

67

you visiting my father?" I demanded, stifled anger emanating through my words.

Bram shrugged as if the answer were of no great consequence to him. He seemed much more interested in just staring at my breasts all night. "I paid him a short visit; yes."

I stood up quickly, banging my knee against the apron of the table. Before I could protest, Bram dismissed my concern with a frown as he reached for my arm, pulling me back down into my chair again.

"Before you conjure up mistruths and fantasy, allow me to explain."

"Why the hell are you still in contact with my father?" I snapped. "You said you were on our side!"

"I am on your side," he answered in a monotone. "But if I suddenly discontinued my role as your father's business partner, you and your cause would both be doomed."

"What do you mean?"

He shrugged as if the answer were obvious, even sighing, like he lacked further interest in the topic. "I cannot afford any suspicion where your father is concerned, my dear. He must believe that my allegiance remains with him, rather than to you or The Resistance."

"Then my father doesn't know you're AWOL?" I asked, frowning while trying to decide if he was telling the truth or not. The one thing I knew about Bram was he was an excellent liar, which I guessed made sense, given he'd had hundreds of years to perfect the skill.

"AWOL?" he repeated curiously. His eyes clouded with confusion as his eyebrows furrowed. "I am unaware of the meaning of the term."

"What I want to know is: does my father know that you're not on his side any longer?" I corrected myself. "Does he have any idea you've joined The Resistance?"

"I did not join The Resistance," Bram answered haughtily.

"You told me you were allied with us." My voice sounded steely.

"I *am* allied with you, my dear," Bram answered with another well-rehearsed grin. "However, I do not wish to dirty my hands. Battling one's nemesis is not in my best interest. Therefore, I prefer to remain on the periphery; but I most assuredly am your ally, as I can provide you with something no one else can."

"Oh, really? And what is that?"

"Information, of course," he said with a smug smile.

At the end of the day, it didn't really matter whether Bram actually fought beside us or not. He was right—privy information was worth much more than magical brawn. But, as to him pulling the proverbial wool over my father's eyes, I couldn't say I completely had my mind wrapped around that one yet. "If my father is still clueless as to your true allegiance, how did he react to what happened between you and Christina? I mean, you basically kidnapped her to get her off the *Bluesliss*, not to mention that you never returned her to Melchior?" He started to answer, but I interrupted him as something else occurred to me. "Speaking of Christina, where the hell is she, anyway?"

"Calm down, please, Sweet. Your litany of questions makes me feel something I imagine you would call anxiety, and I do not appreciate the sensation." He paused for a few seconds and dramatically breathed in for a few counts before breathing out, which was ridiculous since he was already dead, and thus, couldn't breathe. After regaining some sense of serenity, he smiled at me vacantly as if he'd just undergone a lobotomy.

"Okay, I won't ask another question," I muttered. "So answer the ones I already asked."

"As to your leader, she is safely nestled in one of my estates. We shall retrieve her when we return to Lucerne."

"And my father?"

He frowned at me. "I was approaching that discussion, if you would cease interrupting me." He revealed an expression of mild discontent, so I didn't say anything more.

He cleared his throat. "Your father trusts me as much as his nature allows," he started. "And that one arrow in our quiver cannot be jeopardized." His eyes narrowed as his lips grew tighter. "The moment that your father ceases to trust me is the moment of peril for you and your cause."

"So what did my father think when you absconded with Christina?" I asked again.

Bram smiled at me broadly. "Very impressive vocabulary, my dear," he said in a patronizing tone. I honestly thought he thought he was paying me a compliment. Seeing my impatient frown, though, he continued, "Your father showed little or no reaction, as he assumed I was just ... borrowing her."

"Borrowing her?"

Bram eyed me knowingly before sighing again, as if he were bored with our conversation and had more important places to be. "Borrowing her for carnal activities, Sweet."

"Oh my God," I said in disgust, shaking my head as something else occurred to me. Glaring at him, I could feel my jaw tightening. "If you laid one finger on her ..."

"Sweet," he smiled, shaking his head and holding up one hand to silence me. "I give you my word as a gentleman that I was nothing but." Then his gaze dropped to my bust again and he licked his lips. "Where you are concerned, however, gentility abandons me." Then he shrugged. "But no one ever accused a captivated lover of gentility, or did they?"

I had no clue what in the hell Bram was going on about and I didn't even realize I was holding my breath until I exhaled. "So you actually believe my father thinks there isn't anything weird going on with you?"

"That is my belief; yes," he finished succinctly.

"My father is more than a little paranoid," I continued, wondering if Bram was simply deluding himself into believing that Melchior wasn't in the know. "He has his own people followed, as well as their phones tapped."

Bram nodded as if this were old news. "Yes, he does."

I raised my eyebrows in a rendition of "Well?"

"I am not one of his people," he answered while shaking his head as if I were slow. Well, call me slow, but I wasn't going to allow this conversation to end until I fully understood exactly where Bram stood with regard to Melchior O'Neil.

"Then what are you to him?"

Bram cocked his head to the side as he pondered my question. Then he faced me again. "To understand our partnership, it is best to explain from the beginning." He cleared his throat as his eyes focused on something behind me. Pausing another few seconds, he glanced at me again as he sat up straighter, dropping his hands to his sides and clearing his throat again. He looked like he was about to deliver a soliloquy.

"I met your father long before he came into power," he started, and his English accent suddenly sounded more aristocratic. "Melchior and I were first introduced as business associates, something which eventually grew into a partnership. In the beginning, we merely dabbled in importing and exporting, but it later turned into illegal potions smuggling after your father decided to become head of the ANC."

"My father was the head of the ANC?" I asked in surprised disbelief. The connection between the ANC and street potion trafficking was pretty obvious—the ANC was supposed to stop potion smuggling and confiscate all contraband, relinquishing it to ANC custody. My father, as head of the ANC, would obviously have had unlimited access to all the contraband, which he'd obviously chosen to recycle.

Bram nodded. "Of course, Sweet. One cannot become the head of the Netherworld without first becoming the head of the ANC." After another theatrical breath, he continued,

"Once your father achieved his dream as frontrunner of the ANC, he grew quickly bored with it, and later affixed his sights on becoming the leader of the Netherworld."

"So how do you figure into all of this?"

"Once again, you interrupt me, Sweet. I was about to segue into that very subject." He frowned at me, but continued his narrative, thank Hades. "I was already a very wealthy man in my own right, long before I met your father. The truth is that your father never intended to create a partnership with anyone, but he needed my money, and we were both well aware of that fact. Hence, the partnership began and, as the years went by, we both became increasingly well-to-do, although I accumulated much more wealth than he."

"Why was that?" I asked, realizing I was interrupting him, but not really caring.

"Because as an established businessman, and a prudent one at that, I withheld my investment unless I received a larger share of the entire pie."

It was starting to make sense. Melchior needed Bram more than Bram needed Melchior. So while Melchior did all the legwork necessary to rise to the top of the ANC, before becoming head honcho of the Netherworld, Bram simply relaxed and profited from the illegal potions money rolling in. Yep, Bram wasn't lying when he said he was a prudent business man.

"So after becoming leader of the Netherworld, why didn't my father just do away with you?" I asked the obvious.

Bram laughed at the idea, shaking his head as if the question were absurd. "It is not so simple to 'do away with me,' as you so artfully phrased it." His subsequent frown told me he didn't find my question particularly polite.

I, however, couldn't have cared less. "Okay, so from your story, it sounds like you were and still are in the perfect situation," I started, eyeing him narrowly. "So why end it by aligning yourself with us, with The Resistance? Why put an end to something that's obviously benefitted you so nicely?" I finished, glancing around myself and taking in his exquisite home. "I mean, this gorgeous estate, all your cars, No Regrets, all your women … why would you want all of that to end?"

Bram sighed and looked away from me. He tapped his fingernails against the table again as he zoned out on the dark night beyond the window. I followed his gaze and watched the stars twinkling alongside the crescent moon.

"I suppose you might say I turned over a new leaf," he said softly.

"How so?"

He shrugged as he returned his attention to my face. "Yes, this is all fine and well, but even I can be subjected to bouts of … remorse."

I frowned at him, taking a deep breath and shaking my head in disbelief. "You really don't expect me to believe that you feel guilty now, so you want out?" I didn't give him the chance to respond. "Because I don't buy it, not for one second."

Bram chuckled. "I do not know why I bother speaking anything but the truth to you, Sweet."

"Neither do I."

His chuckle faded as he stared at me for a few seconds. Then his jaw tightened and his lips formed a solid line. "I believe your father has grown too hungry for power. He is becoming a threat to everything we worked for," he said finally, with no mirth in his expression. "That is the primary reason I will assist you in his removal from office." He paused for a moment or two. "That and I will never forgive him for the abuse of his sole offspring."

"Here we go with the lying again," I said, unable to conceal the anger in my tone. "You were much more believable when you admitted the sad truth of your own greed, Bram. Don't try to glorify your intentions by throwing me into the mix."

Bram shook his head adamantly, even pounding his fist on the table top. It was a rare display of anger on his part, so very rare that I'd never seen him act like this before. I felt my eyes widening with surprise.

"I apologize," he said instantly as he uncurled his fist and allowed his hand to drop to his side. He leaned back into his chair and studied me. "But on this topic, I have spoken nothing but the truth. Had I been fortunate enough to father offspring of my own, I would never have neglected him or her so carelessly, nor treated my child so cruelly as your father did you. And for that, I shall never forgive him."

I didn't know what to say, so I remained silent. There was something fervently intense about the way Bram had spoken and the way his eyes darkened at the mere mention of my relationship with my father.

"The truth is, Sweet, that you have become quite dear to me."

I wanted to call his bluff, but I couldn't—not when there was something so sincere in his eyes, something that insisted he wasn't lying to me, that there were no tricks, no riddles, nothing I had to discern from his words. It was a rare moment in which I thought Bram was actually baring his innermost soul.

"The gravity of it quite took me by surprise, I am loath to admit," he continued. "I found myself constantly looking forward to your impromptu visits at No Regrets. So when you approached me and asked me to escort you to the Netherworld, I felt such anticipation as I have not known for, oh, a hundred years or more. Yes, of course, I have often said that I would love nothing more than to bed you, but I also must confess now that our … bizarre acquaintance is one of the few joys in my life."

Bram had never been so candid with me, and for the first time ever, I actually felt sorry for him. It suddenly dawned on me, as never before, that living for such a long time had made Bram an island unto himself. The more I thought about it, the more I realized there was no one he was close to—no one he considered his friend.

Except me. Yes, I had to admit that in our own limited and unique way, Bram and I were friends.

"At the expense of turning our last evening together into a maudlin scene, I shall ask that we change the subject, if it pleases you," Bram suddenly said. He cleared his throat and his posture stiffened. "I must confide my unease with anything that defies logic and reason."

I got his gist. Like most men, he wasn't comfortable when facing his inner emotional child. But, to be fair, I wasn't either. "I understand," I said simply.

"Have you no curiosity as to the other person with whom I paid a visit while in the Netherworld?" he asked.

"Oh yeah, that's right," I answered, glancing at him with renewed interest.

Bram smiled smugly as if our last conversation were now a distant memory, something to be locked away in his psyche. I had no idea if we would ever discuss it again. Why? Because Bram had said all he needed to say, and that was that.

"I believe you are acquainted with Caressa Brandenburg?" he asked, flashing me a raised brow expression.

"You visited Caressa?" I asked as shock welled up inside me.

"Yes, does it surprise you that Ms. Brandenburg and I have enjoyed quite a long friendship?"

I nodded. "Yes."

He seemed to like my answer and grinned more widely, apparently enjoying the role of news anchor. "She is quite an attractive woman, do you not agree?" he continued, eyeing me suspiciously.

I could see right through him though. He was obviously trying to make me jealous and it wasn't going to work. "Yes, Caressa is very attractive. No arguments there."

"Are you curious whether I have known her in the way I should like to know you?"

I shook my head and sighed deeply. "For Hades's sake, Bram, get to the damn point!"

"Answer my question, please," he answered with his chin stuck out defiantly.

"No, I'm not curious; and no, I don't want to know about your sex life, or lack thereof, at all!"

He frowned momentarily. "Ms. Brandenburg has informed me that the Netherworld is up in arms regarding a newspaper article your leader ran in *The Netherworlder Today*," he started.

"Really?"

"Yes, and I, too, noticed many handwritten signs posted along roads and highways that supported the fall of the current regime." He cleared his throat as he smiled at me. "By all appearances, the Netherworld seems ripe for rebellion, Sweet. And as such, your father grows more desperate each day. I am certain we both know what Hippocrates had to say about that?"

No, I had no clue Hippocrates had anything to say about it, but I sensed where Bram was going with his point. "Desperate times call for desperate measures?"

"Exactly, Sweet," Bram said and nodded. "Exactly right."

"Then you still think we can win even though the Netherworld Guard outnumbers our own soldiers?"

He was quiet for a few seconds. "Yes, I believe your side can prevail, if you proceed cautiously and correctly."

"I need to know precisely where my father is," I interjected quickly, realizing my father's whereabouts were the crux of the entire matter. "We won't have a chance in hell if we don't know where to find Melchior."

Bram chuckled. "Sometimes I believe you can read my mind, Sweet."

He reached into his pants pocket and produced his pocket watch, handing it to me. I accepted the expensive-looking timepiece as I brushed my fingers against the face of it. I wondered why he'd handed it to me and glanced up at him with curiosity in my eyes.

"Long ago, I found it necessary to my well-being that I track your father's comings and goings," Bram said softly. Pointing to the watch, he added, "This pocket watch will allow you to do the same."

"How?" I asked, glancing down at it again.

"It is a compass programmed to pinpoint your father's location at any given moment." He took it from my hand, placed it flat in his palm, and lifted his palm to eye level. The hour hand began turning counter clockwise before it settled onto the twelve o'clock position. Then the area at the bottom of the watch, which previously showed the date, displayed what appeared to be GPS coordinates.

"West, one hundred twenty-two degrees, by north, thirty-seven degrees," Bram read aloud. Then he faced me with another smile. "It seems your father is close to Splendor, only in the Netherworld, of course."

I dared not believe my own good luck. I'd known Bram would come through and in providing the answer to the problem of finding my father, he'd come through with flying colors, and then some. "Thank you," I said earnestly.

Bram said nothing more as he stood up suddenly. "If it pleases you, there is one more item I would like to unveil to you before your departure this evening."

I figured the business portion of our evening was now finished. And that was fine—there really wasn't anything more I needed to know. "Sure," I said as I clutched the timepiece in my palm, and warned myself not to leave it anywhere. That was the huge bummer about wearing gowns—there wasn't a damn place to put anything.

I followed Bram through the dining room and into the wine cellar where I immediately noticed a painting, covered by a tarp, hanging on the wall. Bram strode up to it, but stopped short before unveiling it. Then he turned to face me with a broad smile.

"I do hope this will please you, Sweet."

He grabbed the tarp and pulled on it gingerly, exposing the portrait he'd had painted of me. At first, I didn't know what to say or think. Maybe it's natural to feel shock when you see yourself reflected back at you in anything other than a mirror. But, I could only say that as far as the artist's ability, he was more than simply talented. The painting looked exactly like me. It was the state in which I'd been represented that threw me for a loop.

SIX

It was a full-scale rendition of me, from head to foot. I was standing on a stretch of grass spotted with bluebells, a forest of pine trees behind me in the distance. The sky was an cerulean blue, interrupted by a few whimsical clouds that looked like white cotton candy. On one side of me was a lake, interrupted by a waterfall that coursed down the face of a craggy mountainside. On my other side, two deer, an owl and a few squirrels looked on curiously. But it wasn't the Winnie the Pooh surroundings that struck me as completely baffling. Instead, it was the fact that nothing about the painting screamed ANC Regulator or law enforcement in general, which was something I'd expected given the title.

"I thought the painting was supposed to be titled 'Fairy Law'?" I asked doubtfully, turning to face Bram who stood in silent appreciation of the portrait, his arms crossed against his chest.

"It is," he insisted in a less-than-interested tone and then proceeded to point to the monogrammed silver plate inlaid at the top of the dark oak frame. The plate proclaimed the "masterpiece" to be The Fairy Law, just as I'd intimated.

The information reinforced, I refocused my attention on the painting, trying to glean some connection between it and the title. It was a little off-putting at first—seeing yourself reflected back at you and in a way that completely defies your own perception of just who and what you are. After a few seconds of trying to make a judgment regarding whether or not I liked the thing, I was left not knowing what to think. I mean, it was me clearly—the artist was obviously a good one because he'd been able to capture everything that made me me pretty well. But, at the same, time, there were definitely details that weren't so much me. For one, my hair

79

was totally off. Even though my hair is naturally long—
ending at just below my elbows—and while I do have some
good hair days when it adopts an inkling of a wave, my hair
as pictured in the portrait was anything but mine. It trailed
down to my butt in bouncy waves of full, golden curl—the
shade a lighter gold with less honey tones than my natural
color. Not only that, but the strands were interlaced
haphazardly with rose, daffodil and lily blossoms, a baby
pink ribbon snaking in and out of the tresses, like some
slithering sea creature.

　　The Dulcie O'Neil I knew and loved so well would
never do flowers in her hair and would never, ever, under
any circumstance, do baby pink. Ever.

　　The expression on my face was neither happy nor sad
but merely contented, the ends of my lips slightly lifted as if
I was going for the Mona Lisa. There was an overall
youthful naiveté to my face—my cheeks were round which
made it look like I was all of eighteen years old. My eyes
were wide and could have portrayed surprise if not for my
eyebrows, which weren't raised but sat idly above my eyes,
appearing haughty with the way they arched so perfectly. As
to the color of my eyes, they were much more of an emerald
green than in real life and my lips were plumper, my nose a
bit more pert and upturned.

　　But what really attracted my attention was the portrait
me's clothing. I was dressed in a lemon yellow gown (that
had more in common with a negligee than a dress) that
seemed like it was made out of chiffon, the material was so
delicate and almost see-through. The dress was very short,
ending at my upper mid-thigh and edged in fine white lace.
My arms appeared to be clasped behind my back, one hand
delicately reappearing at my upper thigh where I inched the
hem of the dress up to the V of my torso. Even though the
viewer wasn't able to see anything he shouldn't have, based
on the angle of where I was holding the dress, it was pretty
obvious panties hadn't been of concern to the artist. And the
fact that the portrait me's arms were pulled back behind me,

in turn, pushed my chest forward and allowed the viewer's attention to wholly focus on my incredibly alert nipples which protruded from the translucent material and were the first things to grab the viewer's attention. I felt myself coloring with embarrassment at just the thought that I was basically unable to stop staring at what were supposedly my own nipples.

As to the rest of "my" breasts, they were in a word: gargantuan. They had to be at least twice their actual size of a full C (which isn't anything to scoff at!). The rest of the "dress" was painted so as to appear clinging to my curves, being both sleeveless and plunging in the front, revealing the swells of each side of my ample breasts. The empire waist flared into a short skirt which, again, was obscenely tiny over one leg. With the way "my" face portrayed a youthful sensuality and the fact that "I" was nearly baring my feminine fruit, it appeared as if the portrait me were beckoning to the onlooker, teasing him seductively. I could just imagine that the follow up to this stunning piece of art would reveal an image of this woman on her back with a man between her legs while the forest creatures continued to look on nosily.

As to the link between the painting and the title, I was still baffled. "I give up. There's nothing about this picture that in any way says law enforcement," I said, shaking my head as I attempted not to be rude because, I mean, it was a portrait of *me* which in and of itself was supposed to be flattering. 'Course, I also couldn't say the sexual way in which I was represented was in any way pleasing, but I also couldn't say I was surprised. I mean, this *was* Bram we were talking about …

The vampire chuckled, facing me with an arched brow of amusement. "You misunderstood, Sweet." Then he glanced at the painting again. "The title refers to the law of nature, my dear, not the law of man."

"I don't get the law of nature from it either," I grumbled, deciding I wasn't a fan of my portrait. "I look like a woodland prostitute."

Bram chuckled again but it didn't appear his attention was in any way focused on me, the real me. Instead, he seemed fully enraptured by and with the painting. The chuckle died on his lips, not even leaving the ghost of a smile in its wake. "It is an absolute masterpiece, the finest specimen of art on which I have ever had the fortune of laying my eyes."

"Then it must also be the only painting you've ever seen period."

But Bram shook his head, still unable to pull his attention away from the portrait. I glanced up at it again and sighed. "Instead of titling it the 'Fairy Law,' you should have called it 'Fairy in need of a bra,'" I finished, deciding I'd now had enough of the painting and of Bram for the evening. Nothing like ruining an evening by being forced to confront a barely clothed rendition of yourself.

"I have stood and admired your portrait more times than I care to remember," Bram said in a level, serious tone. "I must admit I am wholly transfixed by the beauty of the subject, how she teases me and flaunts her feminine loveliness, showing me just enough but not too much."

"Holy Hades, it's getting late, Bram …"

Finally he turned to face me and seemed to study me, as if he were comparing me to the painting. He glanced at my portrait and then at me again, his eyes narrowing. "I will admit the portrait does lack your edge, your feistiness. It is what I imagine Sweet would be had she not experienced the ugliness that exists in this world."

"How poetic," I said with a quick but unconvincing smile. "But I fail to see how that picture has anything in common with me."

Bram didn't shift his gaze, just continued to stare at me as if he could see through me to the other side of the room. There was no expression on his face. "She is the absolute embodiment of you," he whispered.

I shook my head, throwing my hands on my hips as I forced my attention back to the Forest Slut. "She is not. For one, she's coy—I don't do coy. Second, her boobs are bordering on an E and third she looks like a whorish version of Rapunzel because her hair is so ridiculously long. And my eyes are nowhere near that shade of green."

"Then you fail to recognize your own splendor," Bram muttered, unmoved. "She is you and you are she."

"Then I guess we'll agree to disagree," I said quickly, taking a few steps away from the portrait and toward the door in a charade of "I hate that painting and let's get going."

But Bram made no motion to accompany me. Instead, he stood rooted to the same spot. "I have lost count of the evenings I have stood here alone staring into her intelligent and glorious eyes, bemoaning the fact that I do not possess magic, otherwise I should have magicked her into reality, created my very own creature such that Mary Shelley dreamt of."

"A monster Dulcie, that sounds really nice," I grumbled, shaking my head.

"Far from a monster," Bram said sadly and took the few steps that separated us. His lips lifted into a strange smirk that wasn't a smile but hinted that there was something going on in the gray matter between his ears.

"Are you ready to go?" I asked, my voice coming out almost hesitantly. There was just something about his eyes that seemed … different somehow. Really, it was his whole disposition—something was off.

"There have been many moments when I have wished she would inch up her gown just a fraction more, allow me to feast my eyes on her forbidden fruit."

"I've heard enough," I said grumpily, not wanting to point out the fact that he was starting to sound like he was losing his grip on sanity—I mean, there was no way a painting could lift up her skirt but I wasn't in the mood to point out the obvious because I didn't want any part of the direction this conversation was headed.

Bram didn't say anything but continued to stare at me, his eyes boring into mine. What was strange was that I couldn't pull my attention away from his gaze, it was as though I was a deer, locked in the headlights of Bram's eyes.

"It's getting late," I said softly, barely recognizing the sound of my own voice.

I was scarcely aware of Bram taking another two steps toward me and I wasn't sure how many seconds it was until he stood a mere breath away from me but it felt like a split second in the same time that it felt like an eternity. There was just something about his expression, about the way his eyes seemed like deep holes of vivid blue. Even as I stared into them, they began to darken. He said nothing but reached out and took hold of both of my upper arms, as if forcing me to stare into his eyes. His grip was tight but not uncomfortable.

"Wha—" I started but then couldn't finish my sentence. Words failed me because it seemed his eyes had somehow changed color, that their ordinary blue had blazed into a dark navy with specks of gold and those specks appeared to be swirling in a circular pattern. They began to move so quickly, I couldn't see the individual specks any longer, but just a ring of yellow around his eyes.

"Show me your magic," he whispered and although I could recognize the words, I had a difficult time attaching any meaning to them. Unable to do anything else, I just stared into the void of his eyes helplessly. I could feel the cold of his breath against my forehead, but I couldn't focus on it, couldn't pull my eyes from the golden glow of his.

"Create your magic for me, Sweet," he whispered again. Even though I couldn't register his words, my hand suddenly moved of its own accord, my fingers closing into a fist. Without giving myself the direction, I shook my fist until I felt the glittery fragments of my fairy dust in my palm.

"As she is you and you are she, become her for me, Sweet."

I didn't understand what he was asking of me. But it didn't matter because it was as if my body was on autopilot. I felt my arm raise up above my head as I released my fingers and the shimmering dust fell about my hair and face like an ethereal curtain. My eyes shifted to the painting behind Bram and narrowed as I took in every detail of the golden-haired woman who now seemed as if she was smiling. It felt like a swirl of warm air that started at my toes, twirling itself up my legs, my waist, my breasts and higher still, to the crown of my head. I blinked and in the span of that split second, I felt the tendrils of my now incredibly long hair snaking around my body, the kiss of flower blossoms against my cheeks.

Something is wrong! I heard the voice inside my head but, again, couldn't understand the meaning of the words. Instead, I found my eyes stapled to the vision of the man before me. He stared down at me and a smirk lit up his face, a face that was so beautiful, I had never seen its equal. I desperately wanted to reach out and run my fingers across the velvet of his skin, sink my index finger between his lips and feel the wetness of his mouth.

"Remarkable," the deity before me proclaimed as his gaze traveled from my face down to my breasts and down still to my legs, only to arrive back at my eyes again. "You are real."

No! That voice rang out within me. *Fight him!*

But a moment later, the voice was forgotten. Instead, I wanted nothing more than to lose myself in the blue void of the eyes of the magnificent creature before me. He gazed at me and I felt something warm bubble up from within me, it was a feeling of complete happiness, as if nothing could ever harm me, as if I were ensconced in a safe haven. I felt as if I was right where I was meant to be.

"Perhaps I do possess a magic of my own," the being spoke and brought his finger to the side of my cheek. I closed my eyes as soon as I felt his touch and pushed my face into his caress, wanting him to understand how his touch sent shivers down my spine and made it almost difficult to stand.

Dulcie! That angry voice sounded within me and I felt my eyes pop open in response.

The creature smiled as he gazed into my eyes, his canines lengthening. And then the voice was a simple memory, something intangible and, as such, unreal.

"Please," I said, surprised by the words coming off my tongue. The immortal before me seemed to understand my need, as much as I wasn't able to explain it myself. He bowed low and pulled me into him, angling my head back and staring into my eyes as the gold of his irises began to spin even faster, ensnaring me in his web. He brought his lips to mine and I felt my eyelids fluttering closed once I felt the lush softness of his lips and how tender his kiss was.

Knight! The word flashed through my head but I didn't understand the meaning. There was a blankness in my mind that I didn't fully comprehend, something that felt numb and incapable of rational thought. While the void of my thoughts continued to plague me, I felt the deity, the god's, tongue suddenly infiltrating my mouth, mating with my tongue while the points of his fangs indented my lip, not breaking my flesh but threatening to. And I suddenly wanted him to break my flesh, to sink his fangs into me so I could provide his sustenance, so I could, in some way, give back to him the feelings he was engendering in me. I wanted to become his vessel from which he could drink and, what was more, I wanted to become the vessel with which he could vent his masculine need.

Something blossomed within my gut, a feeling I recognized. It was as if a trove of butterflies had suddenly become airborne in the deep recesses of my body, fluttering their gossamer wings in unison until a great maelstrom brewed within me. But there was a sharpness to their wings, a sort of stinging need, a yearning that flooded me deep down in my core. And I knew the only answer to this deeply seated need was to become one with this god, to allow him entrance into my body.

The deity pulled away from me and even though he didn't say anything, I opened my eyes obediently, as if he had silently issued the command.

"You do desire me, after all," he whispered, a broad grin on his face. Then he stepped away and took me in from head to toe again, panting as he did so. All I could do was focus on the deep blue of his eyes, finding the once gold circles were now a deep purple, mesmerizing in the way they circled around his irises so quickly.

Even though I didn't shift my gaze from his eyes, I could see his hand reaching toward me and the touch of his fingers brushing the yellow fabric just above my nipple, was almost too much. I closed my eyes and breathed out.

"Look at me," he said and I immediately opened my eyes again, losing myself in the velvet of his gaze. I felt him brush the strap of the dress down from my shoulder and then his fingertips against my naked breast. He grazed my nipple and I felt the yearning, stinging sensation between my thighs begin pounding, demanding some form of release. He captured my nipple between his thumb and index finger and pinched until I feared I might pass out.

"Dulcie, you must fight me," he breathed but I didn't understand his words, couldn't see through the cloudiness that was consuming me. He brought his other hand to my opposite shoulder and brushed the strap of my dress down my shoulder, baring my other breast as his eyes feasted on it.

Dulcie! That inward voice screamed out again. *Fight!*

"Do not give in to me," the creature said softly as his mouth found my breast and his tongue circled my nipple.

I wanted to tell him that I didn't understand. Why would I fight him when I wanted nothing more than to give in to him? "You don't want me?" I felt the words leave my mouth.

He pulled away from me and his gaze seemed to strip me down to my very core. "You do not understand," he breathed. "I desire you more than I have ever desired anyone or anything."

"Then take me," I crooned, grabbing his hand and placing it on my breast again. "I am yours to do with as you please." The words ricocheted through me, spreading my desire to every corner of my body. "I belong to you."

He didn't say anything but just stared at me, no expression on his face. Then he gripped the back of my neck with one hand and with the other, lifted my body with his incredible strength until I was straddling him. As soon as I felt his tongue in my mouth, the yearning within my belly became an all out fire, consuming me with its fingers of fiery desire. I felt a wind swirling around my legs but couldn't focus on the fact that there were no open windows in the room. Instead, I marveled at the feel of his tongue on my nipple as the wind began whipping up my legs, circling around and around as it danced its way up to my thighs. I undulated against him, rubbing my pelvis into his stomach, wanting him to understand that I was his.

"Dulcie," his voice interrupted the carnal feelings of need ricocheting through me and when he set me on my feet, taking a step back, I felt suddenly cold and empty.

"I do not want you like this," he said almost angrily.

"No," I demanded and grabbed his hand, trying to force it between my thighs. "Touch me and you will want me," I whispered.

He pulled away and clasped both his hands behind his back, as if afraid I might go after them again. "Use your strength and fight me, dammit," he ordered.

I threw my head back and felt a moan break through my lips as the wind suddenly forced its way between my thighs and circled my most sensitive area, breathing against me with a force that made my knees go wobbly. I started to fall and felt his arms suddenly around me but he didn't force me upright, instead he held me at an angle, both of us watching as the wind forced my dress up to my navel. I glanced at his face and found his eyes glued to the feminine flesh between my legs.

"Take me; I am yours," I whispered.

Dulcie, fight his power! The voice rang through my head, this time stronger and clearer than before. I started to glance up at him but the voice stopped me. *Do not look into his eyes!*

The wind seemed to build in intensity and I could feel it pushing my legs apart, intent on burying itself within me.

"Show me your strength," the creature holding me demanded, his tone of voice constricted, almost pained. "I cannot fight this much longer," he finished, shaking his head as he started to trail his fingers down my stomach.

"Don't fight it," I responded, at the same time that pain lodged itself right between my eyes and I had to clench them shut to force it away.

"My desire for you is beginning to cloud my judgment," he whispered.

Dulcie, for fuck sake! The woman's voice inside my head screamed at me. It took me a second or two to recognize it as my own.

I locked my thighs against the power of the wind and clenched my eyes shut tight, the feelings of bliss and harmony slowly beginning to bleed away. I shook my head as dawning realization claimed me. My breathing escalated as the wind began to die down. Even though there was still an overwhelming sense of need within me, something that begged me to open my legs and let the magnificent creature above me take me or, failing him, let the wind take me, there was also something else that rebelled.

Remnants of need and bliss diminishing, I forced myself upright, out of his hold and bent over, with my hands on my thighs as I tried to catch my breath. I shook my head, trying to clear the illusion from my mind and eyes. Within seconds, my grip on sanity returned and with it, the liquid heat of anger. Once I felt like I could stand on my own feet without the risk of falling over, I stood up and turned around to face Bram, who watched me with narrowed but inquisitive eyes. He was panting, his canines indenting his lower lip.

I took the few steps that separated us and without saying anything, unleashed my fist against his face. To his credit, I was more than sure that he saw the blow coming, given his vampire quickness, but he still allowed me to cold cock him.

"You son of a bitch!" I screamed at him, but feeling like I was about to pass out, due to the fact that his vampire glamour still hadn't passed out of my system, I had to lean against the wall and catch my breath.

"You are lucky I have the strength of mind that I do," he said as his canines rescinded. "A lesser man would have succumbed to his more primitive nature."

"I'm lucky?" I laughed acidly. "You just tried to force yourself on me and I'm the one who's lucky?"

Bram shook his head. "I would never force myself on any woman," he argued. "This was merely a test of your strength and power," he said simply and then frowned at me. "And you nearly failed it."

"Don't you ever fucking touch me again," I seethed, still finding it necessary to lean against the wall.

"I did it for your own good," Bram ground out, offering me a raised brow expression that said he was surprised by how I was taking it.

"My own good?" I demanded, trying to find the strength to stand up. I glanced down at myself and found I was still dressed in that awful yellow dress from the painting, only the thing was around my waist, both of my breasts hanging out. Immediately I balled my palm into a fist, sprinkling dust over my head as I imagined myself dressed in jeans, a sweatshirt and sneakers.

"The Netherworld Guard will include vampires nearly as practiced as I am," Bram said stiffly, apparently not appreciating the fact that I'd just denied him access to my nudity.

"Speaking of how practiced you are," I started and peeled myself off the wall. "You've been lying to me about a lot more than my father and the illegal potions industry. You're much older than three hundred."

"My age is of no concern to you, Sweet," he started but I adamantly shook my head.

"Your age is of every concern to me, you bastard." I took a deep breath, trying to calm my frantic heart. "How old are you, Bram?" I demanded. "No three hundred year old vampire could have glamoured me the way you just did."

"I am nearly seven hundred, Sweet," he answered as if it was no big deal.

I shook my head and closed my eyes, trying to keep the stars from clouding my vision. It was amazing I'd even been able to fight him off at all considering the strength inherent in a seven-hundred-year-old vampire. With his ability, he could have permanently damaged my mind because his glamour was so potent. I'd heard of women who had become vegetables after being the unfortunate victims of a centuries-old vampire's glamour.

"What is of greater concern to me, my dear, is that you very nearly gave in to me. Had I not encouraged you to fight me, I am quite certain I would still be enjoying your body as we speak," he ground out, his fangs suddenly lengthening again.

I glared at him. "Do you really expect me to believe that you wanted me to fight you?"

He returned my glare. "Do you not recall me using those exact words?" Then he chuckled deeply as if the whole thing were of no consequence to him at all. "I have had many opportunities to force you into my bed, Sweet. You must ask yourself why I have never sought to glamour you until this moment?"

"Maybe because you know there's a good chance I won't survive this attack on the Netherworld so you figured this was your last chance." I paused. "And weren't you the one to remind me that desperate times call for desperate measures?"

He glanced at me and raised a brow, appearing offended. "As I said earlier, this was a test of your strength. Had you not passed it, I would have attempted to talk you out of joining your brethren in this battle."

"The chances of any vampires seven hundred or older in the Netherworld Guard are slim."

Bram nodded. "Quite true, Sweet, quite true, but why take the chance? I decided I should do you the favor of practicing your resistance against the oldest of my race."

I swallowed hard, somehow surprised but not all that surprised to find out Bram was the oldest "living" vampire. "I want you to take me back to the hotel. I've had enough of you and your games."

"Very well," he said matter-of-factly. "Though I will continue to insist upon my innocence in this instance."

And that was when I lost my temper again. "Bram, did you or did you not kiss me, feel me up and basically see me completely naked?" I demanded, coloring as I remembered the incident with the wind trying to get between my legs while my dress was bunched around my middle. "And I'm also convinced the wind and that fog earlier, were both of your own design."

"I am guilty of all of the above, Sweet," he said and took a few steps closer to me. "And believe me when I tell you that I shall repeatedly replay every memory of your touch and your smell."

"And believe me when I tell you that if you ever touch me again, I'll have your seven-hundred-year-old balls mounted on my wall."

SEVEN

Bram frowned at me, raising his brows in a sarcastic expression, and letting me know in no uncertain terms that he wasn't keen on having his balls mounted on my wall. Well, I wasn't too keen on being glamoured by a horny vampire, so I figured that made us equal.

"As you are so anxious to return to your hotel, I shall endeavor to please you," he said stonily, his frown still evident. "Before we embark on our journey, may I suggest one recommendation?"

I glanced at him and sighed heavily, wondering when he was going to give this charade a rest. "Go ahead," I answered in a tone of unconcealed ennui. There was only so much of Bram and his incessant sexual innuendoes that I could put up with, and I'd definitely had my fill.

The vampire held my attention for a few more seconds before he finally decided to say whatever was on his mind. I wondered if, at some point in his ridiculously long career, he'd ever worked as an actor. All of his dramatic pauses as well as his overall flair for the histrionic suggested he probably would have been a good one.

"Your first attempt to enter the Netherworld should occur at eighteen degrees north, and sixty-three degrees west," he said quickly, as if I had a clue as to what the hell he was talking about.

"What? Wait a second," I started, shaking my head as I held up my hands to tacitly protest "Um, you lost me." But recognizing his calculations as coordinates, I started searching the room for something to write on. I had to admit it more than surprised me that Bram actually had something serious to talk about. I assumed this latest conversation would be merely another bold attempt to woo me into having sex with him.

Unable to find a pen or a piece of paper, I shook my fist until I felt my fairy dust leaking through my fingers. Then I unclenched my fist over my other hand, while imagining a blank piece of paper and a black, ballpoint pen. Within seconds, both appeared in my outstretched palm and I glanced up at Bram again. "Would you please repeat that?"

He did as I requested and I hurriedly scribbled the coordinates on the sheet of paper before looking up at him again with another question. "So why do you think we should enter the Netherworld there? And more importantly, where is 'there'?"

"Those coordinates, when programmed into the portal-ripping device that I already gave to you, will transport you into Squander Valley." He paused and remained silent, apparently presupposing that I would know what in the hell Squander Valley was. I didn't.

"What's that?"

Bram raised his left brow like he was in the process of judging me, and I was coming up short, but I couldn't say I cared. Sometimes his expectations were impossible to meet. I mean, how many times had I been to the Netherworld? All of once.

So put that in your pipe and smoke it, Bram, I thought to myself.

"Squander Valley was the original site for a proposed community," Bram started. "It was a project that had to be aborted once it was discovered that the entire area was sitting atop a *Bregone* swamp."

"A what swamp?"

He shook his head as if he'd just emerged from the realm of being disappointed at my ability to understand him and was now downright exasperated. "I must remind myself that you have not traveled much in the Netherworld," he muttered, more to himself than to me. He brought his eyes to mine and shook his head. "I find it quite tiresome to play the role of teacher at every turn."

"Moving on," I grumbled.

"A *Bregone* swamp is hazardous to the health of any creature unfortunate enough to be within proximity of one. They emit *Brigonnia* fumes, which cause immediate death."

"How?"

"I was about to tell you," he muttered with another arched brow. It was a good thing that as a vampire he remained the same age as he was when turned. Otherwise, his forehead would have been one wrinkly mess, given all his frowns of exasperation. "Once the victim inhales the rancid air of the *Bregone,* the toxin travels through his body, instantly petrifying his organs. Moments later, the deceased organs decompose into nothing but an inky, black mess, which the victim then regurgitates during the final throes of death."

"Sounds fascinating," I said with obvious distaste. "And whose great idea was it to build a community on a *Bregone* swamp?" I asked, trying to banish any further images of death by *Brigonnia* fumes from my mind.

"I do not know for certain, but I do know that it is incredibly difficult to detect a *Bregone* swamp, as they exist within the crust of the earth. An unknowing passerby would not realize he was anywhere near one without proper detection. And even worse, the *Brigonnia* fumes emit no smell. Once you realize you have crossed into the boundaries of one, it is usually too late."

"Thanks for the *Bregone* swamp 101 lesson, Bram," I said as I dropped my hand holding the pen and piece of paper to my side while I gaped at the vampire before moving to my second inquiry. "I think the question now remains why the hell would I want to send my soldiers to a horribly painful death? I'm trying to defeat my father, not lose the battle before it's even begun, remember?"

Bram shook his head, apparently vexed that I wasn't following him. I had a good idea that all this irritation was really stemming from his sexual frustration. Well, he could go on being sexually frustrated for another twenty minutes or so. By then, I was more than sure he'd find some willing woman to appease his frazzled male nerves.

"You would not be sentencing them to death as long as each of them is protected by a gas mask," he said as if the answer were as clear as he was horny. He could have been the horniest person I'd ever met. Well, I guessed Knight could also be in the running for that title …

"As to the reason I advised entering the Netherworld via Squander Valley," the vampire continued, "Squander Valley is a ghost town, and as such, it is safe. The Netherworld Guard does not patrol there despite being relatively close to one of the Guard's training bases."

"You want us to attack their base," I finished for him, smiling. I was beginning to recognize the beauty of his plan. One thing I could say for Bram was that he was smart, even if he drove me crazy, most of the time.

"Ah, behold the Regulator whom I have heard so much about," he said with a patronizing grin. It quickly turned into a lascivious, full-body stare.

"How many soldiers are on that base?" I asked, ignoring his jibe along with his roaming eyes for the moment.

"It is the largest training base in the Netherworld," he answered. Glancing up at the ceiling as if the answer to my question lay there, he replied, "I would estimate perhaps two hundred soldiers live and train there on a regular basis."

"To defeat them, I would need at least two hundred of my own soldiers," I said. The sinking feeling in my gut started to churn as I thought that maybe this sounded a little too good to be true.

"Not if you are the superior strategist," Bram said, crossing his arms against his chest and regarding me coolly. "A few men with the proper artillery could go far."

He thought we should bomb the base—at least, I figured that was his gist. "So we take out this training compound, then what?"

Bram shrugged. "I cannot answer all of your questions, Sweet."

"I'm not asking you to," I replied saucily. "But you know the landscape of the Netherworld way better than I do; and because you rubbed elbows with my father, you also know the structure of the Guard as well as the ANC." I grinned broadly. "Bram, I know you well enough by now to realize you know more than you're letting on."

"The phrase 'never look a gift horse in the mouth' comes to mind," he said, regarding me with effrontery.

I eyed Bram again, wondering if I should tell him about our plan, and how we intended to stage a fake surrender of Loyalist Netherworlders through the airport portal in which I'd first traveled to the Netherworld. But then I decided against it, thinking it was smarter to keep some things under wraps. It wasn't that I didn't trust Bram; but I couldn't say I completely trusted him either. Something in the back of my mind kept niggling at me to be careful where my trust was concerned—that same voice inside my head that previously cautioned me not to put all my eggs in Bram's basket.

"If you use multiple entry points simultaneously and manage to wipe out the largest of the Netherworld Guard's training bases, I believe you would have the advantage," the gallant vampire finished. Then he eyed me pointedly. "Of course, one of your targets should be your father, himself."

I didn't say anything, but simply nodded and Bram continued. "Slay the puppet master and all his puppets shall inevitably fall, do you not agree?"

I swallowed hard, but kept my poker face. So Bram thought along the same lines as I did regarding the assassination of my father. Interesting. And now that I possessed Bram's "Melchior O'Neil GPS timepiece," I expected the job might be entirely easier than what I'd previously imagined.

"Of course, it sounds good in theory," he continued, his words echoing Knight's. At the thought of my Loki, I felt anxiety bubbling up inside me. I had to get back to the hotel and tell Knight everything Bram said, minus the whole glamouring incident, of course. It wasn't that I was trying to protect Bram by not telling Knight, it was because I believed we, The Resistance, still needed Bram. And giving Knight one more reason to despise him wouldn't exactly assist us in our goal of making everyone get along.

Speaking of the vampire, he glanced at me with eyes as sharp as glass. Remembering what happened the last time I dared to gaze into his eyes, I chose to avert mine to the ground.

"It sounds good in theory, but nothing is as easy as it sounds," I finished for him. I could feel my jaw tightening as I realized the enormous battle that awaited us. When I looked up at him again, I found his gaze somewhat less intimidating.

"If removing your father were an easy task, it would have undoubtedly been achieved before now," Bram concluded.

I agreed with a nod that he had a good point. My father was a master at surviving, so really, it didn't matter how many advantages we employed, deposing him would be no easy feat. 'Course, I'd never really managed to convince myself it was easy to begin with, but anyhoo ...

"That is all the advice I have to offer, Sweet," Bram said with finality. He slapped his hands together as if he were ready to move on to bigger and better topics.

"Thanks," I started before he took a few steps towards me. The look of hunger had returned in full force.

Don't look into his eyes! I reminded myself and immediately centered my attention on my shoes. I heard him chuckle, obviously finding it humorous that I preferred not to play the part of lovesick victim again. He didn't say anything, though, but reached forward, taking a tress of my hair between his thumb and forefinger, and rubbing it together as if enjoying the tactile sensation. I started to pull away, but he prevented me from doing so by placing his palm in the small of my back.

"Didn't we just go through this?" I snapped, finally focusing on his face.

"Fear not," he quickly responded, dropping the tendril and releasing his hand so that it surreptitiously brushed past my butt before finding its place at his side. He was definitely an opportunist. "I could not abide your death, Sweet," he said softly.

"Well, we both have that in common."

"Perhaps you should leave the fighting to those who are not so indispensable?" he asked, cocking his head to the side as he studied me. "However, if you do decide to fight and if your little uprising fails, I am more than happy to provide you with shelter and a safe haven from your father." He paused a moment or two. "I could promise you protection, Sweet."

I ignored "the little uprising" statement, but the rest of it couldn't be dismissed so easily. "Thanks for the offer, Bram, and I'm sure our soldiers would love to know you consider them dispensable," I started, shaking my head. It irritated me that he was now trying to discourage me from doing what had to be done. My father had targeted me so it was only fair and just that I set my sights on him. "But this is my fight, and there's no way I'm going to back out of it."

Bram didn't say anything for a few moments, but continued staring at me in an off-putting way that was uniquely his. "I do not know how I would tolerate you losing your life," he began, studying me again as if I were on the auction block. "Although, one part of me might consider it a relief."

"Thanks for that," I said with a frown. I started for the entry to the dining room, having decided there was nothing more that needed to be said. Within a split-second, I felt my cheek slamming against his chest as he materialized directly in front of me, something he only rarely did. I stepped away from him, trying to conceal the shock that was already pumping through me. He gripped each of my wrists and held me in place, staring down at me with an urgency I'd never before seen in his eyes.

"I know you are drawn to me," he started, his voice deep and throaty.

I didn't want a repeat of the whole vampire glamour incident. "Let me go."

"You can no longer pretend not to be attracted to me," he continued. "For we both know the truth."

"Um, let me remind you, fangs-for-brains, that you glamoured me! Whatever the hell you thought I was into had nothing to do with the real me. It was all your own doing."

Bram smiled, revealing his fangs seductively. "Yes, I glamoured you, Sweet, but in order to glamour my prey, she must first come to me of her own free will." He paused for a few seconds while I tried to decide if he was full of shit. Was I truly attracted to Bram? I mean, I had to say he was incredibly good looking, and yes, even sexy on occasion. But when it came right down to it, I had no interest in sex with Bram whatsoever. Especially not when I compared it to the almost bestial appetite I had for Knight.

"It is not possible to glamour someone who does not want to be glamoured, my dear," he continued, smiling like he knew he had me.

"Let go of me, Bram," I repeated in an icy tone.

"Give me one evening, Dulcie," he ground out, his fangs sparkling in the low light. "Allow me to experience your body just this one evening and I will forever refrain from seducing you again."

"No," I said quickly, "and there might not be an again." I shook my head as I realized this was his last ditch effort to shag me, since it appeared he wasn't wholeheartedly convinced of my survival skills.

"Your body reacted to my touch," he continued, his eyes traveling down from my face to my breasts and lower still. He brought his eyes back up to mine and they appeared to darken into navy blue again, his passion overtaking them. I closed my eyes and clenched my jaw, refusing to succumb to his powers again.

"I observed you, Sweet, the twinkle in your eyes, the way you bit your lip. I watched your body respond to me, how you arched your back, how your nipples hardened at my touch." I opened my eyes as he brought his gaze to my face again. "I heard the heaviness of your breathing, and I could smell your desire."

I shook my head emphatically. "You manifested those reactions from me, Bram, and you're damn well aware that none of it was real. You tricked me into feeling what you wanted me to feel."

He shook his head, his eyes now pleading. "Your words only betray you, Sweet. You know as well as I do that you long for me to make love to you."

I closed my eyes, refusing to ponder the possibility that I might have wanted him, as he kept intimating that I had. Was it possible? Was there truth to his insistence that he could only glamour a willing victim?

You know yourself, Dulcie, I thought. *You know yourself well enough to know that if you are attracted to Bram at all, it's only on the surface and you would never act on it if you were in your right mind.*

"Allow me to make love to you just this once," he crooned in words almost as quiet as a whisper.

I gulped down the fear that this situation might go south in a hurry. Was Bram the sort of person to force himself on me? I didn't know. 'Course, he'd sort of come close just a few minutes ago with the whole glamouring incident, but I guessed since he hadn't gone through with it, and I remembered him telling me to fight him, maybe he wasn't the sort?

Well, it looked like I was about to find out.

"No," I said simply, but every fiber of my being was on alert, ready to fight him if he so much as breathed in a way I didn't approve of.

Bram didn't release me right away. Instead, we both just stood there, staring at each other as if we were preparing to duel. Then, just when I began to wonder what he was going to do, and if I could really fend off the advances of such a powerful vampire, he simply released my wrists.

"Very well," he said softly while stepping aside, allowing me more space. I didn't say anything as he headed for the archway that led to the dining room, so I did the same. I followed him through the dining room, down the hallway and into the entryway. His steps were hurried and the silence between us was more than uncomfortable. He reached for the doorknob on the front door before turning around and regarding me with what I can only describe as utter disappointment.

"I wish you much luck," he said as he opened the door and allowed me to walk through it. He closed it behind us and beeped the Rolls-Royce unlocked. Saying nothing, he opened the passenger door wide as I seated myself.

"Thank you, Bram," I said softly with an encouraging smile, not knowing what else I could say or do. After basically admitting that I wanted nothing to do with him romantically, much less sexually, I could only imagine how badly I'd wounded his masculine pride.

He nodded and we both just stared at each other for a few seconds before he broke the silence. "I hope you prevail against your father, Sweet."

After traveling through three portals, we arrived at another of Bram's estates, this one more modern and sitting atop a large hill in Hades only knew where. Bram hadn't managed to say one word to me so I wasn't about to make small talk. Instead, I just wanted to get in, get Christina, and get back to the Hotel Des Balances where Knight was awaiting us.

"I shall return shortly," Bram said as he pulled up in front of the four-story, Spanish styled villa and left the Rolls running. I figured he was going to get Christina so I'd patiently wait for his return. Trying to find something to do, I played with the radio stations but didn't encounter much other than static so eventually turned it off.

When Bram appeared at the front door, he was carrying Christina bride style and she appeared to be either asleep or passed out. I immediately stood up and opened my door, fearing the worst. "What's wrong with her?" I called out as I watched him carry her across the olive-tree lined entryway and up to the Rolls. He opened the car door and plopped her in the backseat. She breathed out heavily and then returned to her previous state.

"There is nothing wrong with her," Bram said quickly as he closed the rear door and opened his door, seating himself. He glanced over at me and frowned. "She is merely in a deep sleep as the *Blueliss* works its way from her body. She will be fully restored by morning."

And that was apparently all he had to say about that because he turned the key in the ignition and we were off. It seemed only moments later that we pulled up to the hotel. Bram put the Rolls in park and then proceeded to act every ounce the undead gentleman. He not only opened my door, but then heaved Christina into his arms and walked us both through the lobby to the elevator.

"I previously made room arrangements for Christina," he announced and then fished inside his pocket, handing me a room key.

"That was nice of you," I said quickly.

Bram didn't respond but simply started down the hallway as soon as the elevator beeped open. I was left with no choice but to follow him and glancing down at the key in my hand, read "304." Christina's room was at the end of the hall and Bram stood outside the door, patiently waiting for me to open the door. Once I did so, he deposited Christina on the bed, covered her with a nearby blanket and then retreated back into the hallway, being careful to close her door behind him. Then he glanced at me and offered me a quick smile before bowing low and kissing my hand. Even though he played up his customary role of gallant vampire, there was definitely something different between us now. That easy affability and informality that used to characterize our relationship was gone, leaving in its place something aloof and awkward. I couldn't allow myself to worry about it though because I had way too much on my mind already.

Tomorrow we would attack the Netherworld and there was still so much information I needed to tell Knight. Not only that, but I was more than sure he had plenty of updates for me too.

Glancing at the clock at the end of the hall, I saw it was nearly two a.m., which meant the dawn was only a few hours away. I gave Bram one last smile as the elevator dinged, announcing it was headed downstairs. Bram wasted no time in entering it and seconds later, the doors closed and I was alone. A moment or so later, my elevator arrived and I entered it with a heavy heart. I expected Knight wouldn't be too happy about the length of time I'd spent with Bram. In my defense, though, Bram had definitely provided more than useful information, but I was sure that Knight was about to read me the riot act.

The elevator doors opened with a "ding" and I hurried down the corridor to our room, knocking on the door sheepishly. Within seconds, the door flew open and an unhappy Loki stood peering down at me.

"Two o'clock in the morning?" he asked, his eyebrows furrowing. Even though he was obviously pissed, just the image of him standing there in his dark jeans and white T-shirt with his hair in disarray was enough for me to want to throw my arms around him and kiss him until my lips hurt.

"I'm sorry," I said with an apologetic smile.

Saying nothing, he held the door open for me and I entered the room, without a word. Instead, I kicked off my sneakers and walked over to the windows, noticing the reflection of the streetlamps on the river. When I heard Knight close and lock the door behind us, I turned to face him.

"Christina is in a room on the third floor, sleeping off the *Bluesliss*," I started. "And I've got a lot of other good information for you," I continued, but I could tell Knight's attention wasn't on that. Instead, he was busily scrutinizing my clothing.

"Why are you wearing a different outfit than you were when you left?" he demanded as he crossed his arms against his broad chest and regarded me angrily.

I gulped, striving to prove my innocence. "As part of our agreement, I have to wear a gown every time Bram and I dine together."

Knight regarded me coolly, but his jaw was so tight, it seemed like he was about to shatter his teeth. "So why not change back into the clothes you were wearing before you put on the gown? Or, better yet, why not wear the gown home so I could enjoy seeing you in it?"

I cleared my throat, unsure of what excuse I could find to explain why I didn't do exactly what Knight was asking. Unfortunately, I was a terrible liar.

"Dulcie, sometimes I can't help but wonder what is going on between you and the vampire," he said softly, shaking his head. "I want to believe you when you say he means nothing to you, but when these situations arise, I find my faith in you challenged."

I knew I had to confess the truth of what happened, whether it meant Knight might hold a grudge against Bram or not. The way I looked at it, the truth was better than having him believe I was having an affair with Bram. "The truth is that Bram isn't three hundred years old," I started.

Knight wore an expression of surprise, which quickly gave way to puzzlement. "What the hell does that have to do …"

"Let me finish and I'll tell you," I snapped with a frown that told him I'd appreciate not being interrupted again. "Bram is actually seven hundred, which is significant because he glamoured me. And his power was so intense, I nearly succumbed."

"What do you mean he glamoured you and you nearly succumbed?"

I took another deep breath, fully aware of how bad my words sounded. "I mean, Bram tried to assert his will on me to prove whether or not I was strong enough to resist him. He claims the vampires in the Netherworld Guard are older than three hundred, and will use their powers of persuasion to throw us, and if we aren't prepared to resist them, we'll lose."

Knight glared at me for a few seconds, his cheeks and the tops of his ears flushing. "So what you're trying to tell me is that you weren't strong enough to resist him, meaning you had sex with Bram?" His eyes began to glow as he dropped his arms from his chest and cracked his knuckles.

"No, that's not what I'm trying to tell you," I protested, throwing my hands on my hips as I grew angry that this whole situation wasn't exactly going as I planned.

"Then get to the point and get there quickly."

"Bram had a portrait painted of me," I said with steely reserve, not appreciating the look of condemnation in Knight's eyes. "He glamoured me into using my magic to dress myself in the same fashion as the portrait. Because of his glamour, I was forced to use my magic to change into this," I finished, with a quick glance at myself.

"Then he didn't try to use his powers and force you into his bed?"

I shook my head, before I nodded. "Sort of. He glamoured me into believing I wanted to be with him, but at the same time, he told me to fight his power. So, to make a very long story short: yes, he glamoured me, and yes, I was eventually able to fight his power. But no, I didn't have sex with him. End of story."

"Did he kiss you?" Knight continued, his eyes now fully white.

I felt my cheeks coloring. "Yes."

He took a step closer to me. "Did he touch you?"

I swallowed hard. "Yes."

"Where?"

I felt my eyes widening the closer he came. "He touched my breast."

Knight didn't say anything but stood merely an inch or so away from me, just staring down at me as I stared back up at him. To avoid letting him think that I'd brought any of this on myself, I decided to further explain. "When I found out what he'd done, I punched him," I whispered, my heart racing as I wondered if he believed me. Not only that, but the way he was staring at me and his close proximity created butterflies in my stomach.

Knight reached forward and ran the backs of his fingers down my cheek. "If anyone ever touches you again without your permission, he will answer to me." He paused a second or two. "And as for Bram, he and I have unfinished business."

"He was testing me, Knight," I started in Bram's defense. "He was trying to prove that if I wasn't strong enough to defend myself against him, I shouldn't be fighting the Netherworld Guard. It was just his way of trying to dissuade me."

"There are other ways he could have tested you," Knight said. When he shook his head, I realized he made a good point. "He took advantage of you when you weren't in the right frame of mind to defend yourself. It's a wonder the bastard didn't take full advantage of the situation."

"At any rate," I started, choosing to change the subject, "I'm sure there are way more important subjects for us to discuss. First off, what is the plan for tomorrow?"

107

Knight shrugged. "We've put the invasion off until ten p.m. tomorrow night because Fagan still needs a little more time with the draft, and we wanted to appease our nocturnal faction."

I figured he meant the vampires. While vampires could be out and about at any time of day or night in the Netherworld, such was not the case here. And since we still had to travel from here to there, it made sense to do so under the cover of night.

"Okay, I have information on where we should enter the Netherworld, and Bram gave me this," I started, fishing for the timepiece inside my pocket. I handed the pocket watch to Knight and watched him study it quizzically. "It's programmed to locate my father's whereabouts at any given second."

Knight's eyebrows rose as he shook his head and brought his gaze to mine. "Bram must really want to see your father taken out."

I nodded as I wondered just why that was.

EIGHT

The sunlight filtered through the blinds, hitting me squarely in the face. I shielded my eyes, opening them just a sliver as my pupils adjusted to the light. Yawning, I sat up and stretched, immediately feeling Knight's big arms encircling my waist as he pulled me into him and planted a chaste kiss on the back of my neck. I glanced down, smiling, and covered his hands with my own, realizing I was still naked.

"Maybe you and I aren't going to make it as a couple," he grumbled.

I frowned. "And why is that?"

He smiled, the grin lighting up his entire face, and reflecting in his piercing blue eyes. "Because you're a morning person and I, most definitely, am not."

"Silly man," I scolded without making any motion to move. I just sat in the bed of our hotel room and admired him. I could only hope Christina wasn't a morning person either because I wanted a little one-on-one time with my Loki.

He leaned up on one elbow while I continued to gaze at him. The blankets fell all the way down to his midsection, baring half of his incredible body. I traced the line of a deltoid, down to his bicep and further down his forearm, relishing the feel of his wiry arm hair and the way it tickled my fingers. Even though Knight's unparalleled beauty was a diversion from my overwrought mind, that's all it was—a diversion. I sighed, dropping my hand as I tried to think of happier times, but my all-consuming thoughts centered entirely on our impending future.

"You're nervous," Knight said softly.

I nodded; there was no reason to try and hide my feelings. Today could possibly be the last day of *everything* as I knew it. Tonight we would invade the Netherworld, and who knew what that meant? Tonight I could lose my life, or Knight could lose his, or my father could lose his. Maybe all three of us would pay the ultimate price, or maybe none of us would. Really, only fate dictated whether we rolled an ace or a deuce. Anyway I looked at it, though, after tonight, nothing would be the same again. And those words weren't easy to think in any way, shape or form.

"Dulcie, we don't have to go through with this," Knight started. He reached over and tilted my chin up until we were eye to eye. "We can remain in hiding while we continue planning. We don't have to act now if you don't feel like we're ready."

I shook my head, refusing to comprehend his words for even one second. "No, we have to do this and we have to do it now. You know it as well as I do."

He nodded but didn't say anything for a few moments, and instead, just gazed at me. He secured a stray piece of my hair behind my ear and picked up my hand, intertwining my fingers in his. "I just hate to see you like this."

I smiled and tried to appear more hopeful, attempting to camouflage my insides, which were roiling with fear, anger and worry. "The situation is what it is."

"I want you to know something," he started, clearing his throat when it sounded like his morning voice snuck in. "You are my number one priority; and no matter what happens, your safety is the most important thing to me."

I adamantly shook my head. "You can't think that way."

"I can't help it," he started, but I brought my fingers to his lips to silence him.

"I'm not the most important person in this and you have to convince yourself of that. The most important thing is our freedom as well as the freedom of *all* Netherworld creatures. They are the reason we're all willing to put our lives on the line." I took a breath, holding his gaze. "I'm a soldier just like the rest of us; and if that means risking my life, I'm doing it."

Knight dropped his eyes to the bed and spanned his fingers across the linens, his mood suddenly more somber. But only seconds later, he eyed me again and the former anxiety and concern that was present merely moments ago totally vanished. "You're right. We need to focus on the positive," he said resolutely. "We need to center all of our energy on our plan of attack." He sighed deeply and then nodded. "Just like you said, we're soldiers, first and foremost."

I nodded as I smiled at him, loving him with every fiber of my being. He stood up, gloriously naked; but before I could bask in his male allure, he pulled on his boxer shorts, turning away from me. He approached the giant windows, opening the blinds and stared at the still river. My attention immediately settled on the scratches covering his back. A blush filled my cheeks when I remembered making love to him the night before. At first, in a mutually ravenous impulse, we tore each other's clothes off. He'd pressed my body against the wall and taken me right there. The scratches on his back reminded me of how I'd allowed my inner wild child to surface. After our first foray of animalistic, sexual instinct, we took a half-hour breather. Then, after crawling on top of him, our love making became much quieter and more serenely intense.

"What's on that beautiful mind of yours?" Knight asked, turning to face me. He stretched his arms above his head and bent over before pushing his palms onto the floor to stretch his hamstrings.

I headed for the bathtub that sat in the middle of the room, and turned on the faucet. Taking a seat on the lip of the tub, I relished the feel of the water running over my toes. I glanced up at him and purposely allowed my eyes to travel down his exquisite form before answering. "Our evening last night flashed in my mind once I saw the scratches all over your back," I said with a smile. "Sorry I got so rough, by the way."

Knight chuckled and shook his head, amused. "Hmm, if I remember correctly, you were like a wild animal."

"Moi?" I asked with mock offense, pointing to myself, as if to say we couldn't possibly be talking about the same person.

Taking the few steps that separated us, he smiled before coming up behind me. His stomach felt warm when he brushed up against my back and I leaned closer to him, shutting my eyes and luxuriating in his warm skin on my back and the hot bathwater, which was now up to my ankles.

"Yes, you," he breathed into my ear. He rested his lips against my neck and cupped my right breast.

"You were the one who was the animal," I laughed. "I mean, aren't you the one with the 'inner beast'?" My eyes opened of their own accord when he gently squeezed my nipple between his fingers.

"Hmm, you don't have to remind me; but weren't you the one begging for it 'deeper and harder'?"

"I guess you have a point," I said, laughing. My laugh died instantly when his fingers descended from my breast to the sensitive area between my legs. He rubbed my nub in tiny circles as I sighed and leaned against him, opening my legs to grant him more access.

"That's right," he whispered into my ear. When his finger entered me, I bucked in response.

Suddenly, a buzzing sound interrupted our sex-capade. It sounded as if it was coming from the top of the dresser, which occupied the corner of the room. With a quick glance, I noticed Knight's cell phone flashing like it was jealous I was getting all of his attention. Knight sighed. The call must have been important, though, because he answered it.

"Sam," he said into the receiver, turning to face me again.

I could hear her voice on the other line, but Knight was too far away for me to make sense of her words. Instead, I just watched him as he continued to stand there quietly. He didn't say much, just listened to her, nodding here and there, although his eyes never left me.

Open your legs, he mouthed. I reached around to turn the water off, but only after realizing it was already dangerously close to overflowing. Remembering his request, I looked at him again and watched as he arched his eyebrows as if to say, *Why aren't you doing what I told you?* I smiled and twirled my hair around my finger as I pretended to feel unhurried or undecided as to whether I should obey him.

He frowned and was about to mouth something else when his attention was redirected to his phone conversation. "Sure, that sounds good," he said to Sam as I made his concentration a bit more difficult by parting my legs, and spreading them wide.

I watched his eyes narrow as he focused on the soft flesh between my legs. He approached me and leaned over, never pulling his gaze from mine as he ran his fingers over me. I closed my eyes and threw my head back, arching against his hand as he pushed two fingers into me.

"Yep," he said into the phone. "Good, I'm glad to hear Fagan's got it under control."

He was quiet for a few more seconds so I opened my eyes, only to find him staring at me. He pushed his fingers deeper inside me and I gasped while he smiled, obviously pleased at the results of his technique.

"Interesting," he said. "Yeah, that sounds fine. Okay. I'll see you in about forty minutes."

Hanging up the phone, he placed it carelessly on the floor and stood up. Then he pulled his boxer shorts down, revealing his erection.

"Sam is coming in forty minutes?" I asked, watching as he grabbed both of my ankles and positioned me so my butt was resting on the edge of the tub. He released my ankles and pushed against the insides of my thighs, spreading my legs apart. Then, holding me close, he rubbed his swollen head against my opening.

"Sam and Trey," he corrected. "Apparently, Trey had a vision, which he wants to discuss with us."

I nodded while pushing against him, enticing him to enter me. He pulled himself away, but smiled, tsking at me for my impatience. "And no word from Christina?" I asked as innocently as possible.

He shook his head. "I expect we have a little time to spend by ourselves." Then he smiled wickedly, and retreated from me when I pushed my pelvis forward, pleading for him to enter. "And I plan to spend it wisely."

"Fagan is all finished with the draft?" I asked, undulating my hips against him, still determined to get my way.

"As far as I understand," he said. Then, without another word, he pushed his entire length inside me. I moaned my surprise and pleasure as I began grinding my hips against him, relishing the rhythm as he pulled out and plunged back in again.

The fleeting thought that this could be the last time we made love shattered my bliss like a sharp blade. I had to forcibly ignore it. I refused to focus on the scary what-ifs that dangled before me. Yes, our future was uncertain; and yes, tonight would mark the end of my familiar world, at least as I knew it; but that didn't exclude one last tryst in the here and now.

As far as I was concerned, here and now were all we had left.

I swallowed down my feelings of fear and despondency, choosing to focus on the beautiful man in front of me. His eyes began to glow as he stared at me and leaned down, grazing my lips with his incredibly gently. Then he pushed inside me as deeply as he could while I gasped with pleasure.

"Everything is going to be all right," he whispered as he pulled his lips away from mine.

Saying nothing, I nodded, all the while hoping and praying he was right.

114

About an hour later, Sam, Trey, Dia, Christina, Fagan, Erika, Rachel and Quillan arrived at our makeshift living room. It was comprised of a two-person couch and two side chairs in the hotel suite. Because there wasn't ample seating space, Trey and Christina sat Indian-style on the ground, while Sam and I relaxed on the bed, and Quill and Knight occupied opposite sides of the room, both standing and neither one making eye contact.

During the reunion between Christina and her team, everyone asked her a bazillion questions, including what happened with the *Blueliss*, as well as Bram and my father. I didn't know who would take over from here on out, Christina or Knight, but I wasn't exactly surprised when Knight cleared his throat, intimating his position as first in command.

"As I understand, Fagan, the draft is complete?" the Loki asked, folding his arms across his chest as he faced the Drow who looked less than happy to be present and accounted for. And I didn't think Fagan's lack of enthusiasm was in response to this meeting—it appeared that was just how he was all the time—miserable.

Knight nodded with an expression of curiosity as he turned to Erika, who was busily chomping a wad of gum. This one smelled grape-flavored. Before Knight could inquire as to where she stood with regard to her responsibilities, she began anxiously nodding, like she was listening to her favorite song.

"All my soldiers are ready and waiting for the go ahead," she said, smiling broadly. "We had a pow-wow this morning where I gave an awesome pep talk and now everything is cool beans."

Knight nodded as he gave Fagan and Erika a congratulatory smile. "Good work. " Then he turned to face the rest of us. "Dulcie and I have uncovered some new

115

information that will be of interest to all of you," he started. Pulling the portal ripper from one of his jeans pockets and Bram's pocket watch from the other, he began explaining what each did. After the oohs and ahhs, Knight then informed everyone of Bram's advice regarding using the portal ripper to create a passage to Squander Valley.

As expected, no one seemed enthused about the *Bregone* swamp part; but once I assured them that wearing a gas mask would ensure their safety, they seemed more on board.

"So that leads us to the next agenda item, which is … Who would like to lead the unit into Squander Valley?" Knight asked.

"I'm going after my father," I said adamantly, not wanting anyone to think that particular job was up for grabs. To me, it all started with my father and that's where it would end.

"It's too dangerous," Quill commented while shaking his head.

"Quill," I started, but he silenced me by holding up his hand, letting me know in no uncertain terms that he intended to voice an opinion on this subject.

"I've held my tongue this whole time, Dulce, but I can't any longer. You make it sound like offing your father is an easy task," he began.

"I never said that," I interrupted, sensing the anger as it churned in my stomach. I've always had an aversion to people telling me what I should and shouldn't do. This time, I was steadfast in my mission to take down my father.

"It's not a matter of cutting a portal with some cool kitchen gadget that Bram gave you," Quill continued. "Your father will have bodyguards, as well as other thugs surrounding him. And these guys don't pussy-foot around. They kill first and ask questions later."

"No one can talk me out of this," I said with steely resolve.

"I'm not arguing that your father shouldn't be taken out," Quill continued. "I am fully onboard with that, but not with you risking your life."

"I appreciate your concern …"

"Between your life and his, Melchior won't hesitate to sacrifice you," Quill interrupted. "Those are odds I'm not comfortable with."

"My mind is already made up," I answered.

Quill shook his head, his eyes showing as much determination as mine. He glared at me while I glared back. "Sometimes you are so fucking stubborn," he whispered. Without waiting for my response, he turned to Knight, who hadn't budged from his position on the opposite side of the room, and was watching us with piqued interest.

"And what about you?" Quill demanded, turning his glare from me to Knight.

"What about me?" Knight asked defensively.

"You supposedly care for her …"

"There's no 'supposedly' about it," Knight rebuffed, his eyes glowing as a warning.

"Then explain to her that what she's doing is insane, and it's only going to get her killed. You said you were familiar with Netherworld politics, so you must know what Melchior's capable of."

Knight nodded. "I'm more than aware."

"So why the fuck are you sending Dulcie to her death?" Quill railed back at him.

Knight didn't respond right away. His jaw seemed incredibly tight and his knuckles turned white, indicating he was probably only seconds away from erupting. "Dulcie is more than capable of taking anyone out," he said icily. "She's the best Regulator I've ever seen."

"I'm not debating her abilities as a Regulator. She worked for me longer than she worked for you. Believe me, I am more than aware of her skills."

Knight's eyes glowed even more brightly and he folded his arms against his chest in an apparent attempt to keep his temper under control. When he didn't say anything, Quill continued.

"Melchior O'Neil isn't just anybody," he finished.

Knight shook his head as he looked at me. I could see the angst in his eyes and realized that he agreed in part with Quill. Part of him didn't want me to fight at all—he wanted to ensure that I was safe. But the other part understood that I *had* to go after my father. I *had* to make him pay not only for what he'd done to me, but for what he'd done to every other Netherworld creature as well.

"I respect Dulcie; and for that reason, I support whatever decision she makes," Knight said finally. I nodded at him, revealing my appreciation.

Despite outward appearances that I was nonchalantly grateful for Knight's words, inside me was another story. Knight's verbal endorsement, despite the fact that I was sure he concurred with Quillan, was one of the reasons I loved him as much as I did. Why? Because Knight always encouraged me to be *me*.

"And you do realize that you could lose her?" Quill continued heatedly. "That we *all* could lose her?"

Knight simply nodded as Quill shook his head angrily. Turning to face me, Quill sighed, then started for the door. "I need some fresh air," he said, throwing the door open and disappearing behind it.

I swallowed hard as I weighed whether or not Quill was right. Maybe my pigheadedness would cost me my life; but on the flipside, maybe it wouldn't. Maybe it would cost my father's life. And those were the odds I was willing to take.

"So who will volunteer to command the attack on Squander Valley?" Knight asked again, eyeing each of us in turn.

"I'll do it," Christina piped up. "Just tell me what to do and I'll do it."

"But you're…" Dia started, no doubt intending to remind Christina that she was the head of The Resistance, and thus immune from volunteering.

But Christina shook her head, with a beaming smile at me. "This fight belongs to all of us. What good is it if we don't fight?"

Dia nodded as she faced Knight again. "Christina's taking Squander Valley, and Dulce is going after her father; so where do you want the rest of us?"

After a few minutes of conversation, we agreed that Christina and Dia would lead the attack on Squander Valley; while Knight, Quill and I would take the most highly trained Resistance soldiers and go after my father. Yes, Knight was less than thrilled to have Quill onboard, but I insisted he take part. I knew Quill could help us find and take down my father. Erika, Rachel and Sam planned to stage a fictitious surrender at the Netherworld airport to create a distraction and draw the Netherworld Guard away from our co-occurring attacks. Finally, Fagan and Trey would lead a raid on the second largest Netherworld Guard base in Tipshaw, only a few hundred miles from Squander Valley.

"So we're good?" Knight asked, looking at each of us pointedly.

I started to nod when I noticed Sam shaking her head. She faced Knight and sighed. "There was something Trey and I wanted to talk to you all about," she said in a despondent voice.

Knight nodded. "That's right—you said as much over the phone. I'm sorry. It escaped my mind."

Sam waved away his concern with her hand and turned to face Trey. "Okay, Trey, the floor is yours," she said. She smiled at him as if he were a five-year-old about to appear in his first play.

As expected, everyone's attention focused on the hobgoblin, who sat on the floor, holding his knees to his chest. His face was pale, beyond its usual pasty white. I suddenly realized that in the course of our discussions, Trey hadn't said one word. Instead, he'd just sat there, holding his knees to his chest while rocking back and forth.

"I, uh … I had a vision," he said softly, exhaling a pent-up breath, and sounding anxious about something. I knew Trey well enough to recognize whatever vision he'd had wasn't a happy one. Trey's visions often stressed him out because they came without warning. Many times, he even channeled the perspective of the evil-doer, which resulted in even more anxiety.

"Are you okay, Trey?" I asked with a reassuring smile.

He shook his head, and his eyes dropped down to his untied sneakers as he rocked back and forth, seemingly to try to console himself.

"What happened?" Knight asked, glancing first at Trey and then at Sam. "What vision?"

Sam shook her head. "He wouldn't tell me; he just asked me to call you to see if we could come over," she said. Facing the hobgoblin again, Sam said, "Trey, you can tell us what happened, what you saw." She flashed her best "mom" expression, which usually coaxed him into confessing. He glanced at her and swallowed hard before facing Knight as well as me.

"I got a vision of something I didn't like," he said, biting his lip.

"What was it?" I asked.

"It wasn't so much a vision," he corrected. With a shrug, he started rocking back and forth again, wobbling like an unbalanced rocking chair.

"Was it more of a feeling?" Sam asked. He nodded, but still made no motion to say anything, and his eyes were filled with worry. It was never easy when Trey got into such moods. Usually, it took days to console him, and even longer still before he resumed his normal, jovial personality.

"Yeah, it was more of a feeling," Trey nodded. "It hit me early this morning. I woke up and everything felt normal, well, as normal as it could feel, considering what's going on," he started. As he continued, his eyes got wider and I could see his hands beginning to shake. "All of a sudden, I just started to feel this really bad feeling in my stomach. At first, I thought the eggs and bacon I had for breakfast were bad or something, but this feeling was different. It wasn't like the stomach ache you get when you're gonna hurl." He took a deep breath and paused for a few seconds before glancing up at me again. "It was a feeling of … like … a really bad dread. Like something bad is gonna happen."

"But we sort of already know that, right, Trey?" I asked, trying to sound sympathetic. "I mean, invading the Netherworld isn't going to be easy, and people will inevitably get hurt." I paused for a few seconds. "Bad stuff *is* going to happen. There's no way around it."

He shook his head like I wasn't getting it. "The feeling wasn't anything like that," he said dismissively. "It wasn't anything in general. It was way worse than that …" his voice faded as he looked away.

"What, Trey?" I prodded, straining to understand what he appeared to be keeping from me.

"It was like I suddenly had this knowledge, like someone let me look into a crystal ball to see the future, only it wasn't something I could see with my eyes. It was something I could feel; and it was this horrible feeling of … loss, like something very important to me was ripped away." When he faced me again, his eyes seemed hollow, wide and filled with fear. "And I knew what it was almost immediately."

"What was it?" Rachel asked.

"It was death," Trey answered softly. "It was an intense feeling that someone is going to die."

Then he became quiet again as he started rocking back and forth, leaving all of us to wonder exactly what his words meant. I was a little baffled because death in wartime shouldn't have come as any surprise. It was expected—if we attacked the Netherworld, creatures would die. That was all there was to it.

Trey brought his pained eyes to mine and at that moment, it was as if the ground beneath my feet suddenly gave out. I instantly understood what he was so reluctant to say.

"You felt it about me," I said softly.

Trey simply nodded, dropping his attention to the carpet as he started rocking back and forth again.

NINE

The whole room became eerily quiet. Maybe the silence wasn't much of a surprise, though, after Trey's announcement regarding the vision he'd had of my death. Although I agreed with everyone else in the room that Trey's news was unnerving, I chose to discount it … slightly. Why? Because it wasn't an actual vision, only a "feeling"; and to me, a feeling didn't carry as much weight as a vision did. Or maybe it was just my wishful thinking. Either way, there definitely was a void building within me that acted like a bulwark, buffering me from any information I preferred not to hear. When it came right down to it, it made no difference whether Trey had a vision of my death or just a feeling about it—my determination to see my father taken down was unaffected. And the more I thought about it, the more steadfast I became. My father had to be removed as Head of the Netherworld; and that's all there was to it.

"Explain this feeling you received," Knight said to Trey in a steely voice, his lips in a tight line, all of his attention focused on the hobgoblin.

Trey sighed, his hands shaking with anxiety, as he glanced from Knight to me, and back to the Loki again. Then he shook his head and chewed on his lip before clearing his throat. "I don't think it's right to talk about it with her standing right there," he said in a small, sad voice. Then, refusing to look at me, he pretended extreme interest in the carpet.

"Trey, I need to know what you saw or felt," I said calmly, but with undeterred emphasis. I didn't want to give the impression that Trey's news in any way disturbed me, because I was afraid any hint of fear on my part would keep him from telling me more. Yep, I had to go for cool, calm and collected, but when I suddenly stood up without even realizing it, it became fairly obvious that I wasn't as untouched by the news as I pretended to be. "Whatever it is, I can handle it," I finished, more as a reminder to myself.

"*We* can handle it," Knight corrected with a quick smile. Even though he wanted to appear encouraging, I could see the storm clouds of apprehension brewing in his eyes. I've only seen Knight visibly bothered a handful of times, and based on those outcomes, I've learned to dread them.

"Dulce," Sam said. She stood up and faced me with pained angst in her eyes, but I shook my head. I couldn't give in now. No matter the consequences, I had to fight for what I believed in—freedom from my father's tyranny.

I nodded at Knight, trying to implant the idea that I could handle whatever Trey had to tell me. "If I don't know what to expect, I won't be able to change it."

Trey remained silent for a few more seconds. It was obvious he was ensconced in a battle of whether to tell me, and it continued to rage inside him. Suddenly, he cleared his throat and faced me, his eyes shiny. "I just have this feeling in my gut that something's gonna happen to you, Dulce. It's real hard to explain, but it's like this big ol' rock dropped right into my stomach with your name on it."

"How did you know it was a feeling about me?" I asked, trying to decipher whether or not his vision really posed a threat. "I mean, you've never had feelings about anything in the past, just visions, so what makes you think you're actually channeling something this time?"

"Because the feeling came from nowhere. It was just like when I get a vision. I was busy minding my own business, doing my own thing, and it just crept up on me like a bad dream."

"That still doesn't really mean much," I said with a half-assed smile, trying not to belittle his abilities.

Trey dropped his gaze to the ground and rocked back and forth, still clutching his knees to his chest. "I felt you," he answered. "Knowing it was you completely filled me. It was like I could see you, hear you and smell you, but I didn't actually see, hear or smell you, if that makes sense."

"Not really," I started, but hesitated when he started shaking his head.

"I'm pretty sure I was channeling the future, Dulcie. And it was warning me about something bad that was centering around you, even though I couldn't actually see anything." He took a deep breath and turned sad, cow eyes on me. "Maybe I'm wrong. I hope to Hades I'm wrong, Dulce. Maybe my mind is so mixed up from all the stress and worry about going to war with your father that I just dredged up some crazy thing that's totally wrong."

Knight shook his head. "When have you ever been wrong, Trey?"

Trey gulped. "Never." Then he nodded with consternation before offering me a consoling smile, as if apologizing that his visions never erred.

"Then you can't go," Sam said in her worried, motherly voice as she brought her big, brown eyes to mine. "There's no other decision to make. "

I turned to face her and shook my head. "I have to go, Sam," I said softly. "This is something I have to do, no matter the consequences."

"But Trey just said," she started, her voice cracking.

"Girl …" Dia started while shaking her head.

"Dulcie," Knight interrupted as he motioned to the corner of the room, obviously begging me for some time alone. I said nothing, but followed him, glancing out at the river, and suddenly wishing I could be as free as the water. If only I could simply flow over rocks and under bridges, carving out my place in the world without conflict, as easily as water shapes the land.

"I know it's important to you to go after Melchior," Knight started. His eyes were fixed on mine, but his expression didn't reveal any of his thoughts.

"Knight, please don't try to talk me out of this."

125

He took a deep breath and expelled it, running his hands through his hair. He was frustrated and worried—I could now see as much in the furrowed lines between his eyebrows. "You won't be dissuaded?"

I shook my head. "Instead of fighting me, give me your assistance."

"You know I've always had your back and I always will."

He said nothing more so I figured there was nothing more to say. Knight would back me just like he always had. I smiled my appreciation and decided to start in on the others again, figuring if I swayed Knight, I now had a room full of people on which I had to do the same. I eyed Trey, who was zoning out on the carpet, before bringing my gaze back to the others. "Whatever Trey felt could just be one version of the future. Maybe I can change my own destiny based on the choices I make." I knew I was definitely grasping for straws, but nothing else came to me so I had to go with it. "Or Trey could have just channeled my feelings and maybe I'll just get hurt in the battle, who knows? It could be that he just channeled my feelings regarding someone else."

"Or maybe Trey channeled exactly what's going to happen," Sam frowned at me, revealing that she most definitely wasn't buying what I was selling.

"My point is that none of us knows for sure what's going to happen, including Trey," I continued, feeling my jaw tighten as I tried to defend my stance. "Either way, I'm not changing my mind and I would appreciate it if all of you would drop the subject," I finished with undeterred resignation.

"You're going to be fine, Dulce," Knight said assuredly, staring at me as his eyes narrowed. "I will make sure nothing happens to you. I'll be at your side the entire time."

I nodded, but was spared the chance to respond when the door opened and Quill sauntered in, returning from his mission to get some fresh air. His eyes were trained on mine, and when we were in earshot of one another, he held his hand out, already turning on his heel toward the door. "Can we talk, Dulce?" he asked with a fleeting look at Knight. "Alone."

I didn't say anything and neither did Knight. I saw the Loki's eyes shift from Quill to me. He simply nodded as if to say he wouldn't put up an argument. Even if he did, I would've insisted on making up my own mind anyway. I firmly believed the only person who should make decisions for me was me.

I took Quill's hand and allowed him to lead me through the hotel room and out the door. Once he closed the door behind us, he didn't falter in his breakneck stride, but led me down the hallway, taking a right, and after another fifteen feet, we T-boned into a large window, overlooking the river below. At the window, he pulled me in front of him so I was parallel with it before taking a deep breath and dropping his attention to my hand, still clasped in his. He just gazed at our hands in silence, and then ran the pad of his thumb across my knuckles.

"Dulce, I heard everything Trey said," he admitted softly, bringing his beautiful amber eyes to mine.

I couldn't say his comment surprised me, even though he wasn't in the room when Trey said what he had. I guessed Quill just used his elfin magic to eavesdrop on the conversation. "So you're going to try to, once again, talk me out of it?"

His eyes seemed to bore right through me, as if he could see the very depths of my soul. He shook his head in frustration. Well, "incensed frustration" might have been more fitting to say. "I don't understand how you would even want to go through with this after what you just heard Trey say." Taking a deep breath, he blew it out loudly, shaking his head again. "You worked with Trey for years, Dulcie, you know his visions are never wrong."

I held my chin up high before answering, "I'm aware of that."

"Why are you still going through with this? Are you trying to prove something?"

"No, I'm not trying to prove something," I snapped.

"So have you completely lost your mind?"

"No, I haven't lost my mind!" I railed back, propping my hands on my hips defiantly. "And I have to admit I'm surprised that you know my father as well as you do, yet you still act surprised that I want to see him taken out." I took a breath and faced him squarely. "You might better ask me how could I *not* go through with it? Especially after everything my father has done! Not only to me, but to you and Christina, Caressa, Knight ... shit, to the whole Netherworld population!"

"Yes, your father is an asshole, Dulce, and yes, he deserves to be removed from office and thrown in prison or even killed," he yelled at me. "I'm not arguing that! What I am arguing is that your life isn't worth his!"

I shook my head. "I'm not fully convinced that Trey's 'feeling' was necessarily a vision," I started, but once Quill began vehemently shaking his head, I quickly got to point number two. "And even if he is right, it still doesn't change my mind."

"Why?" Quill demanded angrily.

"Because it's a moot point, that's why."

"I don't even know how you can consider self-sacrifice a moot point," he said, glaring at me.

"It's a moot point because when I first agreed to join The Resistance and fight, I knew there was a good chance I could lose my life by doing so," I said and sighed. "My sacrifice is no more noteworthy than any other soldier, willing to fight and risk *his or her life*."

"Dulcie, none of those soldiers knows what's going to happen them. But you do!" Quill raged at me. "That's the difference! You know what you're in for! You know that if you go through with this, you *will* most assuredly die!"

I shook my head again, still unconvinced. "I don't know that for sure, and no one can say it's definitely going to happen, not even Trey. If you remember, Trey said he didn't *see* anything. This so-called 'vision' was only based on feelings, Quill, and feelings aren't anywhere near as concrete as images. Maybe he was channeling my sadness about someone or something else? Maybe he had it all wrong to begin with!"

Quill shook his head and ran his hands through his hair. "You're kidding yourself, Dulce, but I'm not going to fall for the same crap. If you're going to go through with this, you need to be honest with yourself about the consequences. This could mean your death."

"Could," I repeated skeptically. Quill glared at me and breathed out deeply, but before he could say another word, I interrupted him. "Nonetheless, I've included you in the mission to depose my father so you can act the part of bodyguard too," I finished hastily, aware of how disingenuous my words sounded.

"I'll do my best," Quill answered, but I sensed how disheartened he was in his tone of voice and expression. "I just don't get you, Dulce, I guess I never did." The anger diminished in his eyes and we were left just staring at one another, our long friendship and shared years of common history hanging between us by invisible threads. He reached for my hand again and squeezed it.

Looking up at him, I smiled, wanting to make amends. Now that the last hours before we invaded the Netherworld were upon us, I didn't want anything ugly between us. "I know where you're coming from with all this, Quill. I know you're just trying to protect me because you care about me."

Quill shook his head and dropped his attention to my fingers. He brushed the tops of them with his own tenderly. When he brought his eyes to mine again, they seemed softer somehow, delicate. "It's more than that, Dulce," he said, his voice growing weaker. He smiled, but it was bittersweet. "Yes, I care about you; and yes, I'm scared to death for you, but I'm not just saying this as your friend. What I feel for you transcends the boundaries of platonic friendship."

129

"Quill," I said in a tone that cautioned him not to go there. I didn't want to go down that road, especially since I couldn't return the sentiments I knew he was on the cusp of revealing to me. Not only that, but I was also on the verge of losing it. I had so many conflicting thoughts raging through my mind: what-ifs and fears that were beyond stressful. I certainly didn't need to add this conversation to the mix.

But he shook his head again, as if to let me know he wouldn't be placated so easily. "I have to get this off my chest, especially now." He took a deep breath and I imagined he figured we probably wouldn't have a chance to have this conversation again. I didn't say anything, but swallowed down the sudden urge to flee. I forcibly held my feet in place. Yes, I wasn't in the right mental state to have a deep conversation where I would undoubtedly disappoint him, but it looked like I had no other choice.

"I know you're with Vander," Quill said gently, almost apologetically. His eyes suddenly appeared downcast, their usual striking amber now the color of autumn maple leaves. "But that doesn't change the fact that ..." he started, bringing his eyes to mine, "I love you, Dulcie."

My eyes dropped to the ground, and I felt incredibly hollow and dejected because I couldn't tell him what he wanted to hear. Most of all, I didn't want to see any pain or disappointment in his eyes. He tilted my chin up and smiled at me.

"I don't expect you to tell me that you love me too, Dulce, in fact, I don't expect anything from you." He smiled more broadly, as if trying to emphasize his sincerity. "This is something that I want to get off my chest because I've never told you how much you mean to me, which I now realize was a mistake." He shrugged. "Well, the truth is, I've known it was a mistake for a long time, but I've never admitted it. So I'm going to make up for lost opportunities now." He inhaled deeply before facing me earnestly. "I want you to know that you are the only person who has ever really been there for me." With a deep breath, he added, "I know we went through some difficult times when you first found out about my involvement with street potions."

"I never stopped caring about you," I said quickly, finally comfortable enough to admit to something. Although I didn't love him the way he wanted me to, I still cared about him as a friend and I always would.

"I know," he answered, grinning from ear to ear as he tightened his grasp on my hand. "You've always been there for me, Dulce, and I want you to know not only how much I appreciate it, but also how much I appreciate you."

"Thanks, Quill."

He nodded, but when he didn't release my hand, I figured there was more on his mind. He smiled again. "I also want you to know that there isn't a day that goes by where I don't kick myself for not snatching you when I had the chance."

The time he referred to was so long ago, it didn't even feel like part of my past anymore. When I worked full-time as a Regulator of the ANC in Splendor, Quillan was my boss, and I had a huge crush on him. That was, of course, before Knight ever wandered into my life, capturing my affections forever. Now that I remembered it, yes, Quill was probably right—if he had shown his feelings for me then, I would have no doubt returned them and then some.

But that time was long past, a fleeting memory that seemed alien to me somehow, like I'd seen it in a movie or something. "How come you never …?" I started.

"Because I knew you would hate me once you found out what I truly was," he interrupted me, shaking his head as he expelled a pent-up breath. "I couldn't stomach the idea that you would eventually find out that I was working for your father." He inhaled again deeply and frowned, his eyes glazing over with what appeared to be pain and frustration. "I just never wanted to see the expression in your eyes if you ever found out who and what I really was."

Well, he was right about that. If we were romantically involved and I found out about Quill's ties to my father, I never would have forgiven him. "I guess we were doomed before we ever even started," I said with a mirthless laugh.

Quill nodded, reflecting the same disheartened expression I gave him. "Yeah, we were." Then he grew quiet as his eyes took on a faraway gaze, like he was recalling places, people and events now long gone. "Just having you in my life was enough for me then," he said gently. "Because it had to be." He nodded and the smile on his lips suggested he was still living in his memories. "Just being able to come by your apartment after work, or bring you dinner when you were sick filled me with so much happiness, Dulcie. Laughing with you about Trey, and working so closely together got me through the reality of the nightmare I was living. I don't know what I would have done if I hadn't had your friendship, or if you hadn't entered my life. Now that I look back on it, you were everything to me, Dulce. You still are." He sighed, but quickly smirked as if something amusing suddenly occurred to him. He glanced at me with a boyish twinkle in his eyes. "And when I found out you were writing a romance novel about me ..."

"Holy Hades," I said, trying to hide my embarrassed smile with my hand as I shook my head. The book *was* a romance novel about a pirate and his lady. I'd fashioned the character of the pirate after Quill, even using his real name in my word document, with the intention of changing it later. Well, as luck would have it, Quill happened to be over one day and the word document was up on my computer screen, so yep, you guessed it—he saw his name. I turned every shade of red then and even now, my cheeks flushed at the memory because the worst part was that the scene I was writing about him was an explicitly sexual one.

"Don't be embarrassed," Quill said with a small laugh. "I was honored. I'm still honored to think you ever had romantic feelings for me, that you ever would have considered the things you wrote about ... with me."

"I definitely did, Quill," I said, shaking my head, mortification still coloring my cheeks. "You don't even

132

know the half of it," I finished, smiling up at him as thoughts about my writing career resurfaced in my mind. Yes, once upon a time, before all this shit with the Netherworld and my father hit the fan, I hoped to become a full-time author, and leave my days in law enforcement far behind me. My pirate romance novel didn't get very far, though, so I ditched it. After putting the kibosh on the Quillan pirate book, I wrote one about Bram that managed to attract the attention of a huge literary agent in New York. Then this mess with my father and the Netherworld fell on my shoulders, and I hadn't even thought about writing for the last month, at least.

If I survive this attack on my father, I promise to pick up where I left off in my writing career, I vowed, suddenly relishing my renewed sense of determination.

"No matter what happens tonight," Quill continued, "I will be with you every step of the way, Dulce, and I swear to you that I will do everything in my power to make sure you're safe."

"Thank you, Quill, that means a lot to me," I answered, glancing up at him while tears started in my eyes.

"Don't get all emotional on me now," Quill said with a chuckle as he wiped the pad of his index finger across my eyelids.

I took a deep breath and clenched my eyes shut, willing the tears back. If there was one thing I hated, it was crying with an audience. "I'm okay," I said as I managed a quick smile.

"I won't let anything happen to you, Dulcie," he whispered before pulling me into him, and kissing the top of my head. I wrapped my arms around him and felt his chin on the top of my head as he held me. His crisp, clean scent filled my nostrils and mind with nostalgia. It reminded me of the old days at the ANC, when things were substantially simpler than they were now. That was when the only dilemma that occupied my thoughts was whether it was wise to have a crush on my boss.

133

How far I'd come.

TEN

I wasn't sure how Quill and Knight were feeling, but I sensed a cold numbness that welled up from deep within me, an overwhelming vacuum that consumed my entire being. I wondered if someone cut me, would I even feel it? In my newly vegetative state, all worries and fears of my impending future were banished from my head until my brain resembled a barren moonscape. And maybe it was a good thing that I felt emotionless at the prospect of ripping a portal opening into the air in order to confront my father, because who knew what that little task might entail? Death was the quick answer, but whose death? Now that was the clincher. Either way, the moment of reckoning was merely seconds away.

Those final seconds slipped through my fingers like cold honey, slow and painstakingly gluey, as if time itself didn't want to pass. But pass it did, and I soon found myself preparing to rip the portal for Erica, Rachel and Sam to stage their mock surrender at the Netherworld airport. Amongst them were nine civilians who would play the parts of innocent victims.

"Good luck," Knight said as he engulfed first Erica, then Rachel and then Sam in a bear hug. Erica just nodded, her meditative mood in complete contrast to her Hawaiian Punch-colored hair. Taking a deep breath, she faced her comrades. She studied them for a few seconds before turning back to us. A gentle wind whipped through her hair until the short strands splayed across her cheeks, looking as delicate as the gossamer threads of a spider web.

"We're ready," she said simply. I couldn't help noticing her usually buoyant personality was definitely turned down a notch or two. In its place was a pensiveness

I'd never witnessed in her before, not that I knew her that well but anyhoo … A general somberness remained hanging in the air, which wasn't surprising, given the enormous question mark hovering over our heads with regard to our impending future.

"Dulce," Sam said softly as I turned my attention from Erica to my best friend. It was as if I could suddenly see Sam for the first time. Was it because this could be the last time? Her beautiful, brown eyes were wider than usual and her skin appeared whiter, suggesting her nervousness. Her brown hair was pulled off her face in a low ponytail and she was wearing khaki pants and brown polo shirt. She looked more like a model for a Gap ad than a witch confronting an unknown future.

"You're going to be just fine, Sam," I said softly, grasping her arms. "No matter what happens, you just play dumb, okay? As far as you know, you're surrendering to my father and that's it."

She nodded and I could see wet pools filling her eyes. "I'm not worried about me, Dulcie."

"Don't worry about me either," I insisted, with a smile that hopefully conveyed a sense of calm and control. "I always come out on top; you know that," I finished jokingly.

Sam smiled and a soft, sad laugh escaped her lips. But only seconds later, her lower lip began to tremble as the tears that were welling in her eyes only moments earlier overflowed and began coursing down her cheeks, soaking into her collar. I pulled her forward and wrapped my arms around her as she rested her cheek against my head because I was so damn short.

"You really do always come out on top," she said with another bittersweet laugh. But the laugh was cut short by a sob.

"Don't cry, Sam," I whispered when her body began to shake slightly. "Everything is going to be fine, and in just a few hours' time, we'll all be reunited again like one big happy family. Except my asshole father will be in custody or, better yet, dead." Obviously, I had no idea what I was talking about and a few hours sounded so optimistic as to be ridiculous, but I wasn't good when it came to soothing people, so what else could I do?

Sam wiped her sleeve across her eyes, drying her tears before smiling again, her lower lip still trembling. "Good luck, Dulce, and make sure you keep those two at your side the entire time," she motioned to Quill and Knight who were standing behind us.

"We'll be like her shadows," Quill said with a quick smile as he approached Sam and hugged her, whispering in her ear, "You'll be fine."

"Whatever happens with the rest of us," Knight started, facing Sam, his expression serious. "You, MJ and Erica just play out the whole surrender thing; you got it?"

Sam nodded and I took a deep breath, feeling some relief at Knight's words. It did sound promising that Sam, Rachel, Erica and their posse could just play at surrendering to Melchior's forces if the rest of us failed in our attempts; but I couldn't help worrying that my father would eventually realize it was feigned. As soon as he put together that all three attacks happened within minutes of one another, he'd know what we were up to. But, since that thought only managed to depress me, I decided to abandon it. After all, wasn't it better to hope for the best, even if the best meant being blissfully ignorant?

"You take care of her," Sam said to Knight as she inclined her head in my direction.

"I will guard her with my life," Knight answered sternly, his eyes reinforcing the statement.

"Girl, you take care of yourself," Dia piped up. She threw her arms around Sam and then followed suit with Erica and Rachel, who stood just behind her. After tears were shed and good-byes were exchanged by all, I held the portal ripper in my hand and followed Bram's directions. As I pulled the device toward me, the air sliced open beneath my fingertips. It looked like I'd ripped clear through one

137

landscape, revealing another. In a manner of speaking, that was exactly what happened. The ripper silently crossed the line between this dimension and the next, blasting a gust of frigid air against my skin in the process.

"No time to waste," I said quickly. Erica nodded at Knight and me while Rachel offered us both a smile and the two simply stepped directly through the portal, and disappeared right in front of us. Three of the recruited civilians quickly followed them. Sam took a deep breath as she offered me a reassuring smile.

"I love you, Dulce," she said softly.

"I love you too," I whispered back and watched as she too disappeared into the Netherworld, just like that. One second she was beside me, and the next, she wasn't. Refusing to dwell on my own emotions, I immediately turned the portal ripper upside-down and "stitched" up the opening to prevent any uninvited travelers from passing through. Once the portal was sutured together, I took a deep breath and thought whatever Sam's fate, I'd just sent her straight into it.

Something inside me broke and all the bravado I'd put on for Sam's benefit dissolved inside me. In no time, the rampart that held back my tears failed as an impenetrable wall and became more of an enthusiastic net.

"Dulce? You okay?" Knight asked, peering at me with concern.

My hands fisted involuntarily and my nails dug into my palms. "Yes, I'm fine," I said, more to fortify myself than to answer him honestly. I took a deep breath and clenched my eyes shut tightly, insisting that I keep it together. I had to be strong—I couldn't give in to my true feelings and collapse into a sobbing heap. If I did, I knew I wouldn't be able to emerge from it. What I needed most now was a clarity of purpose that would allow me to operate like an automaton.

Get in and get out, I told myself. *You need to be calm, cool and collected, not clouded by emotion.*

I opened my eyes to find Quill and Knight staring at me. "I'm fine," I repeated, this time with real authority and even a tinge of anger.

The surrender at the airport was currently underway. Now there were three more portals to rip and three more attacks to stage. Christina stepped forward, with Dia right behind her and one hundred of our soldiers along with one hundred fifty new recruits. They stood in rows of ten creatures across, twenty-five rows in total and looked like a marching band, minus the brass instruments. Instead, they all clutched black gas masks to protect them from the fumes of the *Bregone* swamp.

"Got your radio?" Knight asked Christina. He motioned to his black walkie-talkie, which he held up to prove his was present and accounted for.

"I do," she answered quickly. Her huge smile suggested just how prepared she was for what was about to ensue. In her expression, I could read the weariness of all the trials and tribulations she'd endured fighting in the name of The Resistance. Everything she and Knight had prepared for was about to unfold, and no matter what the consequences, the twinkle in her eye promised that she intended to fight with sword, tooth and nail.

"Let's do this!" she called out.

Knight chuckled and opened his arms wide. She fell into them and hugged him tightly. "Thank you for everything, Knightley," she said softly while gazing up at him. Then pulling away, she took a deep breath before glancing over at me. "You got yourself a good one."

I nodded with a quick smile first to her and then to Knight. "I know."

"Girl, you be careful when you go after that excuse you have for a father," Dia said with a great big grin and that Diva-esque thing she did with her neck. She wrapped her arms around me, suffocating me in the scent of one of Victoria's Secret's body lotions.

"I will, D, you be careful too," I said softly. I could feel the frog returning to my throat as Dia released me. She smiled down at me as if she were my mom and it was my first day of school.

"Now don't go doin' anything heroic, you hear me? Just stay alive," she said confidently, but I could see the trepidation looming in her eyes.

"No heroics for me."

Dia nodded as I took in her bright red pants and purple shirt and hair that settled around her head in myriad sausage curls. With her flame-red lipstick and silvery eye shadow, she looked like she was headed to a dance club rather than an uncertain fate. I shook my head and laughed. "Always the diva."

She nodded and offered me a raised-brow expression, rubbing her nails against her shiny shirt. "Girl, just 'cause you gotta fight, doesn't mean you can't do it lookin' good." Then she glanced down at herself and nodded. "Uh huh, an' if it's one thing I know how ta do, it's lookin' good."

I just smiled at my friend and watched her approach Knight. She gave him the once-over while clicking her tongue against the top of her mouth. "Even when we're headed off into some screwed-up battle, you still look like you should be warmin' my bed," she said with a shake of her head. "If we manage to survive this adventure, you're rewardin' this sistah with a kiss," she finished. Then she inclined her head to me and added, "I'm just sayin'."

Knight chuckled before looking at me curiously. "You've got my blessing on that," I called back, honestly hopeful for Dia to get that kiss since it would mean our victory.

After everyone said their good-byes, Christina faced her soldiers and took a deep breath. "Masks on. Everyone needs to cross into the portal in formation, with all your artillery or magic at the ready."

"That's your go-ahead, Dulce," Knight announced, indicating the portal ripper in my hand. I simply nodded as I strode confidently to the front of the assembled soldiers. They were busily covering their faces with the gas masks until they looked like a troop from the apocalypse. Holding the portal ripper out in front of me, I secured it in place while Christina stood off to one side of her soldiers and Dia the other. Christina nodded, her tacit permission to start ripping the opening to Squander Valley. I rotated myself around so my front was facing the gadget and I started backing up, slicing the air in front of me as I retreated. This task wasn't as quick as the last one, since the portal had to be the width of ten men. But I prevailed, and once the portal was open, the soldiers proceeded immediately, disappearing instantly. After all of the soldiers crossed through, I watched Dia and Christina bring up the rear until they too, vanished into the ether. Without a second thought or word, I sewed up the portal just as I had after Sam's group passed through.

"Fagan and Trey," Knight summoned the Drow and the hobgoblin, who both stepped forward. Fagan looked like he always did—as though a permanent stick up his ass prohibited him from doing anything besides frowning. But I wasn't concerned with Fagan. Instead, I faced Trey, someone who had been a loyal ally of mine for many years.

"You're going to do fine, Trey," I said softly with a smile. I clutched the portal ripper in my palm as he wrapped his pudgy arms around me.

"It's you I'm worried about, Dulce," he whispered against my ear. He pulled away from me, but wrapped my free hand in his own, his skin warm and clammy against mine. If not for the beads of perspiration starting along his hairline, I wouldn't have realized how anxious he was because his hands were perpetually moist. He seemed reserved which was out of character for him. The same sense of foreboding and apprehension was taking hold of everyone.

"Whatever is going to happen will happen," I said, and firmly believed my words, right down to the very depths of my soul. "I can't change the outcome of the future so I'm

141

not going to worry about it. Neither should you. Just do what you came to do. End of story."

Trey nodded, but his eyes remained downcast and his shoulders sagged, telling me he didn't exactly buy my derring-do. "You're a survivor, Dulce, I know that. I'll see you soon." Then, turning to Knight and Quill, he simply nodded at each of them before facing forward. Fagan flanked the opposite side of the rectangular formation of the two hundred soldiers. I didn't fail to notice that Fagan hadn't bothered to say good-bye to anyone. Well, who knew? Maybe that was the better way to go.

Walking to the front of the soldiers, I ripped open the portal just as I'd done for Christina's troop, and watched the rows of creatures stepping forward. They vanished through the portal that would take them to the second largest Netherworld Guard training base of Tipshaw. Once all had crossed through, I zipped up the portal opening with the ripper once again. Then I turned to face Knight, Quill and the forty-one remaining soldiers assigned on our mission to wipe out my father.

"Ready?" I asked, alternating my gaze between Knight and Quill.

"No time like the present," Knight responded with a slight smile. Quill didn't say anything, but simply nodded.

I reached into my jeans pocket until I felt the warm metal of Bram's pocket watch, the navigation unit for my father. I pulled it out and held it at eye level. Then I watched the two hands begin spinning counterclockwise. The hour hand eventually started to slow until it reached the twelve o'clock position, where it stopped, indicating north. The base of the watch, which previously displayed the date, now had new numbers.

"North twenty-nine degrees," I called out.

"What're the coordinates?" Quill asked.

I shook my head to say that I didn't have an answer for him as I faced the watch again. It began to spin counterclockwise again and settled on numeral nine. The numbers at the bottom of the watch's face read eighty-nine. "Twenty-nine degrees north by eighty-nine degrees west," I called out. I dropped the watch back into my pocket while withdrawing the portal ripper from my other pocket.

"Those are the coordinates for Willoughby House," Quill said.

"What's that?" I asked while turning the handle of the portal ripper clockwise to input my first coordinate as north. Then, moving the handle in a circular direction two clicks before rotating it counterclockwise for one click, I proceeded counterclockwise again for the count of nine.

"One of Melchior's many homes. It's located in Southern Netherworld, where the state of Louisiana sits," Quill responded.

"Then you've been there?" Knight inquired. I continued programming the portal ripper with the western coordinates.

"Many times," Quill said, without confidence in his tone.

"Then you'll know the ins and the outs," I said hopefully, adding a quick smile.

"Maybe," Quill started, shaking his head. "One thing I can say for certain is that Willoughby House is the largest of all your father's homes. It sprawls over twenty acres or more of swampland and most notably, it's infested with all sorts of horrible creatures."

"Then we'd better get moving," I said, giving him a smart ass smile. "I wouldn't want to keep my father waiting too long."

When neither Knight nor Quill said anything more, I took their silence as approval. I tilted the portal ripper and began slicing the air in front of me. Once the hole was big enough to fit our troops, I put the device back into my pocket while double-checking my other pocket for Bram's watch. Thankfully, both were there.

"Let the soldiers go in first," Knight said with his hand on my arm, just in case I tried to argue. I simply nodded as

Knight gave the go-ahead to a werewolf who was lined up closest to us. The man started forward, with the rest of the troops moving in kind. They started through the portal, and the sounds of their boots hitting the ground matched the thumping of my heart. Once the last one was through, I faced Quill and Knight.

"We all go in together, side-by-side, with Dulcie in the middle," Knight said with authority.

He stepped up beside me, while Quill did the same. I already knew there wouldn't be anyone to close up the portal on the other side once we went through, but we didn't have any choice. We had to keep the portal ripper in case we needed it. Besides, maybe we'd make a quick getaway through the opened portal, if need be.

With Knight and Quill on either side of me, we stepped through the portal. I felt the familiar, soft mushiness of heavy, wet air just as I did every time I traveled through a portal. My dizziness soon gave way to an overwhelming sense of nausea, but I swallowed the uncomfortable feelings. I blinked a few times as I faced a scene entirely different from the one we'd just left.

All around us were miles and miles of grassland, encircled by an old, rickety, wooden fence that looked as if it had survived centuries. The grassland was enclosed by a forest of pine trees, in which we were now submerged. On the side directly opposite us was the gravelly mouth of a large lake. Looking around myself, I saw that all our soldiers were well hidden by the massive trees of the forest.

"Where's the house?" I whispered to Quill before my feet suddenly levitated and I was rudely reminded that when in the Netherworld, I had wings. Luckily, I was prepared for my wings and wore a halter top with the back cut out. Speaking of my wings, they weren't as cool as they might sound. Why? Because they really weren't that useful. Instead, they seemed like a neurotic lap dog that acted up for no apparent reason, and went into bouts of mindless energy. Sometimes, they flapped maniacally, while at others, they hung as lifeless as a man's spent appendage. At the moment, however, they were anything but languid. They batted against each other repetitively as I continued to rise into the air. I felt a hand on my arm when Knight pulled me back down again.

"Just over that rise of grass," Quill whispered back. He motioned to a hill that was maybe one hundred feet in front of us. He put his hand on my arm to help anchor me to the ground. "There are cameras covering the grassland perimeters as well as the beach, so we can't go that way."

I nodded and whipped out Bram's pocket watch, intent on locating my father. I held the thing out before my eyes and watched it immediately settle on numeral three. The matching coordinates appeared at the bottom of the watch. "Looks like Melchior's off to our right," I said to Quillan.

"We need to talk to the men," Knight interrupted. I was unable to ignore the feelings of awe and admiration that hit me as soon as I allowed my eyes to feast on him. As I've mentioned before, Netherworld creatures, when in the Netherworld, appear differently than they do on Earth. I, for one, get wings, but the most unfortunate part for me in the Netherworld is that my magic doesn't work. Oh, yeah … There's also one more clincher—fairies are like sexual crack in the Netherworld—most other creatures have an irresistible sexual response to me, which, in one word, sucks.

As with most of his abilities, I didn't know how Knight's powers varied in the Netherworld; but one thing I *could* say about the Loki was: despite how gorgeous he was in Splendor, he was even more so in the Netherworld. His skin took on a golden glow, and he appeared even taller and broader than usual. His black hair became a deeper, glossier shade of black and his eyes sparkled like blue prisms.

Looking at Quill, I found the same thing with him— his skin seemed tanner and the amber of his eyes was a deeper gold, and the same color as his hair, framing his face in short, spiky waves. Even though he wasn't as tall as Knight, nor as broad, he appeared powerful in his own right.

145

The swelling of his muscles was readily apparent through his T-shirt.

"I need to tell our soldiers what the plan is and then we have to go after O'Neil separately," Knight finished.

Quillan agreed and we both watched Knight turn around and take the ten steps or so that separated him from our envoy. He brought back a young man, who faced us expectantly.

"The grass isn't safe because it's covered with cameras and so is the lake," Quill started. "If you stick to the forest, you'll find it wraps around the front of the house. There are cameras there as well, but you can avoid them by staying at least a few feet inside the forest. The forest surrounds the house on all but one side."

"So assemble the soldiers in the forest, as far around the house as you can," Knight interrupted, still facing the man. "Then wait for my go-ahead and move in."

The man nodded as he took a deep breath. "Got it. Will wait to hear from you, sir."

Knight turned to face me. "Where is Melchior?"

"Looks like he's in the east wing of the house," I reiterated what Bram's pocket watch had revealed to me. Then I eyed Quillan to see if he wanted to elaborate.

"He's probably in his library," he answered quickly. "It's the only room he frequents on the eastern wing of Willoughby."

"Do you think he's alone?" I asked.

Quill shrugged. "Inside the library, maybe, but there are always two or three guards posted outside, in the hallway."

"We can deal with them," Knight said emphatically.

"What about Dulcie?" Quill asked, his frown marring an otherwise handsome face.

"I can take care of myself."

I pulled the portal ripper from my pocket and programmed it with our coordinates, quickly slicing the air open. Then I lodged the tool back into my pocket, Knight and Quill by my sides, as we stepped through.

When we came out on the other side, I had to find my bearings. I was prepared to land inside a house and was slightly taken aback to find the sun shining down on me as a chill whipped through the air.

"We overshot!" Quill said angrily.

As far as I could see, we were surrounded by swamp. Luckily for us, we'd landed on a stretch of land; but unluckily for us, the land was situated in the middle of the swamp, aka an island. I turned around and noticed a row boat moored to a makeshift dock maybe three hundred feet away.

"We need that boat," I said softly, facing Knight. "I can easily fly to the other side to get it." My wings were already flapping so quickly, I probably looked like an oversized hummingbird. "Or do you think we should try Bram's portal ripper again?"

Knight shook his head. "Not after it sent us here. Who the hell knows where we'd end up if we tried it again."

"Maybe the device just doesn't work when we're in such close proximity to our target," I offered and then shrugged.

Knight nodded. "Maybe." He then glanced at the boat in the distance. "The boat is our best bet."

"It's too dangerous," Quill said, shaking his head.

"My wings are amped and raring to go," I said with a frown. I wasn't sure how else he intended to get across. I, for one, refused to go swimming in some algae-infested swamp with Hades-only-knew-what lurking just beneath the surface.

But, that was just me.

ELEVEN

"There are all sorts of horrible creatures in the swamp and monsters roam the skies," Quill said to me pointedly, releasing my arm from his grip. "In case you didn't notice, there aren't any nets here."

He was referring to the nets that blanketed the skies of most Netherworld cities. The nets discouraged gigantic, winged monsters that soared through the air from preying on Netherworld citizens. Yes, Quill made a good point warning us about the lack of nets in Willoughby House, but I also wasn't exactly thrilled at the thought about what might lurk beneath the swamp. Being stuck on such a small stretch of land didn't fill me with warm, fuzzy feelings.

"How else do you plan to get across the swamp if I don't go after that boat?" I asked with a frown, motioning to the row boat just across the swamp.

Quill didn't say anything, which meant there wasn't any other way across. "Exactly," I muttered as I freed myself from Knight's hold. I immediately started to ascend again, but this time, Knight did nothing to tether me. I effortlessly floated up and in an easterly direction until I was floating over the middle of the swamp, nearing the shore. As I floated nearer the shore, I noticed a mass of oak trees, covered with Spanish moss, just before me. They also housed a whole slew of the biggest, ugliest spiders I'd ever seen. Most of them were perched in large, white webs that stretched from tree branch to tree branch. The spiders were nearly as large as my hands. Their spindly legs were striped brown and cream, and they had orange crests on their abdomens.

Fly yourself around the spiders, Dulcie, I said to myself in an effort to convey the message to my wings.

Instead, they flapped with reckless abandon and drove me right into a spider web. The unsightly behemoth briefly took refuge on my face before jumping down to my shoulder and shooting itself off my arm. Meanwhile, I uncontrollably sailed through the remainder of its web. Fearing the creature's sticky, spindly legs landing all over my skin, I felt myself breaking out in goose bumps, as a shiver raced up my spine. But, it hadn't bitten me so I figured things were better than they otherwise could have been.

After escaping the spider webs, I got scratched by a few oak branches and suffered some minor scrapes before freeing myself from the canopy. Now, a new problem faced me: I was quickly floating up into the sky with no visible way of descending. My wings were flapping on fast forward, and even though they were small, they were powerful in their own right. I tried to tell them that I needed to float down again, especially after overshooting the boat by ten feet or more. But my wings refused to listen and I continued to drift higher.

"Lean over and reach for the tree in front of you!" Knight called out to me, the tone of his voice concerned. But my wings continued to beat incessantly, carrying me even higher.

"Tell yourself to slow your wings down!" Quill yelled, as if I was so dumb I hadn't already told myself exactly that.

As I passed by another oak tree, I reached out, aiming for one of the branches to simply pull myself into the tree. Then I could just climb down, spiders and all. It was probably a long shot, but it was also the only solution I could find.

Leaning toward the tree branch, I suddenly started floating in that direction until I was able to grasp the branch. Then I hand-walked myself down the branch, watching the large, brown, fuzzy spiders disappear into the overgrowth of the trees as I pillaged their webs. Luckily for me, they didn't appear to be territorial.

When I reached the tree trunk, I glanced down and noticed how high up I was. It was probably the equivalent of being on the fifth floor of a building. As soon as I cast my eyes down, though, I felt my wings begin slowing their frantic beating. Hoping to test them, I released my hold on the branch and began to float down toward the ground. So, somehow, my addled brain managed to reach my wings.

"Just take your time!" Knight yelled, he and Quill now fully indoctrinated as the peanut gallery.

Once I hit the ground, I checked my wings once more and then, convinced they weren't going to start up again, I ran the distance separating me from the row boat. I unwound the rope from the dock, pushing the boat into the murky water as I climbed aboard, all the while hoping there wasn't anything larger than my boat lurking beneath the lily pad-covered water. With only a solitary oar that I found in the bottom of the boat, I began paddling first over my left shoulder, then my right. The boat cut through the water and I managed to make it back to the island within a few minutes, despite the infernal aching in my shoulders.

Knight and Quill grabbed the boat's bow and pulled it onto the shore. My wings started to beat again so I gripped the side of the boat as tightly as I could while Knight jumped over the edge and grabbed hold of my arm. Quill hopped over the other edge, and taking up the oar, started rowing.

"The main house is just around the bend of this swamp," he informed us.

I nodded as I reached into my pocket, producing Bram's watch. When I held it up to eye level, the two hands pointed to numeral three, which meant we had to bear to the right, since that's where Melchior was. And, coincidentally, that's also where a gigantic … thing perched on the banks of the swamp, watching us.

The creature was no less than twenty feet tall. Its back was covered with long, broad, brown feathers, and its belly looked like the same rough skin of a crocodile. The thing had been watching us for Hades only knew how long, but as soon as I made eye contact with it, its hunched body sat up straight and it eagerly devoured a midday snack. Stretching out two immense wings that were lined with downy white feathers, the much larger brown feathers comprised the flipside. Whatever had been unfortunate enough to become its lunch was now reduced to red, raw, dripping tissue, the shreds hanging from the creature's talons. It had an ominous, hooked predatory beak and two beady eyes that glowed an eerie yellow.

"Don't look at it," Knight warned softly. "Very slowly, get down on your belly in the bottom of the boat. Dulcie, you go first, and Quillan, you cover her with your body."

Without a word, I moved as slowly as I could, feeling Knight's hand on my back to keep my wings steady, which would, no doubt, only attract more attention. Getting on all fours, I lowered myself down onto the rough, splintery wood, which grated against my cheek. Quillan immediately came behind me and covered my body with his own, but squished me in the process.

"You okay?" he whispered into my ear.

"You're too heavy," I gasped. "I can barely breathe."

He rolled off me until we were lying face-down, side-by-side. Then he draped his arm over me, in order to keep my wings confined. As soon as he did, Knight withdrew his hand from my back, and started to row again. For a few seconds, the only thing to occupy my mind was the sound of my shallow breathing as I tried to get my breath. I just couldn't banish thoughts of the horrible bird creature coming after us. But images of becoming snack number two were disrupted when I felt Quillan's hand as it began to explore my back, following the line of my spine. When he reached the waist of my jeans, he pushed his hand beneath them and started rubbing the top of my butt.

"What the hell are you doing?" I whispered, despite facing the opposite direction.

"Dulce, I'm having a hell of a time fighting your pheromones," he said painfully. His words sounded like he was saying them through gritted teeth. His probing fingers splayed across my backside while his other hand slipped underneath my shirt. Then he rubbed my stomach, coming dangerously close to the bottom of my bra.

"For Hades's sake," I started, fully aware of what was going on. It was just another irritating drawback as a fairy in the Netherworld. Yep, Quill couldn't help falling for my sexual "fairy crack" and there really wasn't anything I could do about it. If I made too much of a ruckus, or sat up, the feathered monster would take notice. I knew Quill was helpless to my feminine power anyway; and now that he was basically on top of me, I was more than sure his resistance was rapidly waning. Reaffirming my suspicion, I felt his hand dip between my thighs on the outside of my jeans.

"I can't fight it when I'm this close to you," he whispered. "I'm sorry."

Knight instantly reached back and forcibly yanked Quill's hand away from my butt. Then, without another word or action, he turned back to rowing again. As far as I could tell, Knight wasn't obeying his own advice regarding taking cover. Instead, he was still sitting up, with no protection or refuge from the daunting monster bird.

"Knight, why aren't you taking any cover?" I whispered.

"Because someone needs to get us to the other side," he whispered back, talking out of one side of his mouth.

"But it's going to see you," I persisted, just as Quillan's hands found my butt again. This time I didn't bother to reprimand him, as I was far too concerned for Knight's safety.

"It's already seen us," Knight responded. "It shouldn't attack me though. It should recognize what I am."

I just sighed and chalked it up to yet another of Knight's mysterious abilities. *How many more*, I wondered,

has he failed to inform me about? Then, I reached around
and ruthlessly removed Quill's hand from my backside.

"Your smell, Dulce! It's driving me crazy," he
whispered. "I can't be this close to you and not touch you."

"Control yourself, Romeo," Knight spat out, "or
you're going overboard." From the corner of my eye, I could
see him glaring at Quill. "I feel it too, but I'm controlling
myself."

Quill didn't get the chance to respond. The loud shriek
of the creature's squawking shattered the stillness of the air.
It sounded like the screech of a cat being tortured—
something that assaulted my ears and made me wish to
Hades I never had to hear it again. The creature's high-
pitched yell was even more discouraging when accompanied
by a swishing sound, which seemed to be getting closer and
closer.

"What's it doing?" I demanded.

"It's flying," Knight said calmly. He didn't sound
especially concerned. "It's telling us that this is its territory."

"Can you tell it that we want nothing to do with it or
its territory?" I snapped back.

Knight chuckled, but didn't say anything more. He
continued to paddle through the encumbering swamp while
Quill started to gyrate on top of me. At least he was keeping
his hands to himself …

The creature continued to squawk and carry on, the
flapping of its wings becoming increasingly louder. I could
feel my heartbeat race as images of myself as the creature's
dinner flashed through my mind.

*Could Trey have been channeling this moment when
he had his vision or feeling?* I wondered. *Could I possibly
meet my end in the jaws of such a horrible beast?* I closed
my eyes tightly to force my brain to eject them at once.
However I would die, I refused to let it be in the beak of a
gargantuan bird.

Hearing another screech, as a shadow passed over our
small boat, I realized the monster bird was swooping down

closer to us. I wondered why it never even attempted to snatch Knight since he was obviously more accessible than either Quill or I. But I also figured it was one of those things I probably would never know the answer to—maybe it was just a Loki thing.

A large "thump!" sounded against the bottom of our boat, next to my cheek that felt as if someone threw something very heavy against it. My heart stopped beating for at least two seconds.

"Oh my God," I whispered. "What the hell was that?"

No one responded, but Quill stopped gyrating against me. I held my breath and tried to convince myself that whatever whacked the bottom of our little boat was no more than a tangle of reeds, or a dirt mound that we'd passed over. It definitely wasn't something as hideously ugly and terrifying as the thing that was currently making its rounds in the sky.

But whatever made the thump wasn't reeds or a random dirt mound because it rammed into the hull again, only this time with more speed and power. It hit us right where my throat lay against the wood. The blow was so jarring, it rocked the entire boat, wobbling it back and forth unsteadily. I started to pull myself up, if only to escape whatever was charging at us from underwater, but Knight shoved his hand onto my back, forcing me back into the boat.

"Knight!" I started.

"Don't say anything," he countered. "It's trying to make you sit up so the *Kegogog* can pick you off. Don't move at all. Just stay the hell where you are!"

I didn't say anything else. I couldn't. My heart rode up into my throat and its frantic beating pulsated throughout my entire body. Then another, even stronger wallop sounded from beneath us. This one hit my collarbone and the entire boat rocked even more violently. Whatever warred beneath us was getting impatient and hence, more forceful in its strategy. Strangely enough, it definitely seemed that the water beast and the bird monster were in cahoots. If I didn't think it impossible, I would have believed the screeches from the bird monster were its way of getting help from the swamp monster to compel Quill or me to sit up.

"Just hold still!" Knight called out. "We're less than twenty feet from the shoreline; and once we make it into the forest, nothing will come after us!"

I swallowed hard and wondered how far it was from the shoreline to the forest. Then I wondered if the thing beneath us could run as well as it swam. 'Course, if the thing below us didn't get us, the thing above us might. The water monster suddenly slammed into the side of the boat, sending the small vessel into a tailspin. Knight's breathing as well as his cursing accelerated as he struggled with the oar to keep us on our trajectory. Nausea began to churn my stomach as the boat circled round and round, but I resisted the urge to heave. Knight finally managed to stop the boat; and with a loud groan, he started rowing forward again. I wasn't sure if it was just my own wishful thinking, but it seemed like the boat was suddenly moving faster.

"Once I give you the go-ahead, you run as fast as you can into the trees; you got it?" he said to both of us. "Quillan, you have to sit up so Dulcie can get out."

"Just tell me when," Quill answered.

Knight didn't say anything else, but continued to paddle. The water beast went eerily quiet. The sudden serenity unnerved me because I knew its attacks were far from over.

"Okay, Beaurigard, sit up and be prepared to jump out in about ten seconds," Knight ordered.

Quill wasted no time in pushing himself off me. A few moments later, I felt the boat skidding on land as we hit the shore. Quill jumped over the side at the same moment the swamp creature charged us full bore, ramming into the stern of the small boat. I was instantly yanked backwards as Knight gripped me by the waistline of my jeans. Just as he wrenched me backwards, the boat exploded and splintered into a thousand pieces. The creature's jaws devoured the boat, and splinters of the wood gouged its gums. Blood filled its mouth and the rows of countless serrated, miniature teeth, mixing with saliva and water, only seemed to cause further outrage in it. Maybe it was the pain inflicted by the splinters of wood, or the taste of blood that sent it into a tizzy, but it made a horrible wailing sound. Then it opened its mouth wider, revealing even more layers of jagged, razor-sharp teeth, all stained red with blood. If Knight hadn't snatched me back when he did, my head would have been inside the creature's bloody mouth.

"Run!" Knight called out as I turned to face Quillan. He was watching the scene in abject horror, but he turned around and ran for the forest line. Knight hoisted me over his shoulder and jumped down from the bow of the boat. We landed on the shore just as the swamp creature vanished under the water.

"It's coming around the boat!" I screamed. The creature swam for the shore, hoisting itself up out of the water onto its two short flippers. Its head looked like a prehistoric dolphin—dark grey with tiny eyes centered in the middle of its forehead, which was huge. Its forehead dominated the upper part of its face, making its small eyes appear sunken and dead, and even more dreadful. But its massive mouth captivated all my attention. From what I could see of its body, it was mammoth—as in the size of a minivan. It definitely couldn't move as quickly on land, but it managed to swivel back and forth like an alligator, using its small fins to gain traction. Knight was too fast for it, though, and dove for the tree line just when it seemed the thing was ready to strike.

When my face hit the ground, my cheeks stung as my skin met the sand. I braced my arms around my head for protection, but luckily, didn't hit anything. Instantly, arms encircled my waist, pulling me upright as I opened my eyes and blinked a few times. Wiping my arm across my face, I attempted to dislodge the grains of sand, which seemed to be caught in my hair as well as my eyes, ears and nose. Once free from as much of the sand as possible, I gazed up into Knight's broad smile and realized we'd made it to the forest and were now bathed in the cover of the tree branches.

"And that, my friends, is the main reason why it's best to avoid swamps when traveling through the Netherworld," Knight said with a hearty chuckle. He acted like everything we'd just gone through was nothing more than an awesome roller coaster ride and now he wanted another turn.

I couldn't even find it within myself to respond, so I didn't. Knight dusted me off as he inspected me.

"Is she okay?" Quill asked, coming up behind me.

"Looks like some minor lesions to her face, but she's a trooper; aren't you, Dulce?"

I shook my head and took a deep breath, trying to regulate my heartbeat. Then I turned to face Quill, before spitting out a mouthful of sand, spit and plants.

"Where to now?" I demanded in a rough voice.

Quill smiled at me and sighed deeply. He appeared to be relieved. He motioned through the trees to the side of Willoughby House, now only thirty feet in the distance. Even though my vantage point didn't allow for much, it was fairly obvious that my father's home was colossal. This particular wing must have been four stories high, with a turret that imbued it with a castle-esque quality. I could see a matching turret on the other side of the house in the distance. As far as my father was concerned, he really did fancy himself a king—well, that is, if Willoughby House was the standard.

"The library is on the third floor in that tower," Quill said, pointing up at the turret.

"We must have been caught on camera?" I started. Seeing how the beach dominated this section of the property, and after Quill's comment that my father had cameras pinned to the grassland as well as the beaches in general, it was the obvious conclusion.

Quill shook his head. "Your father raises those creatures," he started. His expression said just how troubled he was by the information. "He believes they do a better job at deterring unwanted guests than cameras do; well, on the swamp side of the house anyway."

I just looked at him vacantly, traumatized that my father would breed the winged aberrations of the sky. I'd already witnessed one taking out a tourist in line at the airport during my first trip to the Netherworld. Then this one nearly ate us for lunch. Before I could react, Knight's walkie-talkie began buzzing, its white and red lights flashing through the fabric of his jeans. He reached into his pocket and pulled it out.

"Christina," he said in greeting, "over."

"It failed," she said between gasps. She sounded as if she'd been running and was now taking a breather. She panted for a few more seconds. "Somehow, the Netherworld Guard were tipped off that we were coming for them. They were fully prepared for us when we attacked." She took another breath. "Over."

I felt my heart sink as I put the pieces together and realized the gist of what she was saying. Bram had basically backstabbed me. Why? Because he'd instructed us to attack the base at Squander Valley. He'd set me up. He'd set us up. And I'd stupidly walked right into his trap.

"Where are you?" Knight demanded, turning his back on both of us. "Over."

"I … I don't know. I could only get out with about twenty of our soldiers. We made it through Squander Valley and now we're in some nearby forest, just trying to keep ahead of them." Her voice sounded seconds away from becoming panic-stricken.

"You took your gas mask off?" Knight demanded to which Christina coughed, as if on cue.

"It's okay," she said finally. "We're far away from the *Bregone* swamp and its fumes, otherwise this forest wouldn't be able to survive."

"Okay, listen to me very carefully, Christina, you need to find water—optimally, a river—just anything flowing. Once you find one, follow it downstream. Whatever direction the water flows, follow it. And make sure you're on your own, or at least don't have more than one person with you. You'll be harder to find if you're separated from the group." Then he paused for a few seconds. "Where is Dia? Over."

The silence on the line lasted so long, I wasn't sure if Christina was still on the other end. "I don't know," she answered finally, her voice sounding pained. "Over."

I felt my entire body deflate on itself once I heard that Dia wasn't accounted for. And as soon as that news landed in my lap, I concluded that I was the whole reason for the failure of our mission. I should never have trusted Bram. I should have known better. As soon as he'd said he was always in cahoots with my father, that should have been the end of my liaison with him. I should have cuffed him right then and there and taken him to jail where he could have rotted until Kingdom Come.

Knight warned you time and time again that trusting Bram was a mistake! I railed at myself. *Now you could have cost Dia's life. How could you have been so stupid? How could you have gone for Bram's bait so blindly?*

What was more, I was certain that he and my father were sitting back now, laughing as they watched everything crumble that we, The Resistance, had fought so hard for.

"This isn't your fault, Dulce," Quill said softly as he patted me on the back. I turned to face him, but shook my head, unwilling to see the truth in his eyes. Knight wasn't the only person who had warned me about Bram. Quill had many times too. And, yet, I'd insisted the vampire only wanted to help us. How completely stupid I was! All Bram had ever wanted from me was confidential information so he could feed it back to Melchior. Well, information and sex. At least, he hadn't gotten the latter.

159

"I trusted him," I responded, casting my eyes onto the ground, in absolute disgust of both Bram and myself. "Like a total idiot, I trusted him! Now, because of me, who knows how many of our soldiers are dead? And … maybe even Dia."

"How much battery life do you have left on your radio? Over." Knight continued talking to Christina, as if Quill and I were irrelevant.

"Maybe a few hours."

He nodded and didn't say anything for a while. Then he turned around and finally faced Quill and me. Well, it was more fitting to say he finally faced me. When he did, I was surprised not to see any anger or condemnation in his eyes. Instead, his gaze held no semblance of emotion.

"We're going after Melchior," he said with determined resolve. Although he was actually informing Christina, his eyes remained fastened on mine.

"What?" she blurted out on the other side.

"Whatever happens, I'll try to check in with you in a little while, okay?" he continued. "Over."

"Knight, do you think that's a good idea?" she started. "He obviously already knows about our plans. Over."

"We have no choice," Knight said in a hollow tone. He shook his head as he diverted his attention from my face. "We've already made our bed."

Christina sighed heavily and after a protracted silence, she took another deep breath. "Be careful," she said at last. "I'll look forward to your next call."

"You too. Just follow the water downstream and you'll eventually end up in a city somewhere. Stay under the cover of the trees whatever you do, and look out for *smolls*. Over."

"I've got an Op 6 and a 7 so I'm good to go," she responded. I wondered what in the hell *smolls* were but didn't have the strength to ask. "Bye, Knight."

"This isn't good-bye," he responded stonily. "We'll be talking again soon."

Turning off the radio, Knight's eyes bored right into mine. I couldn't read anything in his expression and half wondered if he would yell at me or embrace me. "This isn't your fault," he said at last.

I gulped down my response because at this point, I knew it wouldn't make any difference. Whether or not it was my fault didn't help things. We had to focus on the tactics that would. Knight was right: it was too late now to turn back. We had to push forward and take my father out, even though it was now quite obvious he knew we were coming for him.

TWELVE

"So how much does Bram know?" Knight asked, turning to face me as we hid in the cover of the forest that bordered Willoughby House. I gazed out at the swamp from which we'd narrowly escaped death, and saw the monster bird flying through the air, squawking and screeching as if protesting that its lunch escaped into the forest. There was no sign of the swamp monster.

Facing Knight again, I had to gulp down the burning taste of acid that started up my throat when I thought how easily Bram stabbed me in the back and, worse, how I practically helped him do it. Knowing my anger could only deter me from achieving my goal of going after my father, I tried to answer Knight's question as to what Bram did and did not know. "Obviously, he knows we're gunning for my father, which is why he gave me his pocket watch," I started. "So I predict it's safe to assume he knows we're coming after Melchior."

"And that means it's also safe to assume that Melchior now knows that as well," Quill added while I nodded in agreement.

Knight didn't say anything more as he pulled the walkie-talkie from his pocket and tried to reach Fagan again. As soon as Knight hung up with Christina earlier, he kept trying to reach Fagan through the radio, but the Drow never responded. This time was no closer to being a charm, as there was still no response from the other end. Knight shook his head in obvious disappointment and returned the radio to his back pocket, turning to me again. "When Bram gave you the portal ripper, he instructed you to go after the Netherworld Guard base at Squander Valley, right?"

162

I nodded while wanting to throw up because the taste of acid creeping up the back of my throat was becoming toxic. "Right, so Bram obviously must have helped plan the Netherworld Guard's response."

"Did he know anything about our other attacks?" Knight continued, eyeing me directly. I still couldn't find any anger in his features. And, for some reason, knowing he didn't blame me for trusting Bram, despite his repeated warnings not to, made me feel even worse. It was a guilt I'd never experienced before—it made me want to drop to my knees and cry, while tearing my hair out in mute frustration.

I shook my head and heaved a sigh as I tried to banish the self-disgust from my mind. I just couldn't accept that I, Dulcie O'Neil, was so stupid as to trust the vampire so blindly. I rarely trusted anyone; and it usually took years, sometimes decades, before I allowed someone into my inner circle.

And, yet, you've known Bram for years, a small voice reminded me. *Bram played you like a pro. He waited all these years, pretending to be your ally and your friend, while planning to pull the wool over your eyes at the very end.*

"Bram didn't know anything else about our other strategy," I said finally, concentrating on the subject at hand. "I didn't tell him about staging the phony surrender at the airport, or our proposed attack on Tipshaw."

"So maybe both the airport surrender and Tipshaw went off without a hitch," Knight started as Quill began firmly shaking his head.

"Melchior is a smart man. He would have assigned reinforcements at Tipshaw as well as all the bases in the Netherworld as soon as he learned about Squander Valley," he rebutted, frowning at Knight and then at me. A shadow passed over his face as the bird creature from the swamp flew over the trees.

I nodded at him, reminding myself that the monster bird couldn't find us in the dense forest. And, even if it did, there was no way it could reach us beneath the thick canopy of trees. 'Course, all that did was remind me of all the creatures in the forest that *could* get us …

"Right," I said. "I think it's safest to assume that my father has all his bases covered, no pun intended."

Knight turned his attention from the sky, where he was watching the flying obscenity, to me. "So Bram has no idea how many soldiers we have with us right now?" he asked.

"I never told Bram anything about our numbers," I started. I cocked my head to the side as I considered whether that was a benefit or a hindrance to us. "Bram not knowing our numbers could be good, but it could also be bad."

"How so?" Knight inquired, ever the eager manager.

I shrugged. "Maybe Melchior thinks we're coming with lots more backup than we really are, in which case his battalion here could be huge, leading to our brutal defeat."

Quill shook his head and crossed his arms against his chest. "So far, from what we've seen, there doesn't appear to be much going on here. If Melchior had a whole battalion of soldiers at Willoughby, they'd be assembled everywhere— on all the beachfronts and the forest bordering Willoughby. So far, I've yet to see one soldier."

"That doesn't mean they aren't in the house," I pointed out, and then frowned because it was never a good practice to make assumptions.

Quill nodded. "Your father would have instructed guards to patrol the house, and the property too. My point is, I don't think Melchior stationed more soldiers here than usual simply because we haven't seen nor come into contact with any." He took a breath. "Something I find strange."

"Beaurigard's got a point," Knight piped up as my wings, which lay previously in repose against my back, suddenly started beating furiously. Both Knight and Quill had to grasp hold of my arms to keep me in place. "That issue we had in the swamp would have alerted nearby soldiers if there *were* any," Knight finished.

I couldn't help smiling at Knight's reference to the swamp situation as an "issue." The word was such an understatement to what truly happened. But any feelings of levity quickly vanished as soon as I reminded myself of our current predicament. Really we were stuck between an enormous rock and a hard place, because it was never a good idea to begin an assault without first knowing what you were up against.

"I think it's safe to assume that your father doesn't think we're coming here with much backup," Quill finished. "Because it's not as though he could hide a squadron of soldiers." He shrugged as his eyebrows reached for the sky. "But why doesn't he have an army of reinforcements here? That's the question to which I have no answer."

Knight nodded before turning to face me, his blue eyes flashing. The trees shook with a small breeze, allowing the sun to penetrate the branches in prismatic rays of yellow light. "You said Bram didn't know anything about how many soldiers we brought with us here, but does he know the total number of our soldiers?"

I figured he meant how many soldiers and recruits we'd managed to corral. "No," I said, frowning and inhaling deeply as something else occurred to me. "But don't forget: Bram had Christina in his custody for a couple of days when she was still on the *Blueliss*."

Knight nodded, his eyes sparkling with something that resembled anger as his jaw twitched. "Right, so he could easily have discovered our numbers from her, which he probably did."

Quill faced Knight. "But at that time, The Resistance was only comprised of the three hundred or so soldiers, right? Wasn't Fagan still in the midst of drafting the others?"

"Right," I answered, crossing my arms against my chest as another breeze coiled around my body in an icy embrace. "Which means Bram probably thinks we've only got three hundred soldiers to the Netherworld Guard's four hundred. And, if he does, it's all the better for us since we would still have the element of surprise."

Knight shook his head and arched a brow at me as if disappointed that I hadn't considered some other angle. "But don't forget Squander Valley and Tipshaw equated to four hundred fifty soldiers and recruits, so Bram and your father would be well aware that our numbers exceeded three hundred."

"Well, based on however many creatures they were able to consign," I corrected him as my wings suddenly stopped beating and simply hung there, now exhausted. Knight and Quill released my arms as I remembered Christina mentioning over the radio that many of her group were able to flee from Squander Valley. Since our soldiers hadn't all been caught, Melchior wouldn't know for certain how many of us there really were. Maybe the same thing happened with the attack on Tipshaw. Or maybe I was underestimating us, and our forces had decimated the Netherworld Guard in Tipshaw. Until we reached Fagan, we'd never know.

"At any rate, Melchior must be aware our numbers are larger than three hundred," Quill said.

Knight took a deep breath and shook his head, frowning as he alternated his stoic expression between the two of us. "None of this matters anyway. This discussion is doing nothing, but wasting our valuable time," he said forcibly. "We have two options: we either go after Melchior now, not knowing what we're up against, or we have to surrender. It's too late to beat a path back to Splendor and regroup."

"He's right," I started, facing Quill. "I say we go in," I finished robotically, swallowing hard as I searched Knight's stunning eyes for an answer as to where he stood on the subject. It felt like time stopped as I waited for his response. If he and Quill chose to surrender, I didn't know what I'd do. For my part, I intended to go after my father and that's all there was to it. Whether that meant going in with Knight and Quill was beside the point. I was going in. Period.

"Agreed," Knight said with his jaw tightened and his eyes calculating. "I will never surrender to Melchior. I'd rather die fighting his minions."

I rewarded him with a big smile before turning to face Quill, who was already looking at me. He frowned and I figured his answer wouldn't be quite as clear-cut as Knight's. After a few seconds, he began nodding. "We're here; we might as well go through with our original plan. If we retreat to Splendor, your father would assume he still maintained authority and he'd, no doubt, come after us."

"Either way, there'd be a confrontation," Knight finished.

Quill glanced at the horizon for a few seconds before facing us again. "And, for whatever reason, it seems your father is not very well protected here, which only strengthens our upper hand."

I couldn't agree with them more and nodded. Then, taking a deep breath, I glanced first at Quill and then at Knight. "Our soldiers are already surrounding the house and they're waiting for your word to move forward, Knight."

"Right," the Loki answered. "So we give them the go-ahead, and when they attack the house, all of Melchior's men will be focused on defending the house and its perimeters."

"And we go after my father at the same time," I finished as my heartbeat began to race with peaked adrenaline.

"Your father will have guards surrounding him," Quill cautioned.

"How many?" I demanded.

Quill shrugged. "Probably three. He's always got Manga, Angus and Herrod hovering around him at any given second."

"What are they?" Knight asked.

"Thugs," Quill responded, but seeing Knight's frown, he continued. "Manga is a goblin. He's maybe six-two and he fights street-style."

"Goblin means he has no magic," I said quickly. "We can defeat anyone who doesn't have magic."

"Angus is a warlock," Quill threw back at me. "He doesn't have brawn, but he makes up for it with witchcraft and he's damn good."

"I can take him," I answered quickly, resting my hands on the two Op 6s strapped to my waist, beneath my T-shirt.

"Dulce, your magic won't work in the Netherworld," Quill reminded me.

"I'm aware," I snapped back. "But my Op 6s will."

Knight chuckled behind me as Quill grinned, shaking his head. "Yep, they will," he finished. "It'll help that we're all armed," he added, patting the band of his waistline where he kept an Op 8 loaded and ready to go. "But don't forget that Melchior's men will be armed as well."

"This is nothing new," I said quickly. "We've dealt with this same scenario a thousand times at the ANC." I said it mostly to beef up my own confidence.

"And what is Herrod?" Knight asked, facing Quill.

"Herrod is all brawn. He's a werewolf, but he's bigger and badder than any wolf you've ever seen."

"That doesn't intimidate me," Knight said matter-of-factly.

"Well, maybe their artillery will," Quill shot back. "Each one will be armed with Op 7s and 8s, not to mention automatic machine guns filled with dragon's blood bullets. And that's just what you'll be able to see. They'll also have blades strapped to their bodies beneath their clothes. The main thing to remember is that they're Melchior's thugs for a reason; they're exceptional at what they do."

"Good to know," Knight said, not sounding particularly concerned. "But Dulce is right. It's just another walk in a very familiar park." Then he turned to face me. "When we go in, we go together."

"And how do you propose getting to the top floor of a windowless turret without going through the entryway of the house?" Quill asked, sounding irritated.

Knight replied with a smug smile. "Last I checked, we had a portal ripper."

I nodded, pulling Bram's pocket watch out to pinpoint my father's exact position inside the house. Before I attempted anything, though, I glanced up at Knight. "You realize my father's going to know that we know where he is?"

Knight nodded, not looking especially concerned. "Hopefully, we haven't kept him waiting too long."

After Knight gave his lead soldier the go-ahead to enter Willoughby house, I cut a portal into Melchior's library. Neither Quill, Knight nor I said anything; and the silence hung ominously between us. Standing on either side of me, the three of us stepped forward, entering the portal.

The feelings of wet, balmy air hit me immediately, and I clenched my eyes tightly, suddenly feeling sick to my stomach. Moments later, though, the nausea disappeared and the air became frigid. I opened my eyes and felt myself falling. My wings immediately started flapping wildly to stop me from hitting the ground. Knight and Quill weren't as lucky. Knight smashed into a large, black desk that occupied the center of the room; while Quill fell against a bookshelf in front of the desk.

I didn't have the time nor the wherewithal to take in much, but I scanned the perimeter of the small room anyway. I took in the bookshelves that lined the walls, as well as the desk that Knight so adeptly snapped in two. In only a split second, I realized we weren't alone in my father's library. My eyes focused on a beefy man, looming in the doorway, right behind the bookshelf Quill had bashed into.

"Quill, behind you!" I screamed as I watched the man turn his scowl toward Quill. My ability to differentiate creatures didn't work in the Netherworld, so I wasn't sure if this was the wolf or the goblin. Either way, he was enormous—well over six feet. With his unshaven face and longish, greasy, matted hair, he looked as if he hadn't bathed in weeks. His nose was incredibly wide and uneven, probably broken too many times, and one half of his right ear was missing.

"Beaurigard, you double-crossing son of a bitch," the man bellowed as he rushed forward from maybe ten feet away. Silver daggers shone from both of his hands, and he was missing a finger on his left hand. Quill turned in a split second, though he was still sitting on the floor, and pushed against the ground with his heels, trying to put some distance between the man and himself. Careening into the bookshelf behind him, Quill pulled his Op 8 from the holster around his waist. He fired twice and both bullets hit the man in the center of his chest. He was dead before he hit the ground.

I continued to hover, unable to convince my wings to allow my feet to touch the ground. Unfortunately, there wasn't anything close at hand that I could use to tether myself. Instead, I just snapped my head to the left and right, trying to get a quick recon of what we were up against. There was no sign of my father, and as far as I could see, only these two thugs, one down and one to go. The one to go was already brawling with Knight. The two looked pretty well matched when it came to brawn, both huffing rhythmically as they faced one another with contempt. From the looks of the shiner already forming underneath Knight's eye, he'd obviously suffered a blow. I wondered why he didn't just pull his Op 8 from his holster, but decided he must have wanted to fight the old-fashioned way.

I scanned the room again for any sign of my father or the warlock Quill warned us about. But it seemed there wasn't anyone else in the room. Looking above me, I noticed the library had a second floor that overlooked the first, with more rows of bookshelves lining the walls. But the second floor was also clear.

Somehow, my father must have been forewarned of our attack. He must have known we were coming and fled. I reached inside my pocket for my Melchior GPS device, but before I could pull it out to locate the bastard, I heard the sound of fists meeting flesh. I glanced at Knight, who fell into a bookshelf behind him, after sustaining an incredibly powerful blow. The shelf snapped beneath his weight, sending him, as well as twenty or more books, tumbling onto the floor.

Regarding the thug, I assumed he was the were, Herrod, because he seemed especially hairy and unkempt. More so than the previous thug was. This guy was also immense—built like a wall, thick and wide. Within a split second, he validated my hunch as the man's face began to change. His eyes started to migrate to the center of his face while widening and their color changed to a jaundiced yellow. His nose stretched, growing darker and wetter as it morphed into a snout. Fur began covering his cheeks and chin, overtaking the rest of his face. His human teeth fell onto the floor and much larger, sharper canines replaced them. But that was just his face. Observing his body, I noticed his rib cage seemed to double in size as the sounds of snapping bones accompanied the transformation. His back began to hunch, forcing his abdomen upward and inward. Then a bushy tail emerged from his already shredded pants. His arms elongated while his hands and feet stretched. Razor sharp claws materialized on his fingers and toes. The remnants of his clothing lay in shredded fibers at his feet.

Knight didn't waste any time waiting for the werewolf's change to finish. Instead, he pummeled the were's face and sent the abomination flying into the back wall. It fell into another bookshelf, spraying splinters and books through the room like a tornado. As soon as the creature pushed itself up, it had morphed completely into a wolf.

"Come and get me, you ugly son of a bitch," Knight taunted. He held his hands out by his sides and stared at the gargantuan beast with no trepidation in his eyes. Reaching for my Op 6s, which were strapped to my waist beneath my shirt, I watched the creature jump on Knight. When Knight gripped its arms and rolled over, I realized I couldn't get a clean shot—if I tried, I could just as easily miss the wolf and nail Knight instead.

I eyed Quill, who was already on his feet and staring at me, no doubt trying to figure out how to get me down. It seemed like slow motion as he reached for me, when he suddenly pulled back and gripped his throat like he were choking on something.

"I," he started, still staring at me. "I can't breathe!"

Clawing at his neck, he fell back against the wall as if something were stuck in his throat preventing him from catching his breath. His face started to grow paler as his eyes widened first with fear, and then, panic.

"Quill!" I screamed out, suddenly feeling my wings beating as they took me further and further away from him.

Quill continued to tear at his throat and then leaned over, his hands on his thighs. A few seconds later, he collapsed onto the floor, the color completely drained from his skin. I realized then that he was under the influence of magic. And magic could only mean one thing—that bastard sorcerer was somewhere in the room. Looking back at Quill, I noticed his arms hanging limply by his sides. The need to assist him infiltrated me with an increased sense of urgency and I desperately tried to figure out how the hell I could descend from my ridiculous altitude. I glanced at Quill again. His eyes were closed. Panic spiraled up inside me as I searched for any sign of the warlock, Angus.

Dropping my hands to my waist, I palmed my Op 6s, and pulled them from their holsters, still searching the room. But I couldn't see anything. I wheeled around to my right and left, but found only a destroyed library. My wings continued to beat wildly, carrying me even higher.

Suddenly, a stinging sensation began brewing at the base of my neck. It felt like a very bad sore throat. It soon began to penetrate the entire length of my neck, no doubt the same discomfort that had attacked Quill, rendering him either unconscious or dead. The burning started to dissolve, but left me feeling that my neck was swelling, and restricting my airway. Dropping both of my guns, I didn't even comprehend what I was doing as I brought my hands to my throat instinctively. The guns banged against the ground, and I recognized my mistake instantly, but all I could do was grip my neck, and try to squeeze some air into my lungs. My throat was swelling so much that I could only rasp, and even that ability was quickly dissipating. My wings finally slowed their incessant beating and only flapped every few seconds, allowing me to slowly float to the ground. I continued clawing at my neck, and opening my mouth wide to inhale, but it was useless. When my toes touched the ground, I collapsed against a nearby bookshelf. Then I was confronted by a large-skulled, bald man with a pencil neck and shoulders that were narrower than mine. He must have been invisible earlier, but was now clearly out in the open, and standing before me. He was also clearly the warlock.

"A beautiful fairy," he said with elation, while holding his hands (palms facing me) before him, emitting his power.

His eyes were huge, like disks in his otherwise smallish face, and his nose was long and pointy. It matched his sharp chin. His body was the size of a ten-year-old and he was probably no taller than I was. He narrowed his eyes while he studied me, his face finally lighting up with jubilance.

"A fairy," he repeated again, his eyes glazing over with passion. "It's true what they say about your kind."

While I wasn't sure what "they" said about my kind, I *was* reminded of the power I carried in the Netherworld. Yep, I still had sexual fairy crack that I could turn to. Not that I wanted to, but when I noticed my guns lying uselessly on the floor, I realized they weren't my only option to

173

defend myself. Regardless, I didn't possess enough strength to reach for them. Even if I tried, I knew the warlock would, no doubt, fortify his magical attack, and where would that leave me? Probably dead. I looked past him and saw that Knight was still involved with the were, although neither one looked to be gaining any ground.

"He can't help you," the warlock announced in a nasal, high-pitched voice. "He can't even see us."

So, my hunch was right. The little bastard had made himself invisible before and now he was doing the same, only to both of us. Yep, any way I looked at it, I had no choice but to use my fairy crack. I forced my hands from my neck and ran them through my hair, offering the warlock my best bedroom eyes. His eyes widened as he continued to stare at me, hunger dripping from his expression. He was very obviously about to become ensnared in my trap.

Don't give up now, Dulce, I thought to myself. *You've almost got him!*

Strangely enough, my next thought was of Bram, and how he'd manipulated me by using his powers of vampire persuasion. I remembered how expertly he'd made me do and be something I wasn't. And even though I hated Bram, I recognized the valuable lesson he'd taught me. I realized that I now had the power to do the same.

"I," I gasped, trying to talk even though I couldn't get any air. My voice was barely a whisper. I trailed my finger down to my lips, hoping I had enough air left to maintain my charade. If I passed out, it would all be over. This bastard would do whatever he chose to with me, and then who knew what would happen? No, I absolutely had to stay alert so I could see my plan to fruition.

The warlock continued to gaze at me as I stared into his eyes, running my tongue across my lips. I used my best body language to say, "I want you to make love to me." His hands began to drop, even though his fingers were still actively splayed and his magic was still in effect. The strangulation in my throat began to ease slightly, even though I still couldn't take in a full breath. Once the warlock dropped his hands a little lower, I managed to catch a shallow breath.

Seeing the little bastard's eyes glued to mine, I pursed my lips before running my finger across them. Nearing the grand finale, I dipped my finger inside my mouth, staring at the hideous creature sensuously. The warlock stared at me with ravenous hunger in his eyes and dropped his hands to his side. As soon as he did so, I inhaled fully and I took in so much oxygen, I thought I might pass out. Trying to stay conscious, I continued to gaze at the man, knowing the game was far from over. I had to maintain my act, lest the little cretin snap out of it.

"What do you want?" I whispered, tracing the outline of my breasts above my shirt as I batted my eyelashes at him.

He laughed. "Isn't it obvious?" he asked in his nasal tone. "I want you, my little sexpot."

I giggled, or did my best version of one, because as a rule, Dulcie O'Neil didn't giggle. Hoping the time for giggling would soon be over, I glanced out of the corner of my eye to inquire how Knight was faring. I could see the shape of the wolf, lying in a heap on the ground, and Knight standing above him. The Loki turned to face me and we made eye contact which meant the warlock had ceased his invisibility charm. Knight just watched me for a few seconds, as if trying to understand what the hell I was doing. But then he apparently got it, because he began approaching us stealthily, as if trying to be as quiet as possible.

"If you want me," I continued, spearing the warlock with my full attention. "Tell me what you want to do to me." I finished, trying to channel Marilyn Monroe. I had to keep the little bastard's attention while Knight came up behind him.

The warlock chuckled again, but the laugh soon died on his lips as his eyes narrowed first on my face and then on my bust. "I'm going to tear those clothes off you," he said, his eyes roaming my body.

I giggled again and ran my hands all over myself, attempting to appear turned on. "I like it rough," I said coyly.

"You're going to get it rough as soon as I get hold of you," he said before he jumped at me. He managed to grip my collar before Knight bashed him in the side of the head with the butt of his Op 8, before tucking it back into the waistline of his pants. The warlock collapsed in a heap at my feet.

"Are you okay?" Knight asked as he faced me with concern in his eyes.

"I'm fine, but I'm not so sure about Quill," I said, motioning to Quill's still form, where he lay in the corner of the room.

"He isn't dead," came the voice from above us. Looking up, I saw my father standing on the second floor of the library, leaning on the balustrade lazily and smiling down at us as if we were revered guests. I felt my stomach sour instantly. On either side of him were three guards, each pointing guns at us.

"But Beaurigard's life is most definitely on the line, should you decide to fight us," came an English accent from the opposite side of the room. Glancing over my shoulder, I faced Bram.

THIRTEEN

"Throw your weapons on the floor in front of you," my father said, his stern expression warning us we'd better comply.

I noticed Knight's face was blank, almost like he'd gone into automaton mode. The longer I watched him, the more I realized how well he'd perfected the art of the poker face. It was almost as if his lack of anger, sorrow and defiance was a defense mechanism—something meant to throw my father off in the same way it had thrown me off. Still wearing the façade of someone detached, he reached inside his waistband and produced an Op 8, which he tossed on the floor. Then he faced my father with a look that said, "Okay, what next?"

My father turned his beautiful green eyes from Knight to me as he arched his left brow, and appeared anything but amused. In fact, as soon as his eyes settled on me, he looked disgusted, repulsed and even appalled to see me. "And yours?" he demanded.

I simply pointed at the polished hardwood floors where my two Op 6s lay idly, still in the same place they'd fallen when the warlock magically choked me and I, inadvertently, dropped them.

At the sound of Bram's chuckle, my attention flashed from my father and landed squarely on the haughty vampire. He stood in front of Knight, his expression one of mirth as he regarded us with interest. He was dressed for an elegant soiree, or a funeral. His expertly tailored Italian suit matched the midnight pitch of his hair perfectly. His black ensemble was only interrupted by a charcoal gray dress shirt and the sparkling azure of his eyes. Yes, despite being enraged with

him, even hating him with all my being, I couldn't deny
what a handsome bastard he was.

"All of your weapons, Vander," he said, picking up
Knight's Op 8 from the ground. He stood up and faced the
Loki again. "Allow me to remind you that we have our own
ways of disarming you."

Knight didn't say anything, but reached inside the
waistline at the back of his jeans and withdrew an Op 9,
which he then threw to the ground. "That's it," he muttered.

"Very good," Bram said before daring to assault me
with his arrogant grin. Stepping right up to me, until we
were my face to his lapels, he smiled as if we were old
friends, reuniting after years of separation. I felt my eyes
narrowing as my jaw tightened so much, I was afraid of
shattering my teeth.

"You backstabbing bastard," I ground out at him. I still
found it difficult to speak after basically being strangled by
the warlock's magic. My throat and neck still throbbed and
stung.

The vampire just chuckled with indifference, as if my
trust was immaterial and his betrayal was of no
consequence. Instead, his eyes seemed alight with humor, as
if it thrilled him that I now knew he'd been playing me all
along.

"What did you expect, Sweet?" he asked while
shaking his head at my supposed stupidity. "You, yourself,
remarked that my situation behooved me, so why should I
want to upset it?"

Rage brewed inside me and I could feel my hands
fisting at my sides as I glared at the vampire whom I'd been
thoughtless enough to believe in. But, even now, I couldn't
help the surprise that registered within me, just beside the
anger. Bram had just seemed so genuine when he'd given
me the portal ripper and his pocket watch. Everything he'd
told me about his feelings towards my father had seemed so
authentic, so honest.

Honestly bullshit! He's just a good actor, you moron! I chided myself. But as ridiculous as it sounded, there was still a part of me that refused to fully believe it. Why? Because there was still one piece to the puzzle that didn't make sense. That piece was the reasoning behind why Bram hadn't just killed me or turned me over to Melchior when he'd had the chance. And he'd had numerous opportunities. Furthermore, if Bram was truly allied with my father, why had he returned Christina to us? And why wean her off the *Blueliss*?

They were unanswerable questions, and after struggling with them, I remembered that Bram enjoyed making things difficult for people in general. Being linked to my father didn't mean he would hand The Resistance to him on a silver platter. No, Bram had always made me work for my information, and I was sure he'd do the same to my father, and anyone else, for that matter. That was just the way he was.

Seeing him smiling down at me, rage began building within me until it erupted into a volcano of anger and accusation. When my cheeks flushed, my jaw tightened, and I lurched out at him, pummeling my fists into his face. But I never made contact with him due to the superior speed inherent to his race, which allowed him to easily sidestep me. Losing my balance, I had to ricochet off a nearby wall rather than crash into it.

Once I regained some stability, I heard the sound of weapons being cocked coming from the second story. I kept my attention on Bram, though, who continued to chuckle, while shaking his head like I was making a big mistake.

"You should rein in that famous temper of yours, my pet," he said. Before I could respond, my ears were assaulted by a cacophony. It was impossible to locate the source at first, but it seemed to be coming from right outside the house, or maybe just inside the entryway. The longer I listened, the more I realized it was the noise of battle—bullets being fired and derogatory epithets being yelled. I quickly concluded our soldiers must have invaded

179

Willoughby house and were now in active combat with my
father's guards. I wasn't sure if I'd failed to hear the sounds
before because I was so focused on defending myself against
the warlock, or if our soldiers had just now made their move.
Looking up at my father, I noticed the expression of surprise
in his widened eyes. Hmm, so maybe he hadn't been
expecting us? Maybe our soldiers had just begun their
attack. Either way, it didn't really matter because Melchior
had us exactly where he wanted us.

"I'm tired of prolonging this charade," my father
called out hastily, seemingly alarmed by the sudden surge of
our soldiers. "Vander, call off your men off or I will shoot
my daughter on the spot."

Shifting my murderous eyes from Bram's smug
countenance to my father, I had a fleeting thought that
Bram's immediate reaction to my father's words was angry
shock. Instead, I reminded myself that Bram didn't give a
rat's ass about anyone besides himself, and least of all, me.
Once I'd settled that score in my head, I bit my lower lip as I
faced the monster that was my father. His eyes were riveted
on mine and we just stared at one another for a few seconds,
each of us reading the truth in the other's eyes. In my
father's eyes, I saw that Quillan had been right—I was
nothing to Melchior, but a tool—potentially an arrow in his
quiver, but now gone astray. My father didn't know the
meaning of having a daughter because he didn't possess the
ability to love. Consequently, all people were disposable to
him, even his own kin.

As easily as I could read the truth in my father's eyes,
I genuinely hoped he read the truth in mine … that as much
as I loathed Bram, I despised my father even more. Just in
taking in his expertly tailored grey suit and expensive black
leather shoes, I wanted to throw up. Maybe the biggest
disappointment of all, though, was that I could see him
reflected in me. I had the same wavy honey-colored hair and
the same emerald green eyes that were now alight with fire.
Yes, my father absolutely was a stunningly handsome man,

but to me he was nothing more than a heartless monster. Much worse than either the bird predator or that thing living in the bottom of the swamp.

"I will call off my men," Knight said, his lips a straight line. As I watched him look at my father, I could see the hatred burning behind his eyes. And it was a hatred born from long association, from experiencing just what type of man my father was and despising him for it. Given his boundless loathing for my father, it suddenly surprised me that Knight could love me, especially when the physical similarities between my father and me were so blatantly obvious. I didn't understand how Knight could look at me and not think of the connection between father and daughter every time he saw me. But somehow he didn't, which just spoke to his own magnanimous personality and his strength of character. Not to mention the power of love.

"Yes, you will call off your men," my father stressed, seeming to savor each word. "And then you will remain in my custody, residing in my own personal dungeon, where, I trust, you will not suffer for long."

"You won't touch him!" I screamed out. My father's thugs took a few steps forward, warning me I was the target of their artillery. But I didn't care. There was no way I could stand by and say nothing after my father's words. "No one touches him!"

"It is more than obvious that you and your cabal have been defeated," my father chided, eyeing me hollowly. "I expected so much more from you. I must admit this little uprising has thoroughly disappointed me." Then he laughed heartily, shaking his head as if The Resistance were no more than an anticlimax. "You really believed you could remove me by attacking Squander Valley and then waltzing in here?"

I found it curious that he didn't mention Tipshaw, or the surrender at the airport, but made no comment. Instead, I watched him say to the man on his right side. "Take care of Beaurigard, will you?"

181

The man nodded before disappearing through the doorway of the second floor. It led to a spiral staircase that connected to this one. The man took the stairs two at a time, and reaching Quill, he bent over and hoisted Quill's still body over his shoulder and left the room. Where he took Quill, I had no clue but I intended to find out.

"What are you doing with him?" I demanded of my father. "Where are you taking him?"

"He and your Loki can rot, for all I care," my father spat back at me, his eyes livid. Turning to Knight again, he suddenly smiled, as if he'd completely lost his mind. Who knew—it was probably as close to the truth as anything else. "Believe me when I tell you, Vander, that I will absolutely revel at your death," my father managed between gritted teeth. "You have caused me nothing but trouble, between your silly Resistance and that blasted Sabbiondo."

Hearing my father's words, Knight didn't respond or react. His expression remained completely unchanged. He simply continued to stare at my father, his face a blank slate. "Whatever your gripes with me, I don't care, O'Neil," he said at last, taking a deep breath. His voice sounded heavy, but as melodically beautiful as it always was. "I just don't want Dulcie harmed."

I felt tears stinging my eyes and shook my head, trying to deny the thought that this precise moment was all because of me. Had I never trusted Bram, maybe we never would have gotten into this situation.

If Knight dies, it will be on your conscience, a nasty voice inside me admonished.

I clenched my eyes tightly against the tears welling up because I refused to cry in front of my father. No matter what happened, I wouldn't allow the bastard to see one tear. Once my torn emotions were back under control, I opened my eyes and looked up at my father. Turning to his left, he ordered the man standing there to take Knight into custody. The man came down the same staircase as the previous man, wasting no time in apprehending Knight. As soon as he did, he motioned for Knight to turn around so he could cuff him, but Knight looked at my father instead, with a raised brow expression.

"Do you really think this is necessary, O'Neil?" he asked, holding his hands up as if to say, "I'm surrendering, so why the dog and pony show?"

"I don't want any games, Vander," my father replied matter-of-factly.

Knight laughed dryly. "There are no games to play, O'Neil. You've won." Looking over at me, he shook his head sadly, before returning his attention to my father. "You won as soon as you threatened the life of the woman I love." He took a deep breath and I felt my heart sinking. "Do you really need to rub salt in my wounds by forcing my men to see me in shackles?"

My father looked unimpressed as he shook his head. It appeared he couldn't care less about any of us, which was probably the truth. "Call your soldiers off," he said with ennui, before facing the man beside him. "Assist Taurus in leading the Loki to the holding facility in Belgate Tower," he said. "There's no need for cuffs unless he refuses to go willingly." Then he faced Knight. "And you won't refuse to go willingly, will you, Vander?"

Knight shook his head. "Guarantee Dulcie's safety and I won't fight."

"I give you my word as her father," Melchior replied as if his word meant a damned thing. It didn't—especially after he'd already made it very apparent that I meant nothing to him.

"Do us both a favor and give me your word as the Head of the Illegal Potions Trade," Knight rebuked, his lips a tight line. Apparently, my father's vow offended him as much as me.

"You have my word," Melchior responded with more irritation.

Knight then turned to me and smiled. He seemed to be trying to reassure me, as if he thought this was just a small "blip" in our lives, and we'd be together again soon. "Just stay alive, Dulce, don't do anything stupid that could get you killed … please."

I swallowed hard, my tears threatening to fall again. I just didn't know what to do or whom to turn to.

There is no one left to turn to! I railed at myself. *We've lost!*

We had lost. The words echoed through me, leaving nothing but intense feelings of depression in their wake. The words continued to assault me until they were nothing more than the most devastating words in the English language. We had lost and now there was nothing left for me, but learn what fate my father had in store for me. There appeared to be no other alternatives. As to the here and now, Knight and I were vastly outnumbered, and who knew what was going on outside? The fleeting hope that our men were defeating my father's guards suddenly crossed my mind, but I had to ignore it because the battle was already over. Why? Because Knight and I were in custody, and Christina was lost in a forest somewhere, if not captured or dead. Either way, without a leader, there was no Resistance left.

"I'll do everything I can to make sure you're spared," I whispered to Knight, although I felt the futility of my words right down in my bones.

But there was something in Knight's eyes that threw me, something that seemed out of place. Not worry, rage, disillusionment, or fear, but a jubilance that was inappropriate to the situation. "I just want you to take care of yourself," he said softly, but emphatically. "Whatever you do, whatever decisions you're forced to make, consider only yourself, Dulcie."

I shook my head, unsure why and how he could be thinking of my future when his was so uncertain, or maybe it was more fitting to say his was certain—certainly bad. "Knight," I started, my voice cracking.

"Enough!" my father ordered. Facing the two men on either side of Knight, he added, "Once his men have

184

surrendered, put them all in High Prison. Vander will make his home in the dungeon." Then he took a deep breath as something else occurred to him. "Throw Beaurigard down there too, for that matter."

"Yessir," the man closest to him replied. They each took one of Knight's arms and started to lead him out of the room.

I couldn't even hug him good-bye, or kiss him one last time? I thought as I felt my heart sink. As he walked away, something in his stride caught my attention. His steps were confident and purposeful. And confidence just seemed so out of place considering the situation. In watching him leave the room, it felt as if something inside of me was being trampled to death, as if half of my soul was being ripped apart. Knight turned around and faced me just before he reached the doorway and mouthed "I love you."

Before I could respond, my father's men forced him into the hallway and they disappeared around the corner. I was left with nothing but cold numbness in my gut. Even with an all-consuming sense of loss and desperation, there was still a glimmer of hope deep inside me that defied logic. While I recognized the situation for the piece of total shit that it was, there was something else inside me that still rebelled, something that refused to be silenced. Why? Because Knight hadn't acted defeated. There was a hop to his step and a fire in his eyes that said our fight was far from over. I'd read in his gaze as clear as day the fact that he refused to go down so easily. As to his plan though, I didn't have a clue. I reminded myself of his parting words to me: for me to think only of myself. It was something you'd say to someone if you had a plan for yourself, but were still worried about theirs. The subtle feelings of hope began to surface inside me until they ignited a conflagration of optimism. We hadn't lost. Not yet anyway.

"We find ourselves in an unfortunate situation," my father started. He and the only remaining guard walked down the spiral staircase, taking their sweet ass time.

Hearing my father's voice, I sensed his delusional feelings of supremacy and pride. For the second time in the past twenty minutes, I felt like I wanted to throw up.

I ignored my father and turned my attention to Bram, who was approaching me quickly. His eyes were pools of mystery when he closed the distance that separated us and we were only two inches apart. Instinctively, I wanted to step back, preparing for whatever he was planning to do or say to me. I just couldn't define the look in his eyes and my Spidey senses went on high alert. I'm not sure why I didn't step back, but I didn't. Instead, I stood my ground and watched Bram reach for my hand. I narrowed my eyes, but allowed him to take it all the same. Then I watched as he slipped his hand inside his jacket and pulled out Knight's Op 8 that he'd retrieved from the floor only moments earlier.

He leaned into me, his eyes twinkling like sapphires as he smiled, his fangs in full effect. At first, I feared he was going to bite me, but the look in his eyes wasn't one of hunger. It was the look of victory, or triumph. He brought his lips to my cheek, as if he were going to kiss me, but instead, whispered. "Not everything is as it seems, Sweet." Feeling the cold steel butt of the Op 8 in my palm, I wrapped my fingers around it tightly.

And then I understood.

What happened next seemed as if it took place in a series of still photos. It was as if time stopped and allowed each second to exist as an image snapped by a camera. I closed my eyes and concentrated on the sounds of heavy footfalls on the hardwood floors of my father's library as my father and his bodyguard approached us. My body went into autopilot as I opened my eyes and pivoted on my right foot, turning in my father's direction. I felt a swoosh of wind against my face as Bram dematerialized from where he'd been standing in front of me and reappeared behind me.

My body stayed on autopilot as I did what I'd done hundreds of times before as a Regulator in the ANC. When it came to pure mechanics, this situation was no different than the countless busts I'd made on myriad criminals. Sure, the background was different along with the players, but my response was the same. Strangely enough, I began channeling a moment long ago when I was a lowly cadet, working for the ANC in Splendor and Quill first taught me how to shoot a gun. Remembering his instruction, I placed my feet and hips shoulder-width apart with my knees slightly bent. I raised the Op 8 to my dominant eye, aligning the crosshairs on my father. I didn't realize I was holding my breath until I squeezed the trigger. I never did get to see his response. Instead, my brain alerted me that there was still one threat remaining—my father's bodyguard. With cool ease, I watched the man reach for the pistol sitting in the holster around his waist. I took another breath and simply aimed the Op 8 at him, waiting until I had him in my sights and squeezed the trigger again, watching him go down.

After firing the second shot, time seemed to speed up again and the dreamlike landscape dissolved into cold reality. I dropped my arms to my sides and did nothing but stand still for two seconds, merely allowing my heartbeat to calm as I tried to regulate my breathing. Then, remembering my training, I held the Op 8 out in front of me again and approached the still figures of the two men I'd just shot. Training my gun on the guard, who was closest to me, I bent down onto my knees and reached out to check his pulse. My eyes settled on the enormous bullet hole in his gut, his blood already turning purple after making contact with the dragon's blood my bullets had released inside him. He was pulseless, dead.

Seeing my father, I felt emotionless, which surprised me. Even though I didn't expect to feel any sort of daughterly love toward him, because I never had any, I thought I might feel something. But there was nothing—not even any residual anger, not even relief. It was as if firing that bullet not only released the toxin of the dragon's blood into my father's body, but also wiped out any feelings I had for him. I had nothing left but empty pages toward Melchior.

187

Seeing his pale skin and closed eyes, I assumed he was dead. He hadn't moved and the bullet looked like it entered his heart. Even though I was more than sure he was no longer alive, I reached over and checked his pulse anyway. It was part of my training. I pulled my hand away when I didn't register his heartbeat.

"All is fair in love and war, is it not, Sweet?" Bram said softly, coming up behind me. He offered me his hand so I took it, and allowed him to pull me up from my knees. I shook my head as I looked at him, still trying to figure out his enigmatic persona. I was completely at a loss when it came to his motives. "Why did you rat us out?" I started.

He smiled widely. "I had to maintain appearances, my dear," he answered quickly. "I had to make your father believe I was on his side until the very end. I knew Squander Valley would be a fairly easy blow to suffer, as it was truly the smallest of the Netherworld Guard stations rather than the largest, as I told you."

I felt my eyes widen once Bram mentioned that Squander Valley was the smallest base. Then I remembered my father acting surprised that we would have chosen to attack it. Now his surprise made sense. "Then my father didn't know about Tipshaw?" I asked, unsuccessfully trying to conceal the surprise from my tone.

"No, Sweet, your father knew of no other attacks."

"And you never told him about the pocket watch or the portal ripper that you gave me?" I continued. I was amazed at how thorough Bram was in his subterfuge, even going so far as to convince me he was against us. I didn't allow him to answer my question, though, because I'd already figured out the answer for myself. "Which is why he was surprised when we showed up here and why he didn't have more guards," I finished. "How many guards are there here anyway?"

Bram shook his head. "Perhaps ten or fifteen. I am uncertain. Vander is in the process of arresting all your father's soldiers as we speak."

"Knight," I started, still processing Bram's words before something occurred to me. "Wait. How do you know Knight's arresting …" but I was never able to finish my sentence. Instead, the sound and acrid smoke of a gun firing in the immediate vicinity overtook my senses. I felt the bullet's sting immediately as it entered my lower back and thrust me forward with its impact. My heartbeat began pounding through my ears, sounding like a bowling ball bouncing against a steel wall. As I collapsed, I saw the shock in Bram's eyes. Moments later, my cheek hit the floor and my vision began to blur. In the fuzziness, though, I could make out the smile on my father's face as well as the gun lying beside him. Moments later, I felt wind brushing past my cheek and watched Bram materialize at my father's side. He leaned over Melchior and sunk his teeth into my father's carotid, stealing any whisper of life that remained.

Bram then stood up and approached me, his eyes despondent. "Sweet," he started, as he leaned down and ran his fingers down my face tenderly.

I felt my body began to shake as the poison of the dragon's blood traveled into my bloodstream. I knew I had only a few seconds left before the poison would steal my life away and in those few seconds, I thought only of Knight and how much I would miss him. The blurriness of my vision gave way to black and the last thought to go through my head was that Trey had been right.

FOURTEEN

Despite being shrouded in darkness, I wasn't afraid. In fact, I couldn't register any feelings at all. Instead, I simply existed in a vacuity of space. Inside the void, I was floating, sailing through the atmosphere as if I never was, nor ever would be. I was carefree, boundless, infinite. There was an undeniable buoyancy in my body—the laws of gravity no longer applied to me. Along with the incredible sense of weightlessness, I could feel freedom flowing through me, as if it originated in my very soul and billowed through me in a bubbly cascade of limitlessness.

"Dulcie."

The soft timber of the woman's voice surprised me. In disbelief, I also felt immense happiness as her voice stoked familiar fires deep inside me. Even though I hadn't heard her voice for many years, hers was one I had never, and could never, forget.

"Mom?" I asked, my voice tinged with awe and amazement. As soon as I said the word "Mom," the darkness surrounding me faded and I was bathed in a pure, white light that was so bright, I blinked a few times, and yet still had to shield my eyes. When I was able to see clearly, the feelings of weightlessness were still in effect, although the darkness was gone. Instead, I found myself standing on the top of a mountain, overlooking an immense valley of green. A crystal clear stream flowed through the valley but I lost sight of it when it meandered into a forest of tall pine trees. If I didn't know better, I would have believed I'd been transported to the Swiss Alps. All around me was the green of hillside, punctuated with delicate, bell-shaped, white flowers that blew this way and that in the gentle wind that caressed my cheeks. But where was my mother? I turned around, hoping she was standing behind me, but nothing besides the pristine beauty of the natural world stared back at me.

I shook my head, wondering if I simply imagined her voice, or if it was a trick of the wind. Feeling a renewed dejection, I faced forward again. That was when I saw her. Standing directly in front of me, she embodied the exact picture of how I remembered her before fate snatched her from me so long ago. Her long, platinum blonde hair blew about her face in perfectly straight, silken strands. Seeing the gentle smile on her lips brought fresh tears to my eyes. She was wearing the same, threadbare grey sweatpants she always wore when she returned home from work, along with an oversized T-shirt that proclaimed her "#1 Mom." I'd given her the shirt when I was twelve years old and she'd worn it so often, the fabric was frayed. She wasn't wearing a speck of makeup but she also didn't need to. Her skin was the color and texture of alabaster, warmed by the natural coral blush on her cheeks and the deeper pink tones of her lips.

My mother was just as beautiful as I remembered. Her understanding, light brown eyes were a few shades darker than her hair, framed by eyebrows the color of coffee with cream, and deep, brown eyelashes. I, fortunately, inherited the soft lines of her jaw as well as her high cheekbones and pert, upturned nose. Even though my eyes reflected the same verdant green of my father's, their almond shape belonged exclusively to my mother. The more I studied her, the more I realized how much I was my mother's daughter. And it made my heart sing.

"My beautiful, Dulcie," she said softly. She held her arms out to me and the smile I'd always loved so well deepened into a laugh of pure delight. I fell into her arms instantly, drinking in her scent—something gentle and breezy with whiffs of Tide and Jergens Body Lotion. I held her as tightly as I could, allowing the little girl who had missed her mother so much to surface from my heart. Right

191

then and there, I promised myself I would never lose her again. By some trick or gift of fate, she'd been restored to me and it was a gift I cherished with all the essence of my being.

"Mom? Is it really you?" I whispered, suddenly fearing she might be a hoax created by my mind. Maybe she was really a dream, hallucination, or just an apparition visiting me.

"Yes, it is really me," she reassured. As if to prove it, she ran her hands through my hair just like she'd done a thousand times before. My heart swelled as I snuggled into her embrace and felt blissful tears streaming down my face.

"I've missed you so much, Mom," I whispered.

She kissed the top of my head. "And I've missed you more than you will ever know, my little *Dulcinea*." When she said her nickname for me (borrowed from Don Quixote), a sob surged in my throat. She pulled away from me and studied me for a few seconds, her eyes glowing with pride.

"Why did you have to leave me?" I asked, choking on another sob.

"It was just my time," she said softly. "But I have always been with you, Dulcie, even though you couldn't see me."

I nodded although I didn't understand how she could have always been with me without me ever having seen her or heard her. *But there were so many moments when you felt her*, I thought to myself. I smiled as I realized the truth in my own words. My mom really had always been with me.

I wrapped my arms around her more tightly. "I don't ever want to lose you again."

"You must be strong, Dulcie," she whispered, her voice suddenly sounding pained.

I pulled away from her and regarded her in question, not understanding what her words meant. "Strong?" I repeated.

She simply nodded and dropped her eyes to the grass below our feet. She sat down and patted the grassy spot beside her, asking me to sit next to her. I did and leaned into her when she put her arm around me.

"Where are we, Mom?" I asked as I allowed my eyes to feast on the cornucopia of beauty that surrounded us. I relished the feel of the cool breeze as it toyed with our hair and stirred up the monotony of the otherwise warm, sunny day.

My mother's smile faded slightly. "We're in a place where time stands still," she said gently, running her fingers through my hair as she started to hum the melody of "Golden Slumbers" by The Beatles. It was the same song she used to sing to me when she tucked me in at night.

"Once there was a way, to get back home," she sang.

I wanted to close my eyes and succumb to the beautiful tones of her voice. I wanted to return to a time as a child when she rocked me against her and sang this song to banish whatever nightmare had just awoken me. But I couldn't comprehend her comment that this mountain paradise was somewhere that time stood still. I shook my head. "I don't understand."

She pulled me into her embrace again and I rested my head against her chest. I took a deep breath so I could inhale as much of her wonderful "Mom" scent as possible. "Dulcie, it's not time for you to join me yet."

"But I want us to be together again," I responded, my voice cracking as I gazed up at her. It felt like all the years that separated us were now dissolving into the ether, as if they'd never been. "I've missed you so much. Please don't leave me again."

She smiled down at me, her eyes shining with adoration and unshed tears. "We will be reunited again in time, but now isn't right." She traced the outline of my face, just like she did when I was a child, upset over something.

"Sleep, pretty darling, do not cry," she sang. "And I will sing a lullaby."

I closed my eyes, loving the feel of her index finger traveling along my hairline and then dipping down to the bridge of my nose, only to outline my lips. As my mother sang to me, I realized how much pain I'd been storing inside all these years. I'd never dealt with the feelings of abandonment and heartache after my mother was snatched from me. Holding her now, though, somehow wiped all the pain clean away and I could feel nothing but jubilance.

"You still have a full and rich life to lead, Dulcie," she whispered. "And as always, I will be by your side and I will continue to watch over you." She paused for a few seconds, both of us happy to be snuggling against each another. "I am always with you, Dulcie."

I opened my eyes and pondered her words as dawning reality began to creep into me. I had to catch my breath as images of a library of ransacked books flashed through my delirious mind. They were replaced by one of my father, standing on the second level of his library, leering down at me. I felt a sharp pain in my lower back as I recalled the event that brought me here, the event that had reunited me with my mother.

"I died. My father killed me," I said in a hollow voice. I glanced up at her with shock on my face. "Am I dead now?"

She shook her head. "You haven't traveled into the Forever Valley yet, Dulcie," she said, eyeing the horizon where a forest of trees dominated the landscape.

"Is that the Forever Valley?" I asked. My eyes followed hers and settled on the trees, which seemed so far off in the distance, yet close enough to travel by foot. It was like an optical illusion.

She simply nodded. "I've come from the Valley to help you get back to where you belong, Dulcie."

I sat up and shook my head, suddenly afraid to leave my mother's side. "But what if I don't want to go back? What if I want to stay here with you?"

"We can't stay here," she said quickly. "This is simply the land between here and there."

"Then take me to the Valley with you."

She shook her head, but smiled at me consolingly. "I can't do that yet, Dulcie."

"Why not?" I asked, my tone sounding desperate. "I can't lose you again, Mom," I started shaking my head as tears pooled in my eyes. "Please don't make me go through it again."

My mother silenced me by holding her fingers against my mouth. "You never lost me, Dulcie. I am, and will always be with you."

But I didn't want that sort of relationship with my mother. I wanted the relationship that we had right now—a physical one, where I could see and smell her, hug and laugh with her. A relationship where I could talk to her. "I just want us to be together again," I said, my voice breaking. The tears started pouring from my eyes.

My mother nodded. "We will be together again, but right now, you still have unfinished business that is calling you back."

"Why?" I demanded, suddenly angry. I couldn't understand how fate would return my mother to me, only to yank her away again. It wasn't fair.

"Because he needs you, Dulcie."

"He?" I repeated. At my confused expression, she settled her attention on the ground and ran her palm across the grassy earth between her feet. I watched as the ground began to peel apart beneath her hands, leaving a blackness, an inky abyss of nothing. But after a few seconds, the inky blackness began to brighten and colors started to form against the darkness. The colors morphed into objects and people. I realized I was seeing a picture of another place and time. It was almost like watching a movie. I stared at the images unfolding before us and leaned closer, recognizing the scenery.

It was a library, but the books were strewn across the floor haphazardly, and all the furniture was broken and in disrepair. It looked like the scene after an earthquake, or maybe a burglary. But I didn't get the feeling that either of

195

those events had taken place here. Instead, my memory flashed images of exactly what happened. I shot my father and believed I'd killed him, but my attempt was unsuccessful. Instead, he managed to survive long enough to fire the bullet that entered my back, the dragon's blood poisoning me and bringing me here.

The images playing out on the grass in front of us didn't focus on my father, though. Instead, they zoomed in on the figure of a gallant, handsome man dressed in black. He leaned over the still figure of a woman lying prostrate on the ground, while her honey-gold hair fanned out behind her head and looked like a halo.

"Bram," I whispered as I turned my attention to the woman and recognized her as myself. Icy coldness overtook my entire body and I had to hold back my tears again. I couldn't help but notice the gold of my blood arcing out beneath me, like a river of molten lava. My gaze moved from the puddle of blood to the paleness of my skin. I was as white as the cottony clouds which dominated the sky in this place where time stood still.

I watched the vampire drop to his knees as he hovered over my body. Blood dripped from his mouth, trickling down his chin and vanishing into his neckline. It was my Melchior's blood. Then I remembered how Bram had bitten my father after he'd shot me. Even though I still didn't know my father's fate, I was confident that he was dead and it wasn't just a hunch. It was as if someone inserted the information in my head.

"Melchior," I started, turning to face my mother.

She simply nodded. "He is gone."

"Has he gone to the Valley?"

She shook her head. "He has gone to another place, which we won't discuss." Then she simply motioned to the image of the handsome vampire again. I watched as he leaned over and ran his fingers down the woman's, *down my* cheek. I could hear him whispering the word, "sweet" as if it were an apology. He shook his head in despondent frustration before leaning over and kissing my forehead.

"You do not know how much I will miss you, my sweet," he finished. "May you forever rest in peace, and shine your light wherever you now are. As much as I shall ache from your absence, I also envy you."

I glanced at my mother and shook my head, confusion ringing through me. "But you said I wasn't dead? You said it wasn't my time to go?"

She nodded and offered me a reassuring smile. "You were in the throes of death, Dulcie, but as we are now where time stands still, you have been given a gift. Your gift is the ability to make your choice."

"To make my choice?" I repeated.

"Yes, whether you care to return to your own space and time, or prefer to voyage on to the Forever Valley with me." She took a deep breath and shook her head when I started to open my mouth. "But," she interrupted, "before you make your decision, you need to see more." Then she looked back at the images displayed before us and I refocused my attention.

I watched the gallant vampire as he stood up, averting his eyes from my face. At that moment, the door to the room burst open and a man stood there. His hair was mussed up and his face bore the scars of battle. His clothing was torn, tattered, stained and ripped. He wore a smile of victory, though, as if his bruises and cuts meant little or nothing to him. He seemed to shine from inside out and the smile that beamed from his face made me smile, in turn.

He was the most stunningly beautiful creature I'd ever seen.

"Knight," I whispered, looking up at my mother as the puzzle pieces began to slide into place.

She faced me and smiled knowingly, with a slight nod. "He needs you, Dulcie."

I didn't respond as I watched the images unfolding against the background of the earth. I watched Knight's eyes drop to the floor, where he saw my lifeless body. Instantly, the smile vanished from his face. He hesitated in the doorway, his chest expanding and contracting with his labored breathing.

"Dulcie," he ground out.

"I am sorry," the vampire responded, shaking his head to let it be known that I hadn't survived my wound.

A cry of tortured grief came from Knight's mouth as he ran across the room, throwing himself to the floor. He grabbed my shoulders and pulled me into his embrace, staring at me with eyes that revealed how horrific his loss.

"There was nothing I could do," Bram added softly. Sensing the futility of the situation, Bram showed himself out of the room. Knight never took his eyes off mine.

"Dulcie, no," he moaned into my hair as he rocked back and forth, holding me against him. My arms hung limply by my sides. "This wasn't supposed to happen," he said, shaking his head as he kissed the top of mine. As soon as his lips touched my hair, he buried his face in it and his shoulders began convulsing with sobs. A few moments later, he pulled his face up and strands of my hair stuck to his tear-stained cheeks. "Don't do this to me!" he railed out, in an angry, pained voice. Looking upward, his expression was enraged and threatening. "Don't take her from me!"

Of course there was no response. Dropping his eyes back down to my face, he gingerly placed some strands of my hair behind my ears. "You are so beautiful," he whispered. When he brought his lips to mine, he kissed me so softly, I could barely feel it.

With the thought that I had barely felt his kiss, in the here and now, I ran my fingers across my lips and glanced up at my mother in shock. "I felt his kiss," I said in utter surprise.

She laughed lightly. "Of course you did. You are still there, Dulcie, but only a very small part of you. Your fight isn't over but if you decide to return to that space and time, you *will* have to fight for your life."

Instantly, I knew that there was no decision or choice for me to make. Why? Because it had already been made for me. My mother was right—Knight needed me and I needed him. "I have to leave you," I said softly. My tears choked me as I realized I wouldn't see my mother again for Hades only knew how long. The very thought tore my heart out and snapped it in two right in front of me.

"I know," she said gently, her voice wafting into the breeze as her own eyes filled with tears.

"I love you, Mom," I told her as my voice cracked and a deluge of tears flooded my eyes.

She held me tightly in her arms and we both wept as we hugged one another. Finally, she pulled away from me and rubbed her sleeve against her eyes. "I love you so much, Dulcie," she said. "And you have no idea how proud I am of you, and everything you have accomplished so far." She cleared her throat. "Just remember that I'm always here if you need me. You might not be able to see me or hear me, but I'm always with you, right here," she finished. She leaned over and brushed her hand against my heart.

I clasped her hand and squeezed it tightly, knowing I couldn't waste any more time. Now that I'd made my choice, I had to move forward. I had to fight for what was rightfully mine—my life. I now knew that I did have a lot more to do, especially now that my father was out of the picture. A brand new life awaited me just beyond the horizon. Really, a new life awaited all of us. And I didn't want to miss out on any of it.

"You need to go to him now, Dulcie," my mother said with a bittersweet smile. "It's time for you to leave this place."

I nodded as I stood up and beheld my mother one last time before I was shrouded in darkness again, just as I was after my father shot me. My body still felt strangely buoyant as I floated through the darkness. I tried to sort through the blackness to find the way back to myself, and back to Knight.

199

As soon as the thought crossed my mind, I saw the tiniest glimmer of light, barely the size of a grain of sand in the distance, far, far away from me.

Go toward that light, I heard the words but was unsure whether the command issued from my own mind or someone else's. I forced my arms to swim through the nothingness surrounding me, but it was a difficult chore. I found myself getting nowhere, while the light stayed just as far off as ever.

I closed my eyes and flapped my arms and legs even harder. I focused only on reaching the goal, placing every ounce of energy in my body toward achieving it. Opening my eyes again, I found my effort was useless. To my horror, I was beginning to float even further away, disappearing further into the ether and nothingness that already had a claim on me.

"No!" I said out loud. Tightly clenching my eyes shut, I screamed at myself to resist the darkness and find the light.

My hands flailed as I gritted my teeth and kept swimming through the vacuum surrounding me. Despite being unable to see the light, I imagined it in my mind's eye and moved stridently toward it. With Herculean effort, it felt like trying to swim through thick sludge. My arms suddenly became incredibly heavy, as if weighed down by anvils, but I still forged my way forward, ignoring my intense exhaustion.

You are almost there! Hearing my mother's voice in my head was all it took. I bit my lip as I concentrated solely on reaching the tiny speck of microscopic light. The weights on my arms and legs were now excruciating, but I didn't care. Throwing whatever strength I still possessed into my fight, I refused to fail. This was a fight I had to win. My entire future depended upon it.

When I opened my eyes again, I was surrounded by light, just as when I first saw my mother. I blinked and found myself staring up at Knight.

"Dulcie?" he asked as a tentative smile illuminated his tear-stained face. He shook his head as if he couldn't believe I was alive, as if he thought he was just imagining me. "Dulce?" he repeated.

The sudden heaviness I felt gave me cause for pause. It was so different from the buoyancy of my spirit, which I experienced earlier. I was speechless for a few seconds, and could only look up at the Loki I loved with all my being. I smiled.

"I … I don't understand how you," he started, shaking his head as if the reasons really didn't matter. He pulled me up to him and enveloped me in his large arms. I could hear the acceleration of his heartbeat, and the warmth of his body made me want to close my eyes and just absorb his heat. He pulled away from me, but continued to hold me in his arms. He just stared down at me as if half expecting me to vanish.

"I thought I'd lost you," he whispered, his voice pained and his eyes glassy. "I thought I'd lost you and the agony was so terrible, I didn't think I could go on." He took a deep breath. "I didn't want to go on without you."

"I'm here now," I managed, still finding it difficult to speak. Tears leaked from my eyes and tickled me as they trailed into my hair.

He held me to him again and I relished the feel of his soft hair as it brushed my cheeks. I inhaled deeply, feeling suddenly drunk on the scent that was so uniquely his. He pulled away from me and just smiled down at me. "I love you, Dulcie."

I felt myself beaming as a bright light just behind Knight's head arrested my attention. It was maybe the size of a small plate and glowed incredibly brightly before it simply disappeared into nothing.

Thank you, Mom, I thought to myself before I brought my gaze back to Knight's stunning sapphire eyes.

"I love you," I whispered and then closed my eyes as he kissed my lips.

FIFTEEN

Three hours later, I felt a block away from as good as new. Maybe two blocks away. Yes, I was exhausted, mentally and physically, and my lower back ached like an SOB, but at least, *I was alive*. And being alive made me want to celebrate. As to why I was alive, I had no clue. It wasn't within the realm of fairy magic to die and see your deceased mother who offers you the chance to live again, then "poof!" you're alive. I just chalked it up to another of life's many mysteries, the answer to which I would never know.

Even now, part of me half wondered if the whole Mom thing was a hallucination, while the other half firmly believed I had a vision of the afterlife. Either way, a sense of bittersweet contentment grew inside me, which wasn't there before. Whether my mind fabricated her or she actually came to me was beside the point. All that really mattered was that I could finally make peace with my emotions. My former feelings of anger, depression and abandonment at losing my mother were all stripped from me.

The other situation which gave me an inordinate sense of pride, accomplishment and relief was that we defeated my father. The Resistance prevailed and the time for a new Netherworld order was currently underway. That single feeling, in and of itself, was enough to put the wind back into my sails.

Speaking of my father, we managed to capture all of his remaining thugs, along with the few Netherworld Guard soldiers who happened to still be on my father's estate. Afterwards, we secured them in the holding cells of my father's dungeon, intent on delivering them to a longer term prison in the near future.

Meanwhile, Knight phoned Caressa and informed her she was now officially the Head of the Netherworld. In order to ensure her safety, Knight arranged for fifty of our remaining soldiers to travel to Caressa, lest she become the victim of an assassination attempt. She, however, assured Knight that there were Netherworld Guard forces under her command who weren't corrupt. And she would be quick to instruct this loyal Guard to fan out and infiltrate the various bases throughout the Netherworld, informing everyone of the new order. Anyone who questioned or defied her authority would be instantly arrested with no questions asked.

"Dulce, maybe you should rest for a little while?" Knight suggested as he glanced over at me with concern knitting his brows. After agreeing to use Willoughby House as our ad hoc base, we turned to the enormous task of rallying the rest of our troops, triaging the wounded from the dead from the unharmed.

Knight sat behind an immense desk in the drawing room, with Sam and Erica on each side of him. The three of them examined a list of the names of our soldiers and recruits. They had the unfortunate task of notating next to each name whether that person was wounded, dead, unharmed or simply unaccounted for.

At last call, the only people from The Resistance still unaccounted for were Rachel, Fagan and Trey.

I leaned against the pane of the window seat on which I was sitting, directly across from Knight's desk. "I'm fine," I said with a look that warned him not to argue with me. Then I flashed Sam the same expression as soon as I saw her making "Mom" eyes at me. Usually, those eyes meant a batch of her famous chocolate chip cookies, but now all they said was that I should go to bed and rest. And for me, that was *no bueno*.

Knight glanced at Sam who looked back at him, both of them wearing the expression of "gotta love her but she's stubborn as hell." Turning his indescribably handsome face back toward me, he smiled as he stood up and walked around the desk. He motioned for me to bend down so he could check the bandage he'd affixed to my lower back. I leaned forward, groaning involuntarily, but allowed him to play nurse.

"Looks good," he announced before fluffing the pillow behind me. He was careful to avoid my sore side as he helped me get comfy again. Since my gunshot wound, my wings hadn't flapped once. I actually hoped the bullet might have severed whatever was telling my wings to go Tasmanian Devil all the time. But maybe that was too much to hope for.

"Is Quill conscious yet?" I asked. After my father died, our soldiers quickly removed Quill from the dungeon of Willoughby House. And just as my father mentioned earlier in the library, Quill wasn't dead. He was merely in a trance, a victim of the warlock's magic. Sam did her best to break the warlock's spell and later informed us that Quill would be fine. He just needed to sleep it off.

Knight nodded with a sigh. "Quillan is fine, Dulce," he said, but added hurriedly, "however, you are in no shape to see him. So get that thought out of your mind until your health improves substantially."

I frowned at him, but felt a burning sensation as I shifted and my lower back demonstrated his prognosis. Honestly, I doubted if I could have walked the distance to the doorway, let alone to wherever Quill was recuperating.

"I second that!" Dia called out. She walked through the drawing room entry, her hands on her hips while her neck moved in that diva way, which meant I better not argue with her. "Girl, you need ta take care of yourself, you hear me?"

Luckily, our soldiers had been able to locate Dia about two hours ago when they started their recon missions to recover our missing soldiers. Dia wasn't too far from Squander Valley and had about twenty soldiers with her. As for Christina, she'd managed to get in touch with us over the radio. That was maybe twenty minutes ago. Now Dia was on her way to retrieve our leader. Well, that is, Dia and the jaw-droppingly sexy man who had been by her side from the moment the two were located.

"Don't you have someplace to go?" I grumbled, not liking the idea of one more person playing the part of advice giver. Although I knew I could put Sam and Knight off, when it came to Dia, I wasn't so sure.

"Seems to me that someone got shot on the wrong side of the bed, y'all," she said with a frown, alternating her gaze between Knight, Erica and Sam before she looked back at me as her frown deepened.

Hoping to change the conversation, I drew her attention back to the sex god who stood beside her. "So are you going to introduce me to your stunningly handsome friend or what?" I groaned.

Dia eyed the man standing beside her and flashed him her huge smile, a smile which lit up her entire face as her eyes settled on his. "Oh, him," she said dismissively. She even waved at him with indifference before pretending to examine her fingernails.

"Yeah, him!" the man threw back at her, a smile cresting his sumptuous lips as his eyes told her in no uncertain terms just what sort of carnal appetite he had for her.

Dia grinned at me. "He's just some hot Loki I happened to pick up somewhere along the way," she said, sighing as if it were no big deal.

"A Loki?" I asked with a smile and then looked over at Knight. He wore the same amused expression I did.

"That's right, girl," Dia continued, alternating her gaze between Knight and me. "I mean, there's only so long a girl can wait, an' that Loki (she pointed at Knight) was takin' his sweet ass time." Then she said to me. "This diva was gettin' hungry!"

I just shook my head and started to laugh before my back began to ache and I had to swallow the rest of my amusement. Meanwhile, Knight smiled at the man beside Dia. "Cannon," he greeted him with a friendly tilt of his head.

"Vander," Cannon replied, giving Knight a duplicate of the nod Knight had just given him. On a list of hot men, Cannon would easily have been at the top. As a Loki, he was on the tall side, maybe as tall as Knight, with broad, powerful shoulders and equally striking legs. His skin was almost as dark as Dia's. Whereas Dia's round, chocolate eyes lit up her entire face, Cannon's eyes were a crystalline green. They were so remarkable, I had a hard time prying my attention from them. His face was a blend of chiseled lines. His square jaw, lush, plump lips and high cheekbones almost looked sculpted.

Cannon's back was still toward Dia, and she began fanning herself when her eyes settled on Cannon's perfectly formed butt. After taking Cannon in from head to toe one more time, I returned my attention to Dia. With a simple nod, I let her know she was right on the money. Yep, she'd landed herself a hottie.

"Ms. Robinson," Cannon said as he turned to face Dia again with a sexy grin. "Don't we have places to go and Resistance team leaders to find?"

"Honey, how many times have I told you not to call me Ms. Robinson?" Dia piped up with her hands on her hips. "Diva will do just fine."

Laughing her contagious giggle, she started for the door, wiggling her hips as Cannon came up behind her and swatted her on the butt, their laughter drifting through the hallway as they disappeared around the corner.

No sooner did they exit than one of our soldiers poked his head in the door. "Sir," he said, addressing Knight, who sat on the desk, still trying to reach Fagan through the walkie-talkie.

"Yep?" Knight answered.

"Where would you like us to put the rest of the wounded? The dining room is filled to capacity," the soldier answered.

The living room was our first makeshift ward for the wounded, then the dining room. I could only wonder how many soldiers from each side were wounded because they just kept coming. Although I preferred not to think about it, the dead were temporarily sheltered in the guesthouse, across from the main house. My vantage point at the window seat allowed me to watch body after body being taken inside the house. Not only were we laying our dead soldiers there, but my father's as well.

"Which rooms are still empty on the first floor?" Knight asked.

"There are two bedrooms next to each other at the end of the hall, sir. Also the kitchen and two bathrooms."

"Start filling the two bedrooms," Knight answered as the soldier nodded and left the room. Knight returned to his walkie-talkie, but eventually placed it on the desktop with a defeated sigh, still receiving no response.

A sense of worry brewed inside me while the question of where Trey was continued to gnaw at me, just like it had been for the past three hours. Yes, I was worried about Fagan too, but to a much lesser extent (it wasn't like the Drow made it easy to like him). Regardless, I had to know if Trey was okay, which was why I couldn't adhere to the advice of Sam, Knight and Dia and get some rest. I knew I couldn't sleep if I didn't know where my friend was. Furthermore, I didn't understand how we'd been able to locate the majority of Trey and Fagan's soldiers while both of them remained unaccounted for.

Yes, our attack on Tipshaw was successful, but it had also taken the heaviest toll of our soldiers. It was, after all, the largest of the Netherworld Guard's base camps. Even though we'd suffered our largest losses at Tipshaw, the dead soldiers on my father's side still exceeded ours. Really, all of our attacks had been successful. Even at Squander Valley.

Despite the Netherworld Guard being prepared at Squander Valley, our soldiers were quick to realize they had the upper hand by virtue of their sheer numbers. So they continued to fight, even after many others retreated. In the end, they were victorious.

Christina had rounded up the remaining soldiers who fled Squander Valley. Then they basically made the same decision we had: that nobody was going down without a fight. Refusing to surrender or hide out in the forest, Christina and her soldiers marched on and attacked the base of Granttree. They took control of it in less than one hour, which was right about the same time Knight prevailed at Willoughby. That reminded me of something.

"Knight, "I asked, getting his attention without hesitation. The only good thing about being injured was how much more responsive Knight was, much more so than usual. "How come it didn't faze you when my father's men apprehended you and he insisted you call your men off?" I asked.

He smiled, self-assuredly, as if he couldn't wait to answer my question. "Because I knew Melchior was bluffing. He had fifteen soldiers here at most; we had forty. End of story."

"But how did you know he only had fifteen?" I continued.

"Bram told me."

"What do you mean 'Bram told you'?" I asked, frowning. "I was there the whole time and I don't recall Bram saying one word to you about how many soldiers my father had." So what if I sounded a little more irritable than normal? I mean, I *had* just died before miraculously returning to life. Who said that would be easy?

Knight smiled more widely and gave me a smug expression, hinting that there was something he knew that I didn't. And more, he valued any information he was privy to that I wasn't. "Bram told me in a manner of speaking," he started. "When in the Netherworld, Lokis and their vampire brethren have an interesting relationship."

"Here we go," I muttered, shaking my head, because I'd already guessed the answer was probably "it's just another Loki skill." But when he didn't tell me what exactly, his relationship with Bram was, I had to prod. "So?"

"In the Netherworld, Lokis and vampires share the same telepathic wavelength. If Bram wanted me to know something, all he had to do was think it."

"Really?" I asked, sounding annoyed. It was just unfair that Lokis possessed cool abilities in the Netherworld, while fairies had to deal with reckless wings and sexual crack.

"Really," Knight responded with a boyish grin.

I sighed. "And what did Bram tell you?"

Knight shrugged. "Pretty much the truth. Your father had no security at Willoughby, and as long as I didn't end up in shackles, I could easily lead our rebellion. So that's what I did."

I remembered Knight asking my father not to allow his men to see him handcuffed. I also remembered the hop in his step and how he wasn't the least bit concerned about spending the remainder of his days in my father's dungeon. My father must have been clueless as to how many forces we'd brought with us because if he'd known how vastly overpowered he was, he'd never have agreed to anything Knight requested.

I nodded and my thoughts turned to Bram and the last time I'd seen him, when he believed I was dead. "Any word from Bram?" I asked, facing Knight, a knot of worry tightening my stomach.

He shook his head. "Nothing. I imagine he'll show up sooner or later though."

I just nodded and hoped he was right. I had to see Bram again, if only to thank him for everything he did for me, for us. But mostly, I didn't want him to think I was dead. I wanted him to know that I'd survived. After witnessing the pain in his eyes when he'd believed me dead,

I wanted to correct him. I had to let him know he didn't have to grieve on my account. I couldn't help wondering if I'd ever get the chance.

"I'm okay, I'm okay," I heard a woman's voice coming down the hall and recognized Rachel when she appeared in the doorway, surrounded by our soldiers. Her hair was a mess, blood covered half of her face and dirt colored her entire body. She looked like she'd been crawling through a muddy sewer.

Knight glanced up and immediately smiled with relief. He stood and hurried toward her, gripping her shoulders as he inspected her. "MJ, are you …?" he started.

"I'm okay," she said again, her voice softer this time. She smiled up at Knight, matching his expression of relief. Then she shook her head, implying she'd had one hell of a trip.

"Everything is okay now," Knight said as he opened his arms and she fell into them, wrapping her arms around his waist. They hugged for a few seconds before she looked up at him curiously.

"Is everyone accounted for?" she asked.

Knight shook his head and exhaled a pent-up breath of frustration and concern as he stepped away from her. He looked at his radio, as if hoping Fagan or Trey might call at any moment. "Everyone except for Fagan and Trey. We've recovered most of their squadron, but have yet to locate either of them."

Rachel just nodded and gulped, saying nothing. "I hope you find them soon," she said finally.

Knight sighed. "Me too."

"Was Tipshaw a success?" Rachel asked, her eyes lighting up with hope.

Knight's smile was broad and beautiful. For the first time since everything had gone down, I realized just how much weight was now off his shoulders. He'd waited for this moment for so long, building The Resistance with Christina and taking their time to ensure everything was just so. And now that he'd seen his dreams to fruition, his pride and overarching happiness was beyond obvious. What was more, I was incredibly proud of him—of all that made him him.

"Everything was a success," he said softly.

Rachel studied him for a second or two, astonishment and awe visible in her features. "You mean we won?" she asked in a mere whisper. "We defeated O'Neil?"

Knight smiled and I watched Rachel's shoulders shake as she lost control of herself and started to cry. Knight wrapped his arms around her and held her, patting her on the back while she tried to regain her composure. He eyed me too, I figured to double check that it was okay for him to comfort her. I smiled back because I was more than just okay with it. The bonds between Knight and me had grown too strong for the threat of jealousy to snap them. What pleased me even more, however, was that Knight could be there for Rachel, who clearly needed him.

"Rachel?" Hearing a voice, I looked up to find a striking man standing in the doorway. His eyes bore the expression of someone who'd been incredibly worried. But now, his worry began to vanish as he laid eyes on the woman he, no doubt, loved. He was very tall, maybe six-four, with brown hair and blue eyes. I sensed a kind of sweetness in his disposition. Since we were in the Netherworld, I couldn't determine exactly what type of creature he was. If I had to guess, though, I thought maybe he was an elf—he just had a sort of regality about him.

"Mike," Rachel said as she released Knight and caught the man's gaze for a few seconds. Tears began to build in her eyes again as she ran across the room, before throwing herself into Mike's arms. She continued to cry as he held her tightly. Glancing back at Knight, I found him looking at me. As soon as we made eye contact, he smiled and I could see his love for me gleaming in his eyes.

Neither of us said anything. I just watched him return to the desk where he picked up his radio again and tried to reach Fagan. As with the first zillion attempts, this one was also in vain.

Looking outside, I watched two of our soldiers carrying a cot with a covered body into the guesthouse. Moments later, the soldiers walked outside again, before disappearing through a portal. They were, no doubt, collecting more of the wounded and dead. Exhaling a sigh of despondency, I tried to discourage myself from looking in the direction of the guesthouse again. Observing all the death and destruction of war only depressed me.

"Dulcie," I heard Knight's voice and looked up at him expectantly. His expression was unreadable, but his prior elation was now nowhere to be seen. I brought my attention from Knight's face to the soldier who stood beside him. It seemed like the young man was playing the part of messenger because Knight nodded to him in thanks as the man turned around and left the room. My attention fell on Erica and Sam, who were still busily hovering over the list of soldiers' names. They were in the midst of deep conversation.

"What's wrong?" I asked when I brought my attention back to Knight. He looked as if he'd just seen a ghost. I had to immediately gulp down the rock of apprehension that started climbing up my throat. Knight didn't respond, but approached me, his stride heavy. When he was directly in front of me, he glanced down and there was a gravity in his eyes, which struck me. It was an expression I'd only seen once before—when he'd held me in his arms and thought I was dead.

"They've located Fagan and Trey," he said softly, his tone and words giving nothing away.

I sat up, ignoring the ache in my back. Somehow, I already knew what Knight was about to tell me; I could feel it in the pit of my stomach. And it was a feeling I absolutely detested. But even though I was convinced I knew the truth, I still needed to hear it from his lips. "And?" I asked in a hollow voice.

"Fagan was badly wounded," Knight said, swallowing hard. "Our men are transporting him here now."

There was a dreadful silence that clung to the air. I knew I needed to ask about Trey, but I dared not. I was afraid what Knight would tell me. "And Trey?" I asked finally, my voice breaking.

Knight dropped his eyes to the floor and shook his head. I had to catch my breath while my entire body felt like it was collapsing. When Knight looked back up at me, there were unshed tears in his eyes. "Trey didn't make it."

I shook my head in denial. I couldn't believe that Trey was really gone. A hollowness began to build within me that seemed to fill my entire being. My stomach plummeted to the floor and I couldn't breathe. I also couldn't think, couldn't form one cohesive thought in my head. Instead, it felt like an enormous rock had just flattened me and stolen my ability to breathe, let alone form words.

"I'm sorry," Knight said as I brought my eyes to his. I shook my head, still having a hard time accepting the truth of his words. The horrible feelings of loneliness and grief reminded me of a time long ago … my mother's untimely death. Now as they returned anew, it seemed like I was time-traveling back all those years. My heart was in the process of ripping in two, just as when I'd learned the awful truth about my mother.

At the sound of Sam laughing with Erica, I glanced over at them. My best friend smiled at Erica, completely unaware of Trey's fate. The thought of having to tell her that Trey had been killed remained something I couldn't even conceive of. Why? Because as close as I was to Trey, Sam was even closer. I looked up at Knight again and found his eyes already on mine. As soon as I met his gaze, tears began to flood my eyes, and my body shook with the weight of my sorrow.

Knight immediately dropped to his knees and wrapped me in his strong, capable arms. He was very careful not to disrupt my bandage. "I'm so sorry, Dulce," he whispered.

I shook my head and pulled away from him, blotting my eyes with my arm as I stared up at him.

"Dulce?" Sam asked as she walked up behind Knight with a maternal look of concern. "Are you okay?"

I glanced at her and felt the tears returning again. I shook my head, taking a deep breath, and answered, "Sam, Trey didn't make it." I said it as softly as I could, hating the words as they left my lips.

Sam didn't respond right away, but just stood there, wearing a blank expression. A few seconds passed, during which time I watched the emotions of shock, disbelief and finally anguish overcome her. Then she simply shook her head. Jutting out her lower lip, she lost the battle to restrain her tears. I opened my arms and she fell into them. We clung to each other, both of us grieving over the death of our friend.

SIXTEEN
Three Months Later

We were all very busy. Beyond busy, actually.

After my father's death and our victory, the Netherworld did a complete one-eighty. Caressa took charge of The Resistance, and just as I expected, proved to be an outstanding leader. Strong and confident in her decisions, she also strove to be a direct representative of the Netherworld people. And that wasn't just my opinion. The people already had multiple parades throughout the various cities of the Netherworld, lauding the new order. It didn't hurt that Caressa's first task in office had been rounding up all the flying abominations in the sky created by my father with the purpose of terrifying the public. She'd promptly relocated the creatures to various far off destinations, where there was no chance they could return.

It had been a celebratory day when the nets came down.

As to the illegal potions rings, although they weren't entirely destroyed (something I imagined would never happen, anyway) Caressa was able to curb the amount and availability of street potions brewed in the Netherworld and distributed on Earth. Upon establishing her new position, she insisted that all ANC contraband be destroyed on site. Not only that, but she appointed loyal Netherworld Guard soldiers to make sure the orders were followed.

Now that the Netherworld borders were open again, Knight did quite a bit of traveling back and forth. He still managed to man his post as head of the ANC in Splendor, while also filling the role of second in command to Caressa, with Christina picking up his slack. Together, they were like the A-Team. My part paled in comparison to that of Knight

215

and Christina, but I still did my best to be useful. I accepted Knight's offer to return to the ANC in Splendor, where I basically ran the office in his absence.

Because Knight was so busy organizing the new democracy of the Netherworld, I had quite a bit of downtime on my hands, along with plenty of lonely nights. Although I managed to occupy them with visits from Dia and Sam, I relished my alone time. I guessed it was because it had been such a long time since I had any.

I also kept my promise to continue my writing, and even contacted my agent to pick up where we'd left off. Apparently, one publisher was interested in my Bram books, a revelation which pleased me no end. And the vampire who told me so many colorful stories for my books? I hadn't heard from nor seen him since that final moment in my father's library when he'd left me for dead. I thought about Bram frequently, however, always wondering where he was and what he was doing.

Every time I drove by No Regrets, seeing the "For Sale" sign always made me feel hollow inside. It seemed like Bram had packed up and moved on with his life, which, for all I knew, was the case. Wherever he was, I wished him the best.

When not writing, I spent a lot of my time in quiet repose, just thinking. My thoughts always returned to Trey and I remembered funny situations we'd found ourselves in, along with the various cases we'd worked together while at the ANC. Mostly, though, I recalled all the laughs we shared. My thoughts also centered on my mom, thoughts which brought a contentedness that made me smile. Even though I still missed her, feeling her presence lessened the pain of losing her.

"Dulce, you ready?" Sam called from her living room where we'd been getting dressed for the last two hours. "The party starts in like ten minutes!"

We were on our way to the Netherworld where Caressa was throwing a masquerade party for everyone

216

involved in the defeat of my father. A masquerade to celebrate the removal of a tyrant might sound like an odd pairing, but Caressa was determined to focus on the positive moving forward. She was convinced a masquerade would be the most festive.

Looking down, I shook my head, chiding myself for letting Sam talk me into wearing such a ridiculous costume. It was her idea for both of us to go dressed as Ladies of the Court from the Rococo period. It sounded fine and good, (albeit, a little random) in theory. In practice, however, fine was not the word I would use to describe my getup. I was dressed head to toe in layers of blue and green bows, mint-green netting, blue satin, white lace, and petticoats. Together, they felt like they weighed more than forty pounds. With my enormous skirts billowing out from beneath me, I looked like a very colorful, upside-down mushroom.

Sam was dressed in pretty much the same fashion (only hers was pink and purple), but she seemed to actually enjoy it (she'd primped and preened for over an hour). Our hair was piled high atop our heads (skyscraper-high), with sausage curls and braids to adorn it. Mine was finished off with a little, white, doily-looking thing and an ostrich feather. Sam's had myriad roses and lilies, which matched the print on the parasol she carried with her. I preferred not to carry anything. I was afraid I might collapse beneath the weight of the costume, if anything else was added to it.

"You need some more blush," Sam announced. I was currently trying to fit through her hallway frontwards, but ended up having to go sideways. Even so, I still managed to get caught.

"Some help please," I muttered. Sam giggled and helped me free one of my bows from where it was stuck on the door kick. As soon as she released the fabric, she reached for her blush brush and began dusting my cheeks, the top of my nose, and, finally, my cleavage.

217

"Anymore blush and I'm going to look like a burn patient!" I railed at her, feeling the itch of the contraption Sam invented to keep my wings under control.

"Maybe you need another beauty mark," she said while studying me. She narrowed her eyes and bit one side of her mouth.

"I already have two!" I protested, glancing down at my cleavage where Sam had penciled in a black wart. She'd already painted its twin on my upper lip.

"Okay, I guess we're ready then," she said finally. Holding her palm open, she smiled when I dropped Bram's portal ripper into it. I watched her program the ripper before slicing an opening in the air, obeying my instructions to the last "T."

"You catch on quickly," I said with an approving smile.

"Not as quickly as Knight's fingers will get you out of that costume," she teased. I didn't miss her wink or lascivious smile.

Knight had no clue what to expect from Sam and me, as far as costumes went. It was Sam's idea to make it a surprise. I had no idea what Knight's costume was either, but figured it would be fun to find out. "I'm sure he'll find this extremely amusing," I said with one last look at myself and a sigh. I doubted Knight would find the outfit sexy, except for my ginormous cleavage. Other than that, my costume just looked like a huge waste of fabrics.

"Then we'll agree to disagree," Sam said as she extended her arm. "Shall we?"

"We shall," I answered, taking her arm in mine, and stepping through the portal.

Seconds later, we entered the Netherworld and, more precisely, Bellingvue, the estate Caressa chose to live in after taking on her new role. The place was sprawling and huge, though not quite as expansive as Bram's home in the French Alps. Bellingvue was a two-story, well-appointed home in the style of Cape Cod. The outside was a dark grey with white trim, and the shutters were a charcoal grey. Surrounding the estate were rose bushes of every hue and variety along with enormous poplar trees that made it look like a park.

We landed on the back porch of Bellingvue and as soon as we inhaled the Netherworld air, I felt my wings awaken. I had to smile when they struggled to beat, but stayed restrained, thanks to Sam's creation. The essence of roses perfumed the night air and made me inhale so deeply, I nearly got giddy on the aroma. It was pretty warm with a cool breeze that ruffled the lace of my bodice. Only a few people milled about on the porch, oohing and aahing over the garden; most everyone else was inside.

"Let's go in," Sam said, picking up her skirts. Looking like Marie Antoinette, she forced herself forward, people getting out of her way so as not to trip over her skirts. I walked directly behind her, taking advantage of the path she carved. As we walked inside, many people dressed in costumes passed us, remarking on our costumes while we commented on theirs. So far, the detailed outfits ran the gamut—everything from princesses to knights in armor to wild animals.

"Sexy ladies!" Dia's voice rang out above the harmony of voices, laughter and music. How she managed to spot us in a crowd of one hundred plus costumes was beyond me. Sam and I turned in unison to find Dia standing before us, dressed in a bright red, fitted gown, with glittering red rhinestones that covered its entire surface. She'd paired that with a real diamond tiara and the highest heeled shoes I'd ever seen.

"What are you supposed to be?" I asked, eyeing her quizzically.

"Girl, I'm not supposed to be anythin'," Dia sang back with one of her broadest smiles.

"Then what *are* you?" Sam asked, clicking her tongue against the roof of her mouth as she appeared to be guessing. "'Cause you don't look like the normal Dia."

219

"I'm a diva, of course," Dia answered like we both should have already reached that conclusion. When she did that neck thing again, it almost looked like she was doing an interpretive dance. While she completed her best impersonation of Cleopatra, I saw Cannon slicing through the crowd of people behind her. Carrying two glasses of red punch, one in each hand, he handed one to Dia and smiled at Sam and me in greeting. He wore dark black slacks and nothing above besides a white collar (a la Chippendale dancer) on top. Well, except for the bling-bling he wore around his neck: an enormous pendant that said: "I'm with the diva."

Looking at Cannon's chest (I mean, the pendant) I eyed Dia with a laugh. "Really?" I asked.

"Hey, if you got it, flaunt it, honey," Dia answered with a pretty smile. "That's my motto."

Sam appraised Cannon up and down and whistled before saying to Dia, "I'd say you got it."

Dia nodded as she patted Cannon's stomach. She slid her hand up his chiseled abs and settled it on his defined pecs. "I got it in spades, girl, in spades."

"Dulce!" I heard Quill's voice and glanced behind me to see him decked out in black breeches, an olive-green overcoat, tall black boots and a cravat around his neck. Beside him stood Christina, wearing something similar to Sam's and my costumes only less frilly, way less frilly. I had to admit I was more than a little surprised to see the two of them together. The more I thought about it, though, I decided they actually would make a good couple. But who knew if they'd come here as platonic friends or more …

"Who in the heck are you supposed to be?" Sam asked as she faced Quill skeptically, her brows furrowing in the middle of her forehead.

Quill shrugged as Christina frowned before giving me a raised brow expression that hinted at her lack of enthusiasm regarding their costumes. "We're George and Martha Washington."

"What?" Sam croaked, a wide smile on her lips.

"George and Martha Washington?" Dia repeated with disbelief. She shook her head and raised one brow like she'd just seen or tasted something really bad. "Uh-uh. That is just wrong, y'all."

"The stock was limited at the costume store. I guess I waited too long," Quill apologized as Sam and I started laughing.

"Why didn't you just magick something?" I asked Christina, who seemed the polar opposite of Martha Washington. Being a fairy, she possessed the same abilities as I did. She could have easily become any character she chose.

"Because Quill already paid for them," she said, shaking her head like it was a big waste. Then she gave him a warm smile as he wrapped his arm around her. My previous question as to whether or not they came as friends was thusly put to bed. Maybe even literally. While their mutual show of affection surprised me initially, I was happy for Quill. He deserved a good woman and Christina had definitely earned my stamp of approval.

Getting antsy about where a certain Loki was, I looked past Sam and scanned the mostly masked faces of Caressa's guests, with no clue which one was Knight. I caught the image of Erica, who was fittingly dressed as a nymph. Her hair was now purple to match her floor-length gown. She and the handsome man next to her, who was costumed as a Scottish Highlander, might as well have been alone for all the attention they were paying to everyone around them.

I watched the crowd began to disperse, each faction retreating to the walls as Caressa entered the middle of the crowd, dressed as a cheetah. She was strikingly pretty: long, blondish brown hair flowing around her shoulders and cute little cat ears on top of her head. She'd painted a pink nose and whiskers on her face, and worn a skin-tight, brown spotted body suit with a long tail pinned to the back. She looked exactly like a cat. A pretty fitting costume, considering as a shifter, she took the form of a cheetah.

"Thank you all for coming," she called out, a beaming smile on her lips. "I cannot even begin to tell you how exciting it has been for me to see all the positive changes happening since O'Neil was deposed."

Hearing that, the crowd cheered while Caressa laughed and had to hold up her hands to quiet them. "I am forever indebted to all of you for making this dream, which we *all* shared, a reality. We owe it to your strength and courage or we would not be here this evening." She took a deep breath and her eyes dropped to the floor before she addressed the audience again. "And for those who fought and died in this endeavor, all of us will forever be indebted that they gave the ultimate sacrifice."

Thinking of Trey, I felt Sam's fingers interlacing mine, so I looked over at her. Eyes shining with unshed tears, she looked back at me and I smiled, tightening my grip on her hand. We both faced Caressa again when she said, "In honor of our fallen comrades, I would like to observe a minute of silence."

I dropped my head, but continued to hold onto Sam's hand as the entire room went quiet. I closed my eyes and thought of Trey.

Wherever you are, Trey, I thought to myself, *thank you for giving everything you had and for being the wonderful friend and ally you always were to me.*

I opened my eyes and saw someone handing Caressa a glass of something fizzy. She held the glass up and smiled. "I toast all of you for personally improving the Netherworld and making it safer for all."

There was a round of cheers that rippled through the crowd as everyone downed their libations. Caressa drank the rest of whatever was in her glass, then smiled and the crowd clapped in approval. "Now it's time to get those dancing shoes of yours on!" she called out. Behind her, a band started up, their first song was "Unforgettable" by Nat King

222

Cole. A handsome man wearing a Superman outfit walked up to Caressa and asked her to dance, to which she happily complied.

"Where's Knight?" Sam asked. She pulled her hand from mine and scanned the crowd, looking high and low for the Loki.

"I have no idea," I answered as I watched Quill bow low before Christina, who laughed and then accepted his invitation to the dance floor. Meanwhile, pointing to Cannon with her index finger, Dia beckoned him forward. Turning, they started for the dance floor, while she rested her hand on his taut behind and gave it a little squeeze.

Sam and I eyed each other with surprise before we both started laughing at Dia's nerve.

"Well, she definitely puts the D I A in diva," I said as I shook my head, still smiling.

But Sam's attention wasn't on me. Instead she focused on someone standing right beside me. I turned in the direction she was looking and found a very tall man, wearing the costume of death. The costume included a long black cape, a black hood that obscured his face, and a scythe. He said nothing as he extended his hand to me. I looked at Sam, frowning.

"Looks like you found your Loki," Sam said. She smiled at me with a shrug, as if to say she'd find her own dancing partner.

I stared at Knight, unable to make out his features, and just sighed. "Nice costume, but it's a little macabre, don't you think?" Accepting his proffered hand, I allowed him to lead me to the dance floor.

Without a word, he simply leaned his scythe against the wall before pulling me into him and resting his other hand on the small of my back. I shuddered at the icy cold of his touch.

"Okay, clearly you aren't the person I thought you were," I started. Anxiety was just beginning to build within me. I peered up at him, trying to make out his features

223

beneath the hood. But the darkness absorbed everything, revealing only shadow.

"You are exactly the person I thought you were," Bram responded.

Relief washed over me—just to know Bram was my dancing partner not to mention he was safe and accounted for. I swallowed hard and pulled myself closer to him, to avoid anyone overhearing our conversation. He chuckled when I pressed myself against him, and his hold around my waist tightened. "Where have you been?" I whispered.

"Were you worried about me, Sweet?" the vampire inquired. His icy breath brought goose bumps to the skin on my neck.

"Yes," I answered quickly. "I was very worried about you, if you want to know the truth."

"Touching," he responded in a sincere tone.

"Bram, why did you close down No Regrets?" It was easy to follow him as he paraded me around the dance floor since Bram was an expert dancer.

He took a few seconds to answer. "I felt it was time for me to move on."

I didn't know what to make of his response. Instead, I brought up the subject of what Bram planned to do now that there was a new Netherworld order. "With Caressa in charge now, will that impact you and your ... business?" I asked, hoping the answer would be that he wanted to turn over a new leaf and abandon the ways of his old life.

He chuckled deeply and twirled me around in time with the music. "I suppose I shall have to clean up my act," he said in jest, which pointed to the fact that he would do anything but.

"I guess it was too much to hope that you would end up being a good guy," I muttered without much surprise. Since Bram had never been a "good guy," I wasn't sure what made me hope he'd start now. He'd always lived right on the edge, so I figured that's how his life would continue.

"Ah, but if not, where would the thrill be for you, my pet?" he said with a hearty chuckle. "What is light without the dark, what is good without the bad?"

"I wouldn't call you a bad guy, Bram," I whispered.

"I am not all bad, no," Bram responded slyly. "But as you have often noticed on more than one occasion, I prefer the boundary lines and always avoid choosing sides."

"That I can't argue," I admitted. "I guess it was just wishful thinking on my part to hope that you might have changed your ways."

"I am a creature of habit, Sweet," he said without remorse. "I have lived this way for hundreds of years. I doubt my stripes will change to spots in the near future."

"Well, regardless," I started with a sigh, shaking my head. Some things never did change. "I want to tell you how much we appreciated everything you did for us."

"No need to thank me, Sweet," he answered quickly. He deftly twirled me around again, this time sending my skirts higher on either side. "I only did what I hoped would benefit my own interests," he continued. "It was lucky for you that this time our needs intersected."

"Then I think it's safe to say you're going to continue doing what you've always done?" I asked, meaning that he would continue exporting illegal potions. I felt the truth in my stomach like a lead weight. Even though I expected as much deep down, it was still a disappointment that Bram would never fully be on our side.

"It is all I know," he answered noncommittally.

"And thus begins the game of cat and mouse," I muttered. This was the moment I always knew might come, and now it was happening. Although Bram always provided me with useful information, now it was very clear that we were at odds. "You must realize that if our paths cross again, it will be my duty to arrest you?" I asked.

Bram chuckled again. "If you manage to catch me, my pet, only if you manage to catch me." The song finished and Bram released me. He artfully bowed before reaching for my hand and bringing it to his lips. He then glanced up at me and I could make out the subtle white of his eyes as he stared at me. "And on that note, I believe our game has begun," he said, eyeing me hungrily. "Until we meet again, my sweet."

I couldn't respond because he dematerialized into the atmosphere, leaving nothing but his scent in the air. It took me a second to get my bearings, and as I did, I just stood in the center of the dance floor. I probably looked completely dumbfounded because that's exactly how I felt. Finally, I shook my head and smiled, because deep down I knew Bram and I *would* cross paths again.

"What is such a stunning creature doing all alone out here?" Knight's voice sounded from behind me. I turned on my heel and smiled up at him, taking him in from head to toe. He looked like Henry VIII, with an oversized red coat that ended at his thighs. It gave his shoulders a square shape. Beneath the coat, he wore a long-sleeved white shirt, which matched his white billowing shorts. On the top of his head was a flattish hat with a long feather. Even though he was wearing tights, they were anything but comical. Instead, they only accentuated the incredible muscles of his thighs and calves.

"Is it wrong for me to find your tights so incredibly sexy?" I asked, shaking my head in wonder as I laughed.

Knight chuckled. "I was already devising an opportunity to crawl under your enormous skirts."

Quirking a brow at him, I couldn't hide the smile from my lips. It had been quite a while since I felt Knight inside me. "So, do you expect me to believe that you just happened to dress up like that and we just happened to match?"

Knight shrugged. "Stranger things have happened, right?"

"I think it's more accurate to say Sam has a big mouth."

Knight chuckled and offered me his hand. "Dance with me?" I nodded my acceptance as he pulled me along and kissed my cheek before whispering in my ear, "I made a special request."

As soon as the words left his mouth, the band started playing "Golden Slumbers." I faced him, my eyes wide. "How did you know?" I asked in amazement.

Knight just shrugged, the answer to which I chalked up as just another of his Loki abilities. He seemed very pleased with himself. I wrapped my arms around him, resting my head against his chest, and closed my eyes as I inhaled his scent. His clean, crisp smell suggested something spicy and completely Knightley Vander.

"I'm sorry I've been away so much," he said as he held me. Our feet glided over the dance floor seemingly of their own accord.

"It's okay," I said, opening my eyes to find him staring down at me. "I know how busy you are."

Knight nodded as a pensive expression overcame his face, and I knew that something was on his mind. "Caressa offered me the position of being second in command," he started, taking a deep breath. "If I accept, it will mean that I'd have to live permanently in the Netherworld."

I glanced up at him and my stomach dropped. I'd never considered that all this business with Caressa might possibly lead to Knight moving back to the Netherworld permanently. For my part, I couldn't imagine living here—it was just too different from what I knew and what I was comfortable with. Even though Splendor wasn't exactly Utopia, it was all I'd ever known. Besides, I was happy there. I loved having Sam close by and I enjoyed working at the ANC. Simply stated, I didn't want to move.

"I understand if you want to accept the position," I said softly with a small smile. The Resistance had been his dream for so long, that I knew I had to be supportive and put his needs before my own.

He smiled back at me and shook his head. "I already turned it down."

227

"What? Why?" I asked, narrowing my eyes as I studied him with a frown. "I know how much this new democracy means to you, Knight," I started. "And I know how hard you and Christina worked for it."

But he shook his head again. "Yes, it means a lot to me, and yes I've worked very hard for everything that has happened." Then he smiled at me and ran his fingers down the side of my cheek. "But nothing means as much to me as you do, Dulcie," he finished.

"Knight," I argued, since I didn't want him to abandon something that was so important to him. "We could make it work. It's not like we'd break up if you took the position."

"I know that," he said immediately. "But I don't care. I prefer our own life. I like my position as Head of the Splendor branch of the ANC."

"Are you sure?" I repeated. I had to make sure he wasn't just telling me what he thought I wanted to hear. "Because we can work around it if you do decide to take the position."

"No," he said with more authority. "I want the next chapter of our lives to be about us, Dulce. I want to focus on you and me together, and our future." He took a deep breath. "I told Caressa I would always be here for her, should she need me, but I also emphasized that now my focus was entirely on us."

"Wow," I said, surprised.

"And what's more, I'm hoping you'll move in with me," he finished with a large grin.

I swallowed hard, thinking about this next step. Was I ready to move in with Knight? My first and last thoughts were that the more I thought about it, the better the idea felt. "You really expect me to leave my shithole of an apartment I call home?" I asked, not able to keep from laughing.

"Well, I thought I might be able to convince you if I promised lots of long, lovemaking sessions, massages, and I'll even cook for you, since we both know your cooking leaves something to be desired."

"Hey!" I said in mock effrontery as I playfully swatted him. "Massages and lots of sex?"

"More sex than you can handle," he replied. His eyes began to glow, which automatically started a fire in my core.

"How can I turn that down?" I asked in a breathy voice.

"You'd be a fool to," he answered.

We both quietly attempted to rein in our sexual appetites for one another, which seemed on the verge of becoming out of control.

"Then it's decided," Knight said at last.

"What's decided?"

He chuckled at my inability to follow the conversation. "You are moving in with me and, to that end, I also already recommended Christina for the position as second in command to Caressa."

"And?"

"And Christina accepted it." He wore an amused smile. "Apparently, Quill accepted a position to work at the ANC in the Netherworld, as well."

I felt my eyebrows reaching for the ceiling. "When did this whole dating thing happen between the two of them?" I asked, shaking my head. "Because I totally missed it."

Knight shrugged. "It seems to have taken everyone by surprise." Then he paused for a few seconds and studied me. "Are you ... okay with it?"

"Okay with it?" I repeated, like I was amazed he would even ask. "Of course I'm okay with it. I think Christina is great for Quill and vice versa."

I rested my head against his chest again, savoring his warmth as it seeped into me. I watched the throngs of couples surrounding us talk amongst themselves and hold one another, just as Knight and I were. Rachel and Mike moved past us; she was dressed as a bride and he as a groom. When she caught my attention, she smiled and I returned it. I couldn't help but think about how incredibly lucky I was to hold the man of my dreams while an exciting future awaited us.

"Hey, Dulce?" Knight asked softly.

"Hmm?" I answered.

"One thing I never could figure out," he started, clearing his throat as he smiled down at me. "How were you able to come back after your father shot you? I felt for your pulse, but you didn't have one."

My mother's image flashed into my mind and I felt myself smiling inwardly. It took me a few seconds to answer. "Oh, you know, it's one of my fairy abilities," I answered nonchalantly, even adding a shrug. "Stick around and you might find out what else I'm capable of."

Knight chuckled and pulled me closer into him. "Oh, I plan to, Dulcie O'Neil, do I ever plan to."

THE END

Also Available From HP Mallory:

Turn the page for chapter one!

"Midway upon the journey of our life, I found myself within a forest dark, For the straight foreward pathway had been lost."
--Dante's *Inferno*

ONE

The rain pelted the windshield relentlessly. Drops like little daggers assaulted the glass, only to be swept away by the frantic motion of the wipers. The scenery outside my window melted into dripping blobs of color through a screen of gray. I took my foot off the accelerator and slowed to forty miles an hour, focusing on the blurry yellow lines in the road.

Lightning stabbed the gray skies. A roar of thunder followed and the rain came down heavier, as if having been reprimanded for not falling hard enough.

"This rain is gonna keep on comin', folks," the radio meteorologist announced. Annoyed, I changed the station and resettled myself into my seat to the sound of Vivaldi's "Four Seasons, Summer." *Ha, Summer...*

The rain morphed into hail. The visibility was slightly better, but now I was under a barrage of machine-gunned ice. I took a deep breath and tried to imagine myself on a sunny beach, sipping a strawberry margarita with a well-endowed man wearing nothing but a banana hammock and a smile.

In reality, I was as far from a cocktail on a sunny beach with Sven, the lust god, as possible. Nope, I was trapped in Colorado Springs in the middle of winter. If that weren't bad enough, I was late to work. Today was not only my yearly review but I also had to give a presentation to the CEO, defending my decision to move forward with a risky and expensive marketing campaign. So, yes, being late didn't exactly figure into my plans.

With a sigh, I turned on my seat heater and tried to enact the presentation in my head, tried to remember the slides from my PowerPoint and each of the points I needed to make. I held my chin up high and cleared my throat, reminding myself to look the CEO and the board of directors in the eyes and not to say "um."

"Choc-o-late cake," I said out loud, opening my mouth wide and then bringing my teeth together again in an exaggerated way. "Choc-o-late cake." It was a good way to warm up my voice and to remind myself to pronounce every syllable of every word. And, perhaps the most important point to keep in mind—not to rush.

This whole being late thing wasn't exactly good timing, considering I was going to ask for a raise. With my heart rate increasing, I remembered the words of Jack Canfield, one of the many motivational speakers whose advice I followed like the Bible.

"'When you've figured out what you want to ask for', Lily, 'do it with certainty, boldness and confidence'," I quoted, taking a deep breath and holding it for a count of three before I released it for another count of three. "Certainty, boldness and confidence," I repeated to myself. "Choc-o-late cake."

Feeling my heart rate decreasing, I focused on counting the stacks of chicken coops in the truck ahead of me—five up and four across. Each coop was maybe a foot by a foot, barely enough room for the chickens to breathe. White feathers decorated the wire and contrasted against the bright blue of a plastic tarp that covered the top layer of coops. The tarp was held in place by a brown rope that wove in and around the coops like spaghetti. I couldn't help but feel guilty about the chicken salad sandwich currently residing in my lunch sack but then I remembered I had more important things to think about.

"Choc-o-late cake."

The truck's brake lights suddenly flashed red. The coops rattled against one another as the truck lurched to a stop. A vindictive gust of wind caught the edge of the blue tarp and tore it halfway off the coops. As if heading for certain slaughter wasn't bad enough, the chickens now had to freeze en route. My concern for the birds was suddenly interrupted by another flash of the truck's brake lights.

Then I heard the sound of my cell phone ringing from my purse, which happened to be behind my seat. I reached behind myself, while still trying to pay attention to the road, and felt around for my purse. I only ended up ramming my hand into the cardboard box which held my velvet and brocade gown. The dress had taken me two months to make and was as historically accurate to the gothic period of the middle ages as was possible.

I finally reached my purse and then fingered my cell phone, pulling it out as I noticed Miranda's name on the caller ID.

"Hi," I said.

"I'm just calling to make sure you didn't forget your dress," Miranda said in her high pitch, nasally voice which sounded like a five year old girl with a cold.

"Forget it?" I scoffed, shaking my head at the very idea. "Are you kidding? This is only one of the most important evenings of our lives!" Yes, tonight would mark the night that, if successful, Miranda and I would be allowed to move up the hierarchical chain of our medieval reenactment club. We'd started as lowly peasants and had worked our way up to the merchant class and now we sought to be allowed entrance into the world of the knights.

"Can you imagine us finally being able to enter the class of the knights?" Miranda continued. Even though I obviously couldn't see her, I could just imagine her pushing her coke bottle glasses back up to the bridge of her nose as she gazed longingly at the empire-waisted, fur trimmed gown (also historically accurate!) that I'd made for her birthday present.

"Yeah, instead of burlap, we can wear silk!" I said as I nodded and thought about how expensive it was going to be to costume ourselves if we actually did get admitted into the class of the knights.

"And maybe Albert will finally want to talk to me," Miranda continued, again in that dreamy voice.

I didn't think becoming a knight's lady would make Albert any more likely to talk to Miranda but I didn't say anything. If the truth be told, Albert was far more interested in the knights than he ever was in their ladies.

"Okay, Miranda, I gotta go. I'm almost at work," I said and then heard the beep on the other line which meant someone else was trying to call me. I pulled the phone away from my ear and after quickly glancing at the road, I tried to answer my other call. That was when I heard the sound of brakes screeching.

I felt like I was swimming through the images that met me next—my phone landing on my lap as I dropped it, my hands gripping the wheel until my knuckles turned white, the pull of the car skidding on the slick asphalt, and the tail end of the truck in front of me, up close and personal. I braced myself for the inevitable impact.

Even though I had my seatbelt on, the jolt was immense. I was suddenly thrown forward only to be wrenched backwards again, as if by the invisible hands of some monstrous Titan. Tiny threads of anguish weaved up my spine until they became an aching symphony that spanned the back of my neck.

The sound of my windshield shattering pulled my thoughts from the pain. I opened my right eye—since the left appeared to be sealed shut—to find my face buried against the steering wheel.

I couldn't feel anything. The searing pain in my neck was soon a fading memory and nothing, but the void of numbness reigned over the rest of my body. As if someone had turned on a switch in my ears, a sudden screeching met me like an enemy. The more I listened, the louder it got—a high-pitched wailing. It took me a second to realize it was the horn of my car.

My vision grew cloudy as I focused on the white of the feathers that danced through the air like winter fairies, only to land against the shattered windshield and drown in a deluge of red. Sunlight suddenly filtered through the car until it was so bright, I had to close my good eye.

And then there was nothing at all.

~

"Number three million, seven hundred fifty thousand and forty-five."

I shook my head as I opened my eyes, blinking a few times as the scratchy voice droned in my ears. Not knowing where I was, or what was happening, I glanced around nervously, absorbing the nondescript beige of the walls. Plastic, multicolored chairs littered the room like discarded toys. What seemed like hundreds of people dotted the landscape of chairs in the stadium sized room. Next to me, though, was only an old man. Glancing at me, he frowned. I fixed my attention on the snarly looking employees trapped inside multiple rows of cubicles. Choosing not to focus on them, I honed in on an electric board above me that read: *Number 3,750,045.*

The fluorescent green of the board flashed and twittered as if it had just zapped an unfortunate insect. I shook my head again, hoping to remember how the heck I'd gotten here. My last memory was in my car, driving in the rain as I chatted with Miranda. Then there was that truck with all the chickens. *An accident—I'd gotten into an accident.* After that, my thoughts blurred into each other. But nothing could explain why I was suddenly at the DMV.

Maybe I was dreaming. And it just happened to be the most lucid, real dream I'd ever had and the only time I'd ever realized I was dreaming while dreaming. *Hey, stranger things have happened, right?*

I glanced around again, taking in the low ceiling. There weren't any windows in the dreary room. Instead, posters with vibrant colors decorated the walls, looking like circus banners. The one closest to me read: *Smoking kills.* A picture of a skeleton in cowboy gear, atop an Appaloosa further emphasized the point. Someone had scribbled "ha ha" in the lower corner.

"Three million, seven hundred fifty thousand and forty-five!"

Turning toward the voice, I realized it belonged to an old woman with orange hair, and 1950's style rhinestone glasses on a string. A line of twelve or so porcelain cat statues, playing various instruments, decorated the ledge of her cubicle. What was it about old women and cats?

The cat lady scanned the room, peering over the ridiculous glasses and tapping her outlandishly long, red fingernails against the ledge. Her mouth was so tight, it swallowed her lips. As her narrowed gaze met mine, I flushed and averted my eyes to my lap, where I noticed a white piece of paper clutched in my right hand. I stared at the black numbers before the realization dawned on me.

3,750,045. She was calling my number! Without hesitation, I jumped up.

"That's me!" I announced, feeling embarrassed as the old man glared at me. "Sorry."

"Come on then," the woman interrupted. "I don't have all day."

Approaching her desk, I thought this dream couldn't get much weirder—I mean, I was number three million or something and yet there were only a few hundred people in the room? I handed the woman my ticket. She scowled at me, her scarlet lips so raw and wet that her mouth looked like a piece of talking sushi. She rolled the ticket into a little ball and flung it behind her. It landed squarely in her wastebasket, vanishing amid a sea of other white, scrunched paper balls.

"Name?" she asked as she worked a huge wad of pink gum between her clicking jaws.

"Um, Lily," I said with a pause, feigning interest in a cat playing a violin. It wore an obscene smile and appeared to be dancing, one chubby little leg lifted in the semblance of a jig. I touched the cold statue and ran the pad of my index finger along the ridges of his fur. I was beginning to think this might not be a dream, because I could clearly touch and feel things. But if this weren't a dream, how did I get here? It was like I'd just popped up out of nowhere.

"Last name?"

I faced the woman again. "Um, Harper."

The woman simply nodded, continuing to chomp on her gum like a cow chewing its cud. "Harper... Harper... Harper," she said as she stared at the computer screen in front of her.

"Um, could you, uh, tell me why I'm here?" My voice sounded weak and thin. I had to remind myself that I was the master of my own destiny and needed to act like it. And that was when I remembered my presentation. A feeling of complete panic overwhelmed me as I searched the wall for a clock so I could figure out how much time remained before I was due to sway a panel of mostly unenlightened penny-pinchers on why we needed to invest nearly a quarter of a million in advertising. "What time is it?" I demanded.

"Time?" the woman repeated and then frowned at me. "Not my concern."

I felt my eyebrows knot in the middle as I glanced behind me, wondering if there was a clock to be found anywhere. The blank of the walls was answer enough. I faced forward again, now more nervous than before and still at a complete loss as to where I was or why. "Um, what am I doing here?" I repeated, not meaning to sound so...stupid.

The woman's wrinkled mouth stretched into a smile, which looked even scarier than all the grimaces she'd given me earlier. She turned to the computer and typed something, her talon-like fingernails covering the keyboard with exaggerated flourishes. She hit "enter" and turned the screen to face me.

"You're here because you're dead."

"What?" It was all I could say as I felt the bottom of my stomach give way, my figurative guts spilling all over my feet. "You're joking."

She wasn't laughing though. Instead, she sighed like I was taking up too much of her time. She flicked her computer screen with the long, scarlet fingernail of her index finger. The tap against the screen reverberated through my head like the blade of a dull axe.

"Watch."

With my heart pounding in my chest, I glanced at the screen, and saw what looked like the opening of a low-budget film. Rain spattered the camera lens, making it difficult to decipher the scene beyond. One thing I could make out was the bumper-to-bumper traffic. It appeared to be a traffic cam in real time.

"I don't know what this has to do…"

She chomped louder, her jaw clicking with the effort, sounding like it was mere seconds from breaking. "Just watch it."

I crossed my arms against my chest and stared at the screen again. An old, Chevy truck came rumbling down the freeway, stopping and starting as the traffic dictated. The camera angle panned toward the back of the truck. I recognized the load of chicken coops piled atop one another. Like déjà vu, the camera lens zoomed in on the blue tarp covering the chickens. It was just a matter of time before the wind would yank the tarp up and over the coops, leaving the chickens exposed to the elements.

Realization stirred in my gut like acid reflux. I dropped my arms and leaned closer to the screen, still wishing this was a dream, but somehow knowing it wasn't. The camera was now leaving the rear of the truck and it started panning behind the truck, to a white Volvo S40. *My white Volvo.*

I braced myself against the idea that this could be happening—that I was about to see my car accident. Who the heck was filming? And moreover, where in the heck were they? This looked like it'd been filmed by more than one cameraman, with multiple angles, impossible for just one photographer.

I heard the sound of wheels squealing, knowing only too well what would happen next. I forced my attention back to the strange woman who was now curling her hair around her index finger, making the Cheeto-colored lock look edible.

"So someone videotaped my accident, what does that have to do with why I'm here?" I asked in an unsteady voice, afraid for her answer. "And you should also know that I'm incredibly late to work and I'm due to give a presentation not only to the CEO but also the board of directors."

She shook her head. "You really don't get it, do you?"

"I don't think *you* get it," I snapped as reminded myself more than once that I was the master of my own destiny. The woman grumbled something unintelligible and turned the computer monitor back towards her, then opened a manila file sitting on her desk. She rummaged through the papers until she found what she was looking for and started scanning the sheet, using her fingernail to guide her.

"Ah, no wonder," she said snapping her wad of gum. She sighed as her triangular eyebrows reached for the ceiling. "He is not going to be happy."

I leaned on the counter, wishing I knew what was going on so I could get the heck out of here and on with my life. "No wonder what?"

She shook her head. "Not for me to explain. Gotta get a manager."

Picking up the phone, she punched in an extension, then turned around and spoke in a muffled tone. The fact that I wasn't privy to whatever she was discussing even though it involved me was annoying, to say the least. A few minutes later, she ended her cocooned conversation and pointed to the pastel chairs behind me.

"Have a seat. A manager will be with you in a minute."

"I don't have time for this," I said gruffly, trying to act out a charade of the fact that I *was* the master of my own destiny. "Didn't you hear me? I have to give a presentation!"

"A manager will be with you in a minute," she repeated and then faced her screen again as if to say our conversation was over.

With hollow resignation, I threw my hands up in the air, but returned to the seat I'd hoped to vacate permanently. The plastic felt cold and unwelcoming. It creaked and groaned as if taunting me about my weight. I didn't need a stupid chair to remind me I was fat. I melted into the L-shaped seat and stretched my short legs out before me, trying to relax, and not to cry. I closed my eyes and breathed in for three seconds and out for three seconds.

Lily, stress is nothing more than a socially acceptable form of mental illness, I told myself, quoting one of my favorite self-help gurus, Richard Carlson. *And you aren't mentally ill, are you?*

No, but I might be dead! I railed back at myself. *But if you really were dead, why don't you feel like it?* I reached down to pinch myself, just to check if it would hurt and, what-do-you-know? It did... *So, really, I couldn't be dead. And furthermore, if I were dead, where in the heck was I now? I couldn't imagine the DMV existed anywhere near Heaven. If I'd gone South instead... oh jeez...*

Don't be ridiculous, Lily Harper! This is nothing more than some sort of bad dream, courtesy of your subconscious because you're nervous about your presentation and your review.

I closed my eyes and willed myself to stop thinking about the what ifs. I wasn't dead. It was a joke or something. Heck, the woman was weird—anyone with musician cat statues couldn't be all there. And once I met with this manager of hers, I'd be sure to express my dissatisfaction. That woman deserved to be fired for freaking me out like this.

You are the master of your own destiny, I told myself again.

I opened my eyes and watched the woman click her fingernails against the keyboard. The sound of a door opening caught my attention and I glanced up to find a very tall, thin man coming toward the orange-haired demon. He glanced at me, then headed toward the woman, who leaned in and whispered something in his ear. His eyes went wide; then his eyebrows knitted in the middle.

It didn't look good.

He nodded three, four times then cleared his throat, ran his hands down his suit jacket and approached me.

"Ms. Harper," he started and I raised my head. "Will you please come with me?"

I stood up and the chair underneath me sighed with relief. I ignored it and followed the man through the maze of cubicles into his office.

"Please have a seat," he said, peering down his long nose at me. He closed the door behind us, and in two brief strides, reached his desk and took a seat.

I didn't say anything, but sat across from him. He reached a long, spindly finger toward his business card holder and produced a white, nondescript card. It read:

Jason Streethorn
Manager
Afterlife Enterprises

"We need to make this quick," I started. "I'm late to work and I have to give a presentation. Can we discuss whatever damages you want to collect from the insurance companies of the other vehicles involved in the accidents over the phone?" I paused for a second as I recalled the accident. "I think I was at fault."

"I see," he said and then sighed.

I didn't know what to say, so I just looked at him dumbly, ramming the sharp corners of the business card into the fleshy part of my index finger until it left a purple indentation in my skin.

The man cleared his throat. He looked like a skeleton.

"Ms. Harper, it seems we're in a bit of a pickle."

"A pickle?"

Jason nodded and diverted his eyes. That's when I knew I wasn't going to like whatever came out of his mouth next. It's never good when people refuse to make eye contact with you.

"Yes, as I learned from my secretary, Hilda, you don't know why you're here."

"Right. And just so you know, Hilda wasn't very helpful," I said purposefully.

"Yes, she preferred I handle this."

"Handle this?" I repeated, my voice cracking. "What's going on?"

He nodded again and then took a deep breath. "Well, you see, Ms. Harper, you died in a car accident this afternoon. But the problem is: you weren't supposed to."

I was quiet for exactly four seconds. "Is this some sort of joke?" I sputtered finally while still trying to regain my composure.

Jason shook his head and glanced at me. "I'm afraid not."

His shoulders slumped as another deep sigh escaped his lips. He seemed defeated, more exhausted than sad. Even though my inner soul was starting to believe him—that didn't mean my intellect was prepared to accept it. Then something occurred to me and I glanced up at him, irritated.

"If I'm going to be on some stupid reality show, and this whole thing is a set-up, you better tell me now because I've had enough," I said, scouring the small office for some telltale sign of A/V equipment. Or failing that, Ashton Kutcher. "And, furthermore, my boss and the board of directors aren't going to react well at all." I took a deep breath.

"Ms. Harper, I know you're confused, but I assure you, this isn't a joke." He paused and inhaled just as deeply as I just had. "I'm sure this is hard for you to conceptualize. Usually, when it's a person's time to go, their guardian angel walks them through the process and accompanies them toward the light. Sometimes a relative or two might even attend." His voice trailed until the air swallowed it entirely.

Somehow, the last hour of my life, which made no sense, was now making sense. I guess dying was a confusing experience.

He jumped up, as if the proverbial light bulb had gone off over his head. Then, throwing himself back into his chair, he spun around, faced his computer and began to type. Sighing, I glanced around, taking in his office for the first time.

Like the waiting room, there weren't any windows, just white walls without a mark on them. The air was still and although there wasn't anything offensive about the odor, it was stagnant, like it wouldn't know what to do if it met fresh air. The furniture consisted of Jason's desk, his chair and the two chairs across from him, one of which I occupied. All the furniture appeared to be made of cheap pine, like what you'd find at IKEA. Other than the nondescript furniture, there was a computer and beside that, a long, plastic tube about nine inches in diameter, that disappeared into the ceiling. It looked like some sort of suction device.

With a self-satisfied smile, he faced me again. "We have your whole life in our database."

He pointed toward the computer screen. "My whole life in his database" amounted to a word document with a humble blue border and my name scrawled across the top in Monotype Corsiva. It looked like a fifth grader's book report.

He eyed the document and moved his head from right to left with such vigor, he reminded me of a cartoon character eating corn. Then I realized he was scanning through the Lily Harper book report. With an enthusiastic nod, he turned toward me.

"Looks like you lost your first tooth at age six. Um... In school, you were a year younger than everyone else, but smarter than the majority of your class. You double majored in English and Political Science. You were a Director of Marketing for a prestigious bank."

"'Were' is a fitting word because after this, I'm sure I'll be fired," I grumbled.

The man paused, his eyes still on his computer. "When you were eighteen, you had a crush on your best friend and when you tried to kiss him, he pushed you away and told you he was gay."

I stood up so fast, my chair bucked. "Okay, I've heard enough."

The part about Matt rebuffing my kiss was something I'd never told anyone. I'd been too mortified. Guess the Word document was better than I thought.

"It's all there," Jason said as he turned to regard me with something that resembled sympathy.

"I don't understand..." I started.

He nodded, as though satisfied we'd moved beyond the "you're dead" conversation and into the "why you're dead" conversation. He pulled open his top desk drawer and produced a spongy stress ball—the kind you work in your palm. The ball flattened and popped back into shape under the tensile strength of his skeletal fingers.

"I'm afraid your guardian angel wasn't doing his job. This was supposed to be a minor accident—just to teach you not to text and drive, especially in the rain."

"I wasn't texting," I ground out.

Jason shrugged as if whatever I *was* doing was trivial. "Unfortunately, your angel was MIA and now here you are."

I leaned forward, not quite believing my ears. "I have an angel?"

Jason nodded. "Everyone does. Some are just a little better than others."

I shook my head, wondering if there was a limit to how much information my small brain could process before it went on overload. "So, let me understand this, not only do I have a guardian angel, but mine isn't a very good one?"

"That about sums it up. Your angel…" He paused. "His name is Bill, by the way."

"Bill?"

"He's been on probation for… failing to do his duties for you and a few others."

My hands tightened on the arms of my chair as I wondered at what point my non-comprehending brain would simply implode with all this ridiculousness. "Probation?"

He nodded. "Yes, it seems he's had a bit of trouble with alcohol recently."

"My angel is an alcoholic?" I slouched into my chair, the words "angel" and "alcoholic" swimming through the air as I began to doubt my sanity.

"Yes, I'm afraid so."

Jason parted his thin lips, but that exhausted look resurrected itself on his face. I was quick to interrupt, shock and anger suddenly warring within me until I couldn't contain them any longer. "This is the most ridiculous thing

I've ever heard! Alcoholic angels? I didn't even know they could drink!"

"They can do everything humans can," he said in an affronted tone, like he was annoyed with my outburst.

I sat back into my chair, not feeling any better with the situation, but also figuring my outbursts were finished for the immediate future. Well, until I could come to terms with what was really going on. But flipping out wasn't going to do me any good. I needed to stay in control of myself and in control of my emotions. Wayne Dyer's words, "it makes no sense to worry about things you have no control over because there's nothing you can do about them," floated through my head as I tried to prepare myself for whatever I had coming.

Jason Streethorn, the office manager of death, folded his hands in his lap and leaned forward. "Since your angel, our employee, failed you, we do have an offer of restitution."

Apparently, this was where the business side of our conversation began. "Restitution?"

"Yes, because this oversight is our fault, I'd like to offer you the chance to live again."

I had to suspend my disbelief of being dead in the first place and just play along with him, figuring at some point I'd wake up and Jason Streethorn, the orange-haired woman and this DMV-like place would be nothing more than the aftermath of a cheese pizza and Coke eaten too close to bedtime. "Okay, that sounds good. What do I…"

He rebuffed me with his raised hand. "However, if you accept this offer, you'll have to be employed by Afterlife Enterprises."

I sank back into my chair, suddenly wanting nothing more than to pull my hair out. I had a sinking feeling I probably wouldn't be able to resume my title of Director. "What does that mean?"

He sighed, as though the explanation would take a while. "Unfortunately, Afterlife Enterprises is a bit on the unorganized side of late. When the computer system switched from 1999 to 2000, we weren't prepared, and a computer glitch resulted in thousands of souls getting misplaced."

The fact that death relied on a computer system which wasn't even as good as Windows XP was too much. "The Y2K bug didn't affect anyone."

Jason worked the stress ball between his emaciated fingers, making multiple knuckles crack, the sound imbedding itself in my psyche. "On Earth, it didn't affect anything, but such was not the case with the Afterlife." He exhaled like he was trying to expel all the air from his lungs. "Unfortunately, we were affected and it's a problem we've been trying to sort out ever since." He paused and shook his head like it was a great, big shame. Then he apparently remembered he had the recently dead to contend with and faced me again. "As I said before, due to this glitch, we've had souls sent to the Kingdom who should've gone to the Underground City. And vice versa." He paused. "And some souls are locked on the earthly plane as well. It's been a big nightmare, to say the least."

My mouth was still hanging open. "The Kingdom and the Underground City? Is that like Heaven and Hell?" Why did I have the sudden feeling he was going to start the Dungeons and Dragons lingo?

"Similar."

I rubbed my tired eyes and let it all sink in. So, not only were there bad dead people in Heaven, aka the Kingdom, but there were good dead people in Hell, aka the Underground City? And to make things even more complicated, there were bad and good dead people stuck on Earth?   "Is that still happening now? Or did you fix the computer glitch?" I asked, wondering if maybe I'd been sent to the wrong place. I thought this place seemed like Hell from the get-go. And though I was never a church-goer, I definitely wasn't destined for the South Pole.

"We fixed the glitch, but that doesn't change the fact that there are still thousands of misplaced souls. And the longer those souls who should be in the Kingdom are left in the Underground City, or on the earthly plain, the bigger the chances of lawsuits against Afterlife Enterprises. We've already had a host of them and we can't afford anymore."

I didn't have the wherewithal to contemplate afterlife lawsuits, so I focused on the other details. "So how are you going to get all those people, er souls, back where they belong?"

"That's where you would come in, should you accept this job offer."

"I would bring the spirits back?" I asked, aghast. "I'd be a ghost hunter or something?"

He laughed; it was the first time he seemed warm and, well, alive. Funny what a laugh will do for you.

"Yes, your title would be "Retriever" and we have thousands who, like you, are currently retrieving souls."

An image of the Ghostbusters jumped into my mind and I had to shake it free. Whatever this job entailed, I doubted it included slaying Slimer. "And if I don't agree?"

Jason shrugged and turned to the computer again. After a few clicks, he faced me with a frown. "Looks like you'll be on the waiting list for the Kingdom."

"The waiting list?" I said, shocked. "I think I've led a pretty decent life!"

He shook his head and faced the computer again. "I show three accounts of thievery—when you were six, nine and eleven."

"I was just a kid!"

He cleared his throat and returned his attention to the Word doc. "I also show multiple accounts of cheating when you were in university."

Affronted, I launched myself from the chair. "I've never cheated in my life!"

He frowned, looking anything but amused. "No, but you aided a certain Jordan Summers by giving him the answers in your Biology class and I show that happened over the course of the semester."

I sat back down and folded my arms against my chest. "I would think helping someone wouldn't slate me for a waiting list!"

"Cheating takes more than one form." He glanced at the screen again. "Shall I go on?"

"No." I frowned. "So how long will I be on the waiting list?"

He leaned back in his chair and resumed working the stress ball. "You're fairly close to the top of the list since your offenses are only minor. I'd say about one hundred years."

"One hundred years!" I bit my lip to keep it from quivering. When I felt I could rationally conduct myself again, I faced Jason. "So where would I be for the next one hundred years?"

"In Shade."

I frowned. "And what is that? Like Limbo?"

"Yes, close to it."

"What would I do there?"

He shrugged. "Nothing, really. Shade exists merely as a loading dock for those who are awaiting the Kingdom… or the Underground City."

I didn't like the sound of that. "What's it like?"

"There is neither light nor dark, everything exists in gray. There's nothing good to look forward to, nor anything bad. You just exist."

"But if those people who are going to Hell," I started.

"The Underground City," he corrected me. "Those destined for the Underground are kept separate from those destined for the Kingdom," he finished, answering my question before I even asked it.

I felt tears stinging my eyes. "Shade sounds like my idea of hell."

Jason shook his head while a wry chuckle escaped him. "Oh, no. The Underground City is much worse." He paused. "The good news is that if you do become a Retriever and you relocate ten souls, you can then go directly to the Kingdom and bypass Shade altogether."

"So I wouldn't have to go to Shade at all?"

"As long as you relocate ten souls, you bypass Shade," he repeated, nodding as if to make it obvious that this was the choice I should make.

"What does retrieving these people mean?"

He started rolling the stress ball against his desk. "We'd start you with one assignment, or one soul. With the help of a guide, you'd go after that soul and retrieve it." He paused. "Are you interested?"

I exhaled. Did I want to die and live the next century in Shade? The short answer was no. Did I want to be a soul retriever? Not really, but I guessed it was better than dying.

"Okay, I guess so."

"We could start you out and see how you do. You can always decide not to do it."

"But then I'd die?"

"I'm afraid that's the alternative."

"Why can't you let me go back to my old life?"

He shook his head. "It's not possible. Your soul has already left your body. Once the soul departs, the body goes bad within three seconds. Unfortunately, you are way past your three seconds. That and the coroners have already pronounced you dead and the newspapers are preparing your obituary. Your mother was notified, as well."

Mom has been notified... Something hollow and dreadful stirred in my gut and started climbing up my throat. I gulped it down, hell-bent on not getting hysterical. Tears welled up in my eyes and I furiously batted them away.

"I never got to say goodbye," I managed as I tried to wrack my brain to remember the last conversation I'd had with my mother, the only person (besides Miranda) with whom I was close. Truly, my mother and Miranda were my best friends. And right about now, both of them had to be traumatized.

Jason nodded, but it wasn't a nod that said he was sympathizing. It was a hurried nod. "I'm sorry; but you need to make a decision soon. Time is of the essence and Shade will be calling soon to find out if you're joining them."

I forced my tears aside and focused on his angular face, trying to ignore my grief so I could come to a decision which would completely change the course of my life... or afterlife. "So, if I take this job and choose to live, I can't do so in my own body?"

It wasn't like I was thrilled with my appearance: I was short, overweight and plain. I was the woman who no one ever noticed—the one always behind the scenes. I'd had one major boyfriend in my life and that had lasted all of two months. Yep, anyway I looked at it, I was basically hopeless—a twenty-two year old workaholic virgin with nothing but the redundancy of a stress-inducing job to force me to wake up each morning. But, I was me, and the idea of coming back in another body left me cold. No pun intended.

"You would not be able to come back as yourself," Jason said. "You'd have to come back in another body."

I glanced down at myself. As far as I could tell, I still looked the same. "But, I'm in my body now."

"You're here in spirit only."

The phone on his desk rang and he faced me with impatience etched in his eyes and mouth. "That's probably Shade calling."

He picked up the phone. "Jason Streethorn, Afterlife Enterprises, how can I help you?"   After a few nods, he glanced at me. "Yes, she's here. She's just deciding what she wants to do. Yes, I understand it's been over an hour."

He muffled the end of the phone with his palm and faced me again. "You need to decide now." He faced the phone again. "Yes, I've informed her. You're going to send someone over within the hour?"

"Wait," I said. "Tell them I'll take the job. I want to live."

Available Now!

Also Available From HP Mallory:

Turn the page for chapter one!

ONE

It's not every day you see a ghost.

On this particular day, I'd been minding my own business, tidying up the shop for the night while listening to *Girls Just Wanna Have Fun* (guilty as charged). It was late—maybe 9:00 p.m. A light bulb had burnt out in my tarot reading room a few days ago, and I still hadn't changed it. I have a tendency to overlook the menial details of life. Now, a small red bulb fought against the otherwise pitch darkness of the room, lending it a certain macabre feel.

In search of a replacement bulb, I attempted to sort through my "if it doesn't have a home, put it in here" box when I heard the front door open. Odd—I could've sworn I'd locked it.

"We're closed," I yelled.

I didn't hear the door closing, so I put Cyndi Lauper on mute and strolled out to inquire. The streetlamps reflected through the shop windows, the glare so intense, I had to remind myself they were just lights and not some alien spacecraft come to whisk me away.

The room was empty.

Considering the possibility that someone might be hiding, I swallowed the dread climbing up my throat. Glancing around, I searched for something to protect myself with in case said breaker-and-enterer decided to attack. My eyes rested on a solitary broom standing in the corner of the Spartan room. The broom was maybe two steps from me. That might not sound like much, but my fear had me by the ankles and wouldn't let go.

Jolie, get the damned broom.

Thank God for that little internal voice of sensibility that always seems to visit at just the right time.

Freeing my feet from the fear tar, I grabbed the broom and neared my desk. It was a good place for someone to hide—well, really, the only place to hide. When it comes to furnishings, I'm a minimalist.

I jammed the broom under the desk and swept vigorously.

Nothing. The hairs on my neck stood to attention as a shiver of unease coursed through me. I couldn't shake the feeling and after deciding no one was in the room, I persuaded myself it must've been kids. But kids or not, I would've heard the door close.

I didn't discard the broom.

Like a breath from the arctic, a chill crept up the back of my neck.

I glanced up and there he was, floating a foot or so above me. Stunned, I took a step back, my heart beating like a frantic bird in a small cage.

"Holy crap."

The ghost drifted toward me until he and I were eye level. My mind was such a muddle, I wasn't sure if I wanted to run or bat at him with the broom. Fear cemented me in place, and I did neither, just stood gaping at him.

Thinking the Mexican standoff couldn't last forever, I replayed every fact I'd ever learned about ghosts: they have unfinished business, they're stuck on a different plane of existence, they're here to tell us something, and most importantly, they're just energy.

Energy couldn't hurt me.

My heartbeat started regulating, and I returned my gaze to the ectoplasm before me. There was no emotion on his face; he just watched me as if waiting for me to come to my senses.

"Hello," I said, thinking how stupid I sounded—treating him like every Tom, Dick, or Harry who ventured through my door. Then I felt stupid that I felt stupid—what was wrong with greeting a ghost? Even the dead deserve standard propriety.

He wavered a bit, as if someone had turned a blow dryer on him, but didn't say anything. He was young, maybe in his twenties. His double-breasted suit looked like it was right out of *The Untouchables*, from the 1930s if I had to guess.

His hair was on the blond side, sort of an ash blond. It was hard to tell because he was standing, er floating, in front of a wooden door that showed through him. Wooden door or not, his face was broad and he had a crooked nose—maybe it'd been broken in a fight. He was a good-looking ghost as ghosts go.

"Can you speak?" I asked, still in disbelief that I was attempting to converse with the dead. Well, I'd never thought I could, and I guess the day had come to prove me wrong. Still he said nothing, so I decided to continue my line of questioning.

"Do you have a message from someone?"

He shook his head. "No."

His voice sounded like someone talking underwater.

Hmm. Well, I imagined he wasn't here to get his future told—seeing as how he didn't have a future. Maybe he was passing through? Going toward the light? Come to haunt my shop?

"Are you on your way somewhere?" I had so many questions for this spirit but didn't know where to start, so all the stupid ones came out first.

"I was sent here," he managed, and in his ghostly way, I think he smiled. Yeah, not a bad looking ghost.

"Who sent you?" It seemed the logical thing to ask.

He said nothing and like that, vanished, leaving me to wonder if I'd had something bad to eat at lunch.

Indigestion can be a bitch.

~

"So no more encounters?" Christa, my best friend and only employee, asked while leaning against the desk in our front office.

I shook my head and pooled into a chair by the door. "Maybe if you hadn't left early to go on your date, I wouldn't have had a visit at all."

"Well, one of us needs to be dating," she said, knowing full well I hadn't had any dates for the past six months. An image of my last date fell into my head like a bomb. Let's just say I'd never try the Internet dating route again. It wasn't that the guy had been bad looking—he'd looked like his photo, but what I hadn't been betting on was that he'd get wasted and proceed to tell me how he was separated from his wife and had three kids. Not even divorced! Yeah, that hadn't been on his *match.com* profile.

"Let's not get into this again …"

"Jolie, you need to get out. You're almost thirty …"

"Two years from it, thank you very much."

"Whatever … you're going to end up old and alone. You're way too pretty, and you have such a great personality, you can't end up like that. Don't let one bad date ruin it." Her voice reached a crescendo. Christa has a tendency towards the dramatic.

"I've had a string of bad dates, Chris." I didn't know what else to say—I was terminally single. It came down to the fact that I'd rather spend time with my cat or Christa rather than face another stream of losers.

As for being attractive, Christa insisted I was pretty, but I wasn't convinced. It's one thing when your best friend says you're pretty, but it's entirely different when a man says it.

And I couldn't remember the last time a man had said it.

I caught my reflection in the glass of the desk and studied myself while Christa rambled on about all the reasons I should be dating. I supposed my face was pleasant enough—a pert nose, cornflower blue eyes and plump lips. A spattering of freckles across the bridge of my nose interrupts an otherwise pale landscape of skin, and my shoulder length blond hair always finds itself drawn into a ponytail.

Head-turning doubtful, girl-next-door probable.

As for Christa, she doesn't look like me at all. For one thing, she's pretty tall and leggy, about five-eight, and four inches taller than I am. She has dark hair the color of mahogany, green eyes, and pinkish cheeks. She's classically pretty—like cameo pretty. She's rail skinny and has no boobs. I have a tendency to gain weight if I eat too much, I have a definite butt, and the twins are pretty ample as well. Maybe that made me sound like I'm fat—I'm not fat, but I could stand to lose five pounds.

"Are you even listening to me?" Christa asked.

Shaking my head, I entered the reading room, thinking I'd left my glasses there.

I heard the door open.

"Well, hello to you," Christa said in a high-pitched, sickening-sweet and non-Christa voice.

"Afternoon." The deep timbre of his voice echoed through the room, my ears mistaking his baritone for music.

"I'm here for a reading, but I don't have an appointment ..."

"Oh, that's cool," Christa interrupted and from the saccharin tone of her voice, it was pretty apparent this guy had to be eye candy.

Giving up on finding my reading glasses, I headed out in order to introduce myself to our stranger. Upon seeing him, I couldn't contain the gasp that escaped my throat. It wasn't his Greek God, Sean-Connery-would-be-envious good looks that grabbed me first or his considerable height.

It was his aura.

I've been able to see auras since before I can remember, but I'd never seen anything like his. It radiated out of him as if it had a life of its own and the color! Usually auras are pinkish or violet in healthy people, yellowish or orange in those unhealthy. His was the most vibrant blue I've ever seen—the color of the sky after a storm when the sun's rays bask everything in glory.

It emanated out of him like electricity.

"Hi, I'm Jolie," I said, remembering myself.

"How do you do?" And to make me drool even more than I already was, he had an accent, a British one. Ergh.

I glanced at Christa as I invited him into the reading room. Her mouth dropped open like a fish.

My sentiments exactly.

His navy blue sweater stretched to its capacity while attempting to span a pair of broad shoulders and a wide chest. The broad shoulders and spacious chest in question tapered to a trim waist and finished in a finale of long legs. The white shirt peeking from underneath his sweater contrasted against his tanned complexion and made me consider my own fair skin with dismay.

The stillness of the room did nothing to allay my nerves. I took a seat, shuffled the tarot cards, and handed him the deck. "Please choose five cards and lay them face up on the table."

He took a seat across from me, stretching his legs and rested his hands on his thighs. I chanced a look at him and took in his chocolate hair and darker eyes. His face was angular, and his Roman nose lent him a certain Paul Newman-esque quality. The beginnings of shadow did nothing to hide the definite cleft in his strong chin.

He didn't take the cards and instead, just smiled, revealing pearly whites and a set of grade A dimples.

"You did come for a reading?" I asked.

He nodded and covered my hand with his own. What felt like lightning ricocheted up my arm, and I swear my heart stopped for a second. The lone red bulb blinked a few times then continued to grow brighter until I thought it might explode. My gaze moved from his hand, up his arm and settled on his dark brown eyes. With the red light reflecting against him, he looked like the devil come to barter for my soul.

"I came for a reading, yes, but not with the cards. I'd like you to read … me." His rumbling baritone was hypnotic, and I fought the need to pull my hand from his warm grip.

I set the stack of cards aside, focusing on him again. I was so nervous I doubted if any of my visions would come. They were about as reliable as the weather anchors you see on TV.

After several long uncomfortable moments, I gave up. "I can't read you, I'm sorry," I said, my voice breaking. I shifted the eucalyptus-scented incense I'd lit to the farthest corner of the table, and waved my hands in front of my face, dispersing the smoke that seemed intent on wafting directly into my eyes. It swirled and danced in the air, as if indifferent to the fact that I couldn't help this stranger.

He removed his hand but stayed seated. I thought he'd leave, but he made no motion to do anything of the sort.

"Take your time."

Take my time? I was a nervous wreck and had no visions whatsoever. I just wanted this handsome stranger to leave, so my habitual life could return to normal.

But it appeared that was not in the cards.

The silence pounded against the walls, echoing the pulse of blood in my veins. Still, my companion said nothing. I'd had enough. "I don't know what to tell you."

He smiled again. "What do you see when you look at me?"

Adonis.

No, I couldn't say that. Maybe he'd like to hear about his aura? I didn't have any other cards up my sleeve ... "I can see your aura," I almost whispered, fearing his ridicule.

His brows drew together. "What does it look like?"

"It isn't like anyone's I've ever seen before. It's bright blue, and it flares out of you ... almost like electricity."

His smile disappeared, and he leaned forward. "Can you see everyone's auras?"

The incense dared to assault my eyes again, so I put it out and dumped it in the trashcan.

"Yes. Most people have much fainter glows to them— more often than not in the pink or orange family. I've never seen blue."

He chewed on that for a moment. "What do you suppose it is you're looking at—someone's soul?"

I shook my head. "I don't know. I do know, though, if someone's ailing, I can see it. Their aura goes a bit yellow." He nodded, and I added, "You're healthy."

He laughed, and I felt silly for saying it. He stood up, his imposing height making me feel all of three inches tall. Not enjoying the feel of him staring down at me, I stood and watched him pull out his wallet. I guess he'd heard enough and thought I was full of it. He set a one hundred dollar bill on the table in front of me. My hourly rate was fifty dollars, and we'd been maybe twenty minutes.

"I'd like to come see you for the next three Tuesdays at 4:00 p.m. Please don't schedule anyone after me. I'll compensate you for the entire afternoon."

I was shocked—what in the world would he want to come back for?

"Jolie, it was a pleasure meeting you, and I look forward to our next session." He turned to walk out of the room when I remembered myself.

"Wait, what name should I put in the appointment book?"

He turned and faced me. "Rand."

Then he walked out of the shop.

~

By the time Tuesday rolled around, I hadn't had much of a busy week. No more visits from ghosts, spirits, or whatever the PC term is for them. I'd had a few walk-ins, but that was about it. It was strange. October in Los Angeles was normally a busy time.

"Ten minutes to four," Christa said with a smile, leaning against the front desk and looking up from a stack of photos—her latest bout into photography.

"I wonder if he'll come," I mumbled.

Taking the top four photos off the stack, she arranged them against the desk as if they were puzzle pieces. I walked up behind her, only too pleased to find an outlet for my anxiety, my nerves skittish with the pending arrival of one very handsome man.

The photo in the middle caught my attention first. It was a landscape of the Malibu coastline, the intense blue of the ocean mirrored by the sky and interrupted only by the green of the hillside.

"Wow, that's a great one, Chris." I picked the photo up. "Can you frame it? I'd love to hang it in the store."

"Sure." She nodded and continued inspecting her photos, as if trying to find a fault in the angle or maybe the subject. Christa had aspirations of being a photographer and she had the eye for it. I admired her artistic ability—I, myself, hadn't been in line when God was handing out creativity.

She glanced at the clock again. "Five minutes to four."

I shrugged, feigning an indifference I didn't feel. "I'm just glad you're here. Rand strikes me as weird. Something's off …"

She laughed. "Oh, Jules, you don't trust your own mother."

I snorted at the comment and collapsed into the chair behind her, propping my feet on the corner of our mesh waste bin. So I didn't trust people—I think I had a better understanding of the human condition than most people did. That reminded me, I hadn't called my mom in at least a week. Note to self: be a better daughter.

The cuckoo clock on the wall announced it was 4:00 p.m. with a tinny rendition of Edelweiss while the two resident wooden figures did a polka. I'd never much liked the clock, but Christa wouldn't let me get rid of it.

The door opened, and I jumped to my feet, my heart jack hammering. I wasn't sure why I was so flustered, but as soon as I met the heat of Rand's dark eyes, it all made sense. He was here again even though I couldn't tell him anything important last time, and did I fail to mention he was gorgeous? His looks were enough to play with any girl's heartstrings.

"Good afternoon," he said, giving me a brisk nod.

He was dressed in black—black slacks, black collared shirt, and a black suit jacket. He looked like he'd just come from a funeral, but somehow I didn't think such was the case.

"Hi, Rand," Christa said, her gaze raking his statuesque body.

"How has your day been?" he answered as his eyes rested on me.

"Sorta slow," Christa responded before I could. He didn't even turn to notice her, and she frowned, obviously miffed. I smiled to myself and headed for the reading room, Rand on my heels.

I closed the door, and by the time I turned around, he'd already seated himself at the table. As I took my seat across from him, a heady scent of something unfamiliar hit me. It had notes of mint and cinnamon or maybe cardamom. The foreign scent was so captivating, I fought to refocus my attention.

"You fixed the light," he said with a smirk. "Much better."

I nodded and focused on my lap. "I didn't get a chance last time to ask you why you wanted to come back." I figured it was best to get it out in the open. I didn't think I'd do any better reading him this time.

"Well, I'm here for the same reason anyone else is."

I lifted my gaze and watched him lean back in the chair. He regarded me with amusement—raised eyebrows and a slight smirk pulling at his full lips.

I shook my head. "You aren't interested in a card reading, and I couldn't tell you anything … substantial in our last meeting …"

His throaty chuckle interrupted me. "You aren't much of a businesswoman, Jolie; it sounds like you're trying to get rid of me and my cold, hard cash."

Enough was enough. I'm not the type of person to beat around the bush, and he owed me an explanation. "So are you here to get a date with Christa?" I forced my gaze to hold his. He seemed taken aback, cocking his head while his shoulders bounced with surprise.

"Lovely though you both are, I'm afraid my visit leans more toward business than pleasure."

"I don't understand." I hoped my cheeks weren't as red as I imagined them. I guess I deserved it for being so bold.

He leaned forward, and I pulled back. "All in good time. Now, why don't you try to read me again?"

I motioned for his hands—sometimes touching the person in question helps generate my visions. As it had last time, his touch sent a jolt of electricity through me, and I had to fight not to lose my composure. There was something odd about this man.

I closed my eyes and exhaled, trying to focus while millions of bees warred with each other in my stomach. After driving my thoughts from all the questions I had regarding Rand, I was more comfortable.

At first nothing came.

I opened my eyes to find Rand staring at me. Just as I closed them again, a vision came—one that was piecemeal and none too clear.

"A man," I said, and my voice sounded like a foghorn in the quiet room. "He has dark hair and blue eyes, and there's something different about him. I can't quite pinpoint it … it seems he's hired you for something …"

My voice started to trail as the vision grew blurry. I tried to weave through the images, but they were too inconsistent. Once I got a hold of one, it wafted out of my grasp, and another indistinct one took its place.

"Go on," Rand prodded.

The vision was gone at this point, but I was still receiving emotional feedback. Sometimes I'll just get a vision and other times a vision with feelings. "The job's dangerous. I don't think you should take it."

And just like that, the feeling disappeared. I knew it was all I was going to get and I was frustrated, as it hadn't been my best work. Most of the time my feelings and visions are much clearer, but these were more like fragments— almost like short dream vignettes you can't interpret.

I let go of Rand's hands, and my own felt cold. I put them in my lap, hoping to warm them up again, but somehow my warmth didn't quite compare to his.

Rand seemed to be weighing what I'd told him—he strummed his fingers against his chin and chewed on his lip. "Can you tell me more about this man?"

"I couldn't see him in comparison to anyone else, so as far as height goes, I don't know. Dark hair and blue eyes, the hair was a little bit longish, maybe not a stylish haircut. He's white with no facial hair. That's about all I could see. He had something otherworldly about him. Maybe he was a psychic? I'm not sure."

"Dark hair and blue eyes you say?"

"Yes. He's a handsome man. I feel as if he's very old though he looked young. Maybe in his early thirties." I shrugged. "Sometimes my visions don't make much sense." Hey, I was just the middleman. It was up to him to interpret the message.

"You like the tall, dark, and handsome types then?"

Taken aback, I didn't know how to respond. "He had a nice face."

"You aren't receiving anything else?"

I shook my head. "I'm afraid not."

He stood. "Very good. I'm content with our meeting today. Do you have me scheduled for next week?"

I nodded and stood. The silence in the room pounded against me, and I fought to find something to say, but Rand beat me to it.

"Jolie, you need to have more confidence."

The closeness of the comment irritated me—who was this man who thought he could waltz into my shop and tell me I needed more confidence? Granted, he had a point, but damn it all if I were to tell him that!

Now, I was even more embarrassed, and I'm sure my face was the color of a bad sunburn. "I don't think you're here to discuss me."

"As a matter of fact, that's precisely the reason I'm …"

Rand didn't get a chance to finish when Christa came bounding through the door.

Christa hasn't quite grasped the whole customer service thing.

"Sorry to interrupt, but there was a car accident right outside the shop! This one car totally just plowed into the other one. I think everyone's alright, but how crazy is that?"

My attention found Rand's as Christa continued to describe the accident in minute detail. I couldn't help but wonder what he'd been about to say. It had sounded like he was here to discuss me … something that settled in my stomach like a big rock.

When Christa finished her accident report, Rand made his way to the door. I was on the verge of demanding he finish what he'd been about to say, but I couldn't summon the nerve.

"Cheers," he said and walked out.

AVAILABLE NOW!

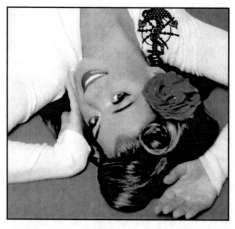

H. P. Mallory is the author of the Jolie Wilkins series as well as the Dulcie O'Neil series.

She began her writing career as a self-published author and after reaching a tremendous amount of success, decided to become a traditionally published author and hasn't looked back since.

H. P. Mallory lives in Southern California with her husband and son, where she is at work on her next book.

If you are interested in receiving emails when she releases new books, please sign up for her email distribution list by visiting her website and clicking the "contact" tab: www.hpmallory.com

Be sure to join HP's online Facebook community where you will find pictures of the characters from both series and lots of other fun stuff including an online book club!

Facebook: https://www.facebook.com/hpmallory

Find H.P. Mallory Online:

www.hpmallory.com

http://twitter.com/hpmallory

https://www.facebook.com/hpmallory

THE JOLIE WILKINS SERIES:

Fire Burn and Cauldron Bubble
Toil and Trouble
Be Witched (Novella)
Witchful Thinking
The Witch Is Back
Something Witchy This Way Comes

Stay Tuned For The Jolie Wilkins Spinoff Series!

THE DULCIE O'NEIL SERIES:

To Kill A Warlock
A Tale Of Two Goblins
Great Hexpectations
Wuthering Frights
Malice In Wonderland
For Whom The Spell Tolls

THE LILY HARPER SERIES:

Better Off Dead

CPSIA information can be obtained at www.ICGtesting.com
Printed in the USA
LVOW05s0227250913

353922LV00016BB/504/P